THE
SALTWATER
MURDER

A POSIE PARKER MYSTERY #7

L. B. HATHAWAY

WHITEHAVEN

WHITEHAVEN MAN PRESS

London

First published in Great Britain in 2019
by Whitehaven Man Press, London

A CIP catalogue record for this book is
available from the British Library.

ISBN (e-book:) 978-0-9955694-2-3
ISBN (paperback:) 978-0-9955694-3-0

For Flora

Also by L.B. Hathaway

The Posie Parker Mystery Series

PROLOGUE

It had been a shock.

The girl.

Seeing her again after so many years. He'd been thinking about her a lot lately, had wanted to ask her one special favour.

He wished he'd been better prepared. Wished he'd been wearing his wig and black gown. That feeling of power they gave him would have come in handy.

But the London Courts were closed for the holidays, and even he, Amyas Lyle, King's Counsel, wouldn't have donned his heavy legal costume for the sheer sake of it. He frowned as he crossed dusty Serle Street and swung under the red-brick gate of Lincoln's Inn, that secret enclave of London's lawyers. He looked like an angry raven with one of its wings clipped. Dark and dangerously handsome.

Tetchy. Thundery.

He walked on slowly, cautiously, past the huge grassy quad of New Square, surrounded by its tall Victorian buildings, reminding him of his days at Cambridge, and on past the Gothic Great Hall. There was no-one about. Most lawyers disappeared off to the coast for a month, all of them anxious to escape the thick pollen-filled city air. But Amyas Lyle KC was a workaholic; he was famous for it. He never left Lincoln's Inn in the summertime: this was his world.

Amyas was the top barrister in London, and he dealt with financial fraud, defending men whose actions had led to misery for hundreds of people. He was also one of the richest self-made men in town, and Head of his Chambers. Not bad for a man just approaching his thirty-fifth birthday. No holiday could ever compare to *that*.

And just before the summer recess he had received the news he craved above everything: a vacancy had arisen among the tiny handful of High Court Judges, and he had been asked to fill it. In the autumn he would become the youngest ever High Court Judge.

Life was becoming exciting, and wonderful in so many ways. He'd packed off his wife and rowdy twin boys to France on holiday, and things should have been good.

But things *weren't* good. There was no use denying it.

The fact was that Amyas Lyle was receiving a barrage of weird threats.

Not that there was anything new in *that*. He'd had threats before, of course; it went with the job. Grubby messages from sad people who'd hated how Amyas had successfully defended the fraudulent criminals who had ruined their lives. But those threats had never amounted to anything and he'd laughed about them in the Clerks' Room, made fun of the people who had sent them.

But this post was different. Spooky. Strange. Anonymous postcards and notes which drivelled on about odd things. Inexplicable things: tears, secrets, saltwater. The notes had started off innocently enough, but just recently they'd turned sinister.

On top of which he'd now had this sudden shock.

The girl…

Amyas Lyle replayed over in his mind the events of just fifteen minutes ago.

He'd lunched at his usual Italian restaurant on Sicilian

Avenue after his morning's business at nearby Bedford Row and had been walking back through Lincoln's Inn Fields, that green expanse of park in Holborn where folk came for a picnic or to sunbathe. He'd crossed the baking tarmac at the centre, with its tennis courts and accompanying rickety little café. And that's where he'd seen her. And *she'd* seen him.

They'd both stopped in their tracks, frozen.

He, in his foolishly informal grey summer suit, carrying an armful of papers. And she, rising from her chair at the tennis club café, almost spilling her pink lemonade, bursting away from the company at her table like a ship cut adrift. She was a beautiful woman, just past her youth, but grown richer for it, bold in the choices she made: a careful silk dress the colour of a bruise, an expensive bobbed haircut, no hat.

He had to stop himself staring like the boy he had been when he had loved her.

'Why, it's Mr Lyle, isn't it? How delightful! But I'm not sure if you remember me? It was a long time ago.'

A dry, warm handshake. A smile. The scent of Parma Violet.

Even now, so many years on, those cornflower-blue eyes still sparkled like a perfect summer's day, even if they *were* surrounded by tiny lines; even if they had seen too much. He'd kept track of her. Had heard she'd had a rough time of it in the war. Worse than most. That she'd lost most of the people dear to her.

'Posie? Miss Parker? Of course I remember you. I was sorry to read of Richard's death in the war. It was tragic.'

A curt nod.

Amyas Lyle had known Richard Parker at school. But the best thing about Richard Parker had always been his little sister.

Two years younger, Posie had been a dreamy, cream-skinned girl, long dark hair in plaits, easy on the eye. The focus of many a schoolboy's attentions. Amyas, like the others, had seen Posie at various speech-days and sporting events. A mere sighting of her could make his day back then, give him something to think about for weeks on end. He'd felt obsessed by her for years. Once, in 1910, when she was about eighteen and he was in the last year of his legal degree at Cambridge University, he had found the courage to ask her out to tea. But it had proved unsuccessful, and he'd not seen her since.

'I've followed your cases in the newspapers, Mr Lyle.' The grown-up Posie was smiling. 'Congratulations.'

'I have followed you, too, Miss Parker.' Of course he knew that Posie was now a successful private detective in her own right. Famous, really. *Who in London didn't?*

'Would you like to join my friends and I for a drink, Mr Lyle? You might know Chief Inspector Richard Lovelace, of New Scotland Yard?'

'Thank you, no. I won't interrupt. But this is a real coincidence, Miss Parker. I was meaning to get in touch with you. A mere trifle, a legal thing. Perhaps best explained at my office? It's confidential, and becoming rather urgent, actually.'

'Oh?' A raise of a perfect eyebrow.

And suddenly, quite inexplicably, because he never asked anyone for anything, he found himself wanting to tell Posie all about the strange messages he was receiving. Messages which made him feel unaccountably panicky, which kept him awake at night. He felt like asking her for help. *I'm out of my depth.*

But he managed to swallow down the panic, stick to the matter at hand. 'Could you see your way to telephoning me in my Chambers, 20 Old Square? Later today or tomorrow? The sooner the better.'

'Of course.'

She was cool as a cucumber, he'd give her that. She didn't show any surprise at his request. Just a calm professionalism. 'Actually, I'm just about to go on holiday, Mr Lyle. So you've caught me just in time.'

'Going anywhere nice, Miss Parker?'

'The north. Whitley Bay.'

He tried not to gasp but felt the blood and heat drain from his face.

'You know it, Mr Lyle?'

'No. Not at all. Not at all.'

And now here he was in Old Square, outside his Chambers, standing dawdling like a fool under the shady cover of the ancient plane tree. Unsettled and uncertain. Not quite sure what he was doing involving Posie Parker in all of this.

Whitley Bay…

Amyas Lyle felt slightly sick.

He pushed open the glass door to the Chambers. It was very quiet inside, with everyone away. Only George, the Head Clerk, could be seen in the Clerks' Room, slotting slim papers into the pigeon-holes which honeycombed an entire wall. George turned, unsurprised at seeing the boss back promptly from his lunch. Amyas headed to his own large office over on the right, moving over the red plush carpet as silently and carefully as a cat.

His calm cream-painted office with its view over Old Square was his private sanctuary, and the afternoon sunlight which flickered over the walls, dappling the room in green, seemed more than usually restful. It took Amyas a moment to realise that all of the windows had been opened and yet no wind blew through the room. It was boiling hot and airless.

But *something* here was different. Panic caught again in Amyas' throat.

He looked about him, but could see nothing amiss. The red leather-bound legal volumes lining the walls, and the dark-wood desk with its neat stack of case-notes were exactly as he'd left them that morning.

So what was it that was wrong?

He felt a sort of sickness washing over him. Like being at sea.

A movement behind him in the doorway caused Amyas to swing around, heart hammering in his chest.

But it was only George, the Head Clerk.

Amyas exhaled in relief, grabbing at the back of his chair. 'You startled me, you fool. What d'you want to go creeping up on me like that for?'

'I'm sorry, sir.' The slight man darted forwards. He gestured around, before pointing at the desk. 'I took the liberty of opening all the windows, sir. On account of that there *delivery*.'

'Delivery?'

'Aye, sir. That box there. Stinks to high heaven, it does. A Porter bought it, sir. A Fish Porter. Not half an hour ago. Came from Billingsgate Fish Market, in the East End.'

Amyas couldn't now take his eyes off what he had previously missed. A white, enamelled metal box, the size of a large shoebox, similar to those which pathologists keep samples in, sat centrally in pride of place on his desk's blotting-pad. The legend 'BILLINGSGATE MARKET' was stamped roughly all along one side in blue.

It hit him all of a sudden, his senses catching up. *That* was what was different: the smell of fish. The smell of the sea. Of saltwater.

'I supposed it was a delivery of fish, sir. From the smell. In my opinion whatever's in that box doesn't smell too fresh.'

'I don't need your opinion on things.' Amyas' voice came out as a bark. 'Just tell me: was there a note with it?'

'Aye, sir. A white envelope with your name on it. Sealed and lying beside that there box. Looks the same as those others you've been getting recently, sir.'

George shuffled awkwardly. He was only being paid for working mornings in this temporary, unsatisfactory arrangement, and he was anxious to be off. 'Is there anything else, sir?'

'That will be all. Now clear off.'

'Very good, sir.'

And now, alone, Amyas Lyle found himself reaching unaccountably for the brand new High Court Judge's white horsehair wig and the red gown which had arrived last week from Ede & Ravenscroft and which hung proudly on a brass wall hook just behind his desk. It was as if he felt he had to be properly dressed to receive this missive. He put the items on carefully and sat himself down at the desk chair where he normally felt so comfortable.

He looked at the envelope which had been addressed to him.

George was right: it was the same handwriting as all the other strange notes which had preceded this one, all summer long. Nothing particularly special about the writing: black ink, plain curving letters which were clear to read but uninteresting on the eye.

Amyas ripped it open and read the note inside. And then read it again.

It made no sense, a bad attempt at rhyming:

> *A lifetime of tears is what you caused me.*
> *A gallon of saltwater will be your undoing.*
> *Just wait and see.*

Amyas frowned. That mention of *saltwater* again.

He found himself gingerly holding the white box, both palms flat on the cool metal top. He felt his heart hammering madly in his chest, his throat tight with fear. Sweat was beading on his brow in the boiling room and he wiped it away impatiently. What horror could the box contain? What mad crank was he dealing with here?

Should he simply pick up the telephone and call the police? Hadn't that man over at the tennis club café been something to do with Scotland Yard? An Inspector or something? Shouldn't he go to *them* for advice, rather than asking for a visit from a woman who was as intangible to him now as she had been fifteen years before?

Without further ado he opened the lid. Breathed a deep sigh of relief.

Nothing.

No fish, anyway.

The metal box contained nothing more sinister than water. Brackish water with a very strong salt-briny smell.

Amyas sniffed suspiciously and bent his head a bit lower. He looked at the note again: the writer seemed to have been quite literal about things; the amount of water in the box was probably about a gallon.

And it was definitely saltwater. Sea water, probably.

Looking closer, Amyas saw that sand seemed to move in a strange swirl through the liquid. Was it his imagination or was the water fizzing somehow? Starting to react?

Suddenly he found his eyes were stinging like mad. *What on earth?*

He drew a deep angry breath of air, but now his nose was running and when Amyas touched it he saw his hands were bright red with blood. Suddenly he felt as if his face was blistering and his ears were ringing, too. He couldn't move.

It was as if he was glued to his chair.

His nostrils flared and then his throat and mouth dried up and he fought for air in a panic. Amyas couldn't shout out. And anyway, who was there to hear him? He'd sent his Head Clerk home.

He couldn't feel his hands anymore. There was an intense heat tearing up through his whole being. Amyas was vaguely aware that the liquid in the white box was not just fizzing now, but steaming and hissing. An odd white mist was rising up from it.

A poison?

It reminded him of some nightmarish experiment from those days at school in the hateful chemistry labs. When Richard Parker had known all the answers.

But Richard Parker was now dead and long gone. Dead in the mud of France.

A gallon of saltwater will be your undoing…

As Amyas lost consciousness, he had the uncanny sensation of being a small boy again.

He was running along a pale beach somewhere, a holiday-place, a lighthouse in the far distance, feeling the sand beneath his toes. The strong stinging smell of the cold North Sea was filling up his nostrils; the sound of a small child's laughter, finding something hysterically funny, and a woman shouting a warning in response rang out now clear as day. And then there was the suck of the sand giving way to the tide, pulling him in with the waves…

As he breathed his last and the poison did its worst, his white wig fell off onto the desk in front of him.

And Amyas Lyle toppled over, smiling.

* * * *

PART ONE
LONDON
Tuesday 8th July and
Wednesday 9th July, 1924

One

Posie Parker, London's premier female detective, slouched against the gleaming oak reception desk of the deserted barristers' Chambers, a feeling of foreboding washing over her. She had been summoned here urgently and she was hungry, too. Just at this moment she could easily have wolfed down two hot bacon breakfast rolls and still had room for another.

A highly-polished grandfather clock announced that it was exactly nine-thirty in the morning.

There was no-one in the small unlit Clerks' Room behind the reception desk, and Posie found herself staring at the honeycomb of wooden shelves which lined the walls, filled with documents all tied with the same pink ribbon. Legal cases, probably. All manner of problems, all awaiting solutions. There was an odd chemical smell lingering in the air. And she was sure she could smell recent burning, from over in the fireplace in the Clerks' Room. But that would be crazy. Who would light a fire on such a hot July day?

'Ah, Posie. Nice of you to join us. Better late than never, eh?'

Richard Lovelace, Chief Inspector of Scotland Yard, closed a door firmly behind him and stepped into the red-carpeted room. He was holding a strange grey contraption which Posie recognised immediately as an old gas mask from the trenches of the Great War. The Inspector was well known to Posie, and the pair had worked on several cases together, but today she fancied he looked especially pale beneath his smattering of coppery freckles, fatigued.

However, Lovelace proved to be on form, as ever, and his keen green eyes took in Posie's crumpled purple outfit from the day before, her soft suede dancing shoes, and her lack of any make-up. He raised an eyebrow mock-comically.

'Good night out, was it?'

Posie gulped, smoothing down her mussed-up hair, then held her smart silver notepad and pencil just a little bit higher than was quite necessary, like a shield. 'I came just as soon as I got your telephone message at the office. I jumped in a motor-cab and sped over here. I know you must have rung my flat beforehand but if truth be told I haven't been home yet.'

'Really? You don't say!' The Inspector laughed for a split-second, raking his fingers through his thick red hair. 'Well, it's none of my business where you spend your nights, Posie.'

He didn't add *or with whom*. But the notion hung palpably in the air between them.

'You said in your message that this was about Amyas Lyle, sir?'

'So I did.'

'Is he dead?'

'Indeed.'

Posie clicked her tongue, resisting panic, halting the tides of fear and guilt which threatened to break over her. 'But dash it all, what a coincidence! I saw Amyas very briefly yesterday in the park. You probably saw me get up and greet him? I take it something is amiss, hence *your* presence here. You suspect foul play?'

'Absolutely. It was murder.'

Posie exhaled, pulling on her professional mantle. 'And this is where Amyas worked?'

The Inspector gestured around him. 'Yes. He was Head of Chambers here, the big boss. Amyas Lyle ran the place like a tight ship, apparently. He was in charge of about twenty barristers, and some clerks. Apparently Mr Lyle also had a small flat here, above us, on the very top floor. Perk of the job.'

Lovelace stopped suddenly, puzzled. 'But surely you know all of this? Wasn't the fella some sort of pal of yours? It certainly looked that way yesterday...'

'No, we'd lost touch.'

'I see.'

Posie crossed her arms, defensive now. 'Is that why you called me in, sir? Because you hoped I knew Amyas Lyle in a *personal* capacity? Or is it because you need my help on the detecting front? Whichever it is, I'm not finding my position with you very clear-cut.'

For a split-second Richard Lovelace looked away, out through the long sash windows to the green magical light in Old Square beyond. There was a flicker of pain, twisted with amusement, playing briefly on his face. When he spoke his voice was very low:

'Since when has your position with me ever been clear-cut, Posie? Not just *today*. And I don't mean only with work.'

Posie felt trapped, as if all the air in the room was being used up. She rushed on desperately, ignoring him. *Please, not this, not now.*

'Where did Amyas die, sir?' She gestured behind him. 'In there? Was that his office?'

Her eyes darted to the room Lovelace had exited. The closed door.

Lovelace nodded without giving any further explanation. There were muffled banging sounds coming from within which were getting louder now and proving hard to ignore. The scene-of-crime chaps were busy: Posie had seen their ominous black vans parked outside, awkwardly grouped together around the tree at the centre of Old Square.

There had been a man standing under the tree, too, dressed like a tourist in a straw boater hat, watching. You always had weird hangers-on at a new crime scene. Posie had been running in so fast, fearful of being later than she already was, that she hadn't looked at him properly.

But something else was odd here. Why was Lovelace standing, sentry-like, in front of Amyas' office door? Normally Posie would have been given access by now.

'Shall we go in? So I can see the crime scene as it still stands?'

There was a grimness in the Inspector she had never witnessed before. 'No. I don't advise it.'

'Really? That's a first, sir.'

Posie had seen many terrible things. Her work as an ambulance driver on the Western Front during the Great War had toughened her up no end, and she knew Inspector Lovelace normally relied on her for her strong stomach and her nerves of steel.

At his continued silence she shrugged. 'Well, it must be bad, then.'

'Yes, it is. Worst thing I've ever dealt with, Posie. By far. The Forensics chappies are crawling over everything, and Dr Poots the Pathologist is in there now, practically speechless. He concurs: worst scene of crime he's worked on.'

She held her nerve. 'A mess then. Shot gun? Sawn-off barrel? Poor Amyas.'

'I wish it was only that. Although the result's the same: the fella's lost most of his head. No, this was downright nasty. Someone sent Mr Lyle a metal box filled with poison. Of the liquid variety.'

'And he was stupid enough to drink it?'

'No. It was clever. It was white nitric acid. The poison needs to be carried, or diluted, in another liquid in order to work. Simply opening the box on a hot summer's day like yesterday was a death sentence in itself. The stuff is lethal apparently: it reacts with heat. It starts to fizz and foam and causes a loss of consciousness if you as much as catch a whiff, not to mention causing heart and multiple organ failure. Amyas Lyle most likely died in his seat before he toppled head-first into the concoction.'

Posie gasped at the horror of the thing. 'How dreadful.'

'It *is* dreadful. Mr Lyle is barely recognisable, and the wooden office desk he was sitting at has also been burnt away quite fearsomely. It's a bally mess in there.'

Posie fought back unprofessional tears. 'Who found him, sir? It strikes me there's nobody about.'

'George, the Head Clerk. He found Amyas sitting here dead this morning, about seven-thirty. That's when he called us. He's had a helluva shock. I've stationed Sergeant Rainbird with him, in a quiet room along the corridor, with plenty of strong tea and a tot of brandy.'

'And did George know anything about the mysterious box of poison?'

'Yes, he did, as it happens. It came with a note.' And Lovelace flicked open his black leather notebook. 'See here? I copied down the words. Old Poots wouldn't let me take the real note away for love nor money. It was still clamped tightly in Amyas' hand. One of the only things left intact.'

Lovelace moved closer to Posie. So close she could smell the tang of sandalwood shaving soap on his skin.

Posie frowned as she read the short message, uncomprehending.

A lifetime of tears is what you caused me.
A gallon of saltwater will be your undoing.
Just wait and see.

'Tears, sir? A gallon of saltwater?'

She read it again, puzzled. 'I don't understand. What's all this got to do with how Amyas died? With nitric acid?'

'*You* tell me. Although George the Head Clerk said the box smelt of seawater. It's possible that the liquid carrying the nitric acid was exactly that: a gallon of saltwater. We may have a very literal murderer on our hands, eh? But we'll have to wait for the test results. And George says he recognised the black handwriting on the envelope. Apparently Amyas Lyle has been receiving the same notes all year long. We got George to search Amyas Lyle's office with us briefly for any more of the notes, but there was nothing to be found. Nothing personal at all, in fact. We couldn't even find Mr Lyle's wallet or his keys. No safe, no locked cupboard. Bally odd, what?'

Lovelace broke off suddenly as the door to Amyas' office opened again and a party of five gas-masked men in thick oil-cloth aprons stumbled out, carrying black boxes and cases. A police photographer laden down with his camera, tripod and flash equipment, shuffled behind them, shaking his head in disbelief.

Posie craned her neck to see what was happening inside the room. Fat little Dr Poots, immaculate in his usual black suit and red dickie bow-tie, was well known to Posie, and he was pacing back and forth, also masked, shouting at a couple of undertaker's men as they tiptoed about, trying to load their grisly cargo onto a stretcher. Posie was quite relieved she couldn't see the actual corpse, or the desk at which Amyas had been sitting.

She bit her lip nervously.

Inspector Lovelace's voice cut into her thoughts: 'I can't figure you out, Posie, old girl. You seem jittery as hell about this fella's murder but you claim not to have known him well. What's the story? Are you upset at his death? *Personally*, I mean? Too upset to work the case with me?'

'Upset?' Posie thought how the word sounded so trite.

'Golly, of course I'm upset, sir. But most of all I feel *guilty*.'

They turned to watch in respectful silence as the mortal remains of Amyas Lyle were carried solemnly out of the Chambers, the undertaker's men having wrapped the body on the stretcher carefully in black rubber sheeting. From outside in Old Square came the sudden sounds of the slamming of doors, and men shouting. An engine started up, vehicles moved away. Posie peered out, but there was no-one standing under the tree anymore. No more ghoulish spectators.

The Inspector perched against the window-sill, visibly more relaxed now that the body had gone. 'Enlighten me, if you feel you can. Why do you feel guilty?'

Posie sighed, vaguely aware of the Inspector lighting up a Turkish cigarette and taking a deep drag, envious of its easy comfort.

'Yesterday was the first time I'd seen Amyas Lyle in about fifteen years.'

She stopped, but the Inspector stayed silent, smoking out of the half-open window, allowing her time to tell the story in her own way.

'Amyas Lyle was at school with my brother, Richard, but they were never friends. In fact, from what my brother said, I'd be surprised if Amyas Lyle had *any* friends. He was hated, and nicknamed "the Vampire". Amyas was known to be the worst sort of competitive boy: boastful, sneering, not patient of anyone else's weaknesses. He wasn't a boy to work as part of a team; a real loner. It wasn't surprising to my brother that Amyas had set his cap at becoming a barrister, where he could work all alone on legal cases, every day of the year.'

The Inspector raised his eyebrow. 'Your brother seems to have known the murder victim quite well, for one who wasn't his pal. How's that?'

'Every year at the school there were a handful of scholarship boys, perhaps only four or five in total. Boys

19

who were outstandingly clever but whose parents couldn't afford the fees. My brother Richard and Amyas Lyle were both scholarship boys, so they were lumped together for everything, and the hatred grew and grew. You might remember that my father was a none-too-wealthy Vicar, and I believe Amyas' father was a small-time lawyer, but of the provincial sort; certainly not a London lawyer who could afford to pay big fat school fees.'

'So how come *you* met up with Mr Lyle fifteen years ago? A *Romeo and Juliet* story, was it? Similarly ill-fated?'

Posie found she was flushing red; wished she'd had the presence of mind to stick some good thick pan-stick and lipstick on her face before hurrying over.

'Sort of. It wasn't my finest hour, sir, if I'm honest. I literally bumped into Amyas in Cambridge. It was October, some years before the Great War, and I was down with my father visiting Richard at the University for the weekend. I had a couple of hours to myself on the Saturday morning, and I remember I was wearing a new mauve autumn hat and coat, and I felt very grown-up; ready for a romance. I was only eighteen and very impressionable. Richard and Amyas were both almost twenty-one. Impossibly old…'

Her voice tailed off, and Lovelace studied her face, beautiful with not a scrap of make-up on it, and he saw how she was peeling back the years, placing herself back in the surrounds of that Cambridge autumn day.

Posie smiled sadly. 'I was in a bookshop on Trinity Street, Heffers, killing time and sheltering from the rain, when suddenly this wonderfully handsome man with honey-coloured eyes appeared alongside me, and it was Amyas! He asked me to join him for afternoon tea. I felt swept up by the whole thing, like I was a character in a novel. I said yes immediately and then rushed back to my hotel to get ready.'

'Even though your brother hated him?'

'Perhaps *because* of that. Forbidden fruit, you know?

Besides, I said that Amyas was hated, but that was just by the boys at school. He was incredibly handsome, sir. *More* than handsome. I'd always spied him at speech-days and been intrigued. Those sort of dark good-looks don't go unnoticed by bored teenage girls, I can tell you! And when I saw him again in Cambridge he'd grown even more handsome: he looked like a film star. I could see the way other women were looking at him, catching their breath. I wanted to be part of that, no matter his character. To be honest I was flattered he had asked me out. Flattered he noticed me. That he *remembered* me.'

Lovelace grinned. 'So how did it go? This tea with the Vampire?'

'It didn't.'

Posie grimaced. 'That's why I feel guilty. Still. As I was about to leave my lodgings my brother arrived, and upon hearing where I was going, he promptly banned me. Richard went crazy: telling me that Amyas would be the worst thing that ever happened to me, that he had no moral compass, that he held people and their lives very cheaply. That Amyas would ruin me. I didn't understand it at the time and I confess I still don't understand it, but Richard must have had some reason for saying those things, surely? He wasn't the dramatic sort. Richard said he'd send Amyas a note to say I was sick. Looking back I think I should have lied to my brother about where I was going. I'm ashamed to say I regret my honesty.'

'I sense a tragedy looming. Did Richard send the note?'

'No.' Posie shook her head in disbelief. 'I loved my brother, and I miss him terribly now he's gone. But there are one or two things he did which I still can't quite forgive, and *that* is one of them. I'm sure Amyas Lyle had women queuing up left right and centre for his attentions at Cambridge University, but the thought of him standing there, at the Copper Kettle, which is where we agreed to meet, looking up and down King's Parade in the rain, checking his watch, waiting for a silly girl who didn't come… it still makes me feel ashamed.'

She cleared her voice which had gone husky for a second, aware her face was still very flushed and pink. 'I'd hoped, when I saw him yesterday, to try and explain, after all these years, what had happened that afternoon; to apologise for Richard's bad manners. But in those few moments I somehow couldn't bring it up. When Amyas said he wanted to speak to me again about a legal thing, I resolved I would clear it all up when we met again, once and for all. I was supposed to have called his office, you see. It seemed important, almost urgent.'

Lovelace kept his face entirely blank. 'You *do* know that Amyas Lyle was married?'

He looked down again at his notepad, as if checking the price of some rather boring till receipts. 'He married one Antonia Roade. *Lady* Antonia Roade, as was, it says here. She has kept her title. The daughter of Lord Justice Roade, the famous High Court Judge. You'll have heard of him, eh? He's a "hanging" Judge; famous for always whipping out the old black hat and sentencing those found guilty in his Courts to death. Dreadful fella.'

Posie nodded. 'I've heard of him. Hasn't he got some gallows-humour nickname?'

Lovelace grinned. 'You mean "*End of the Road, Roade*"? Yep, that's quite right.' He sighed. 'I gather Lady Antonia is currently in Paris, watching the Olympics with their twin boys. She's been contacted already by one of my lads. We're expecting her back in London this afternoon.'

Posie waited, sensing the Inspector was weighing up some delicate situation.

'I'd like you to be with me when we speak to Lady Antonia. But a word of advice: don't mention the *Romeo and Juliet* connection with her husband, will you? I've been told Lady Antonia is "jittery" by nature, whatever that means. Who knows what sort of state the woman's in after hearing the news this morning? Your little story might just send her over the edge.'

Posie blushed again. 'I didn't mean to rekindle a romance which never was, sir. There was never anything between us; no story, no connection, just one lost encounter. I dare say Amyas Lyle never gave me another thought. Let alone mentioned me to his wife.'

'And the legal thing he wished to speak to you about urgently? What was that?'

'I don't know. But I sensed he needed help.'

'Mnnn.' Lovelace looked thoughtful, and ground out his smoke on the outside window-ledge. 'Could be something, but could be nothing, eh?'

The Inspector sat, cracking each knuckle in turn, a habit he only indulged in at points of the highest tension, and which Posie secretly loathed. 'I've already told you that this is the worst case I've ever dealt with, Posie. But in addition, I'm going to have to work quickly, solve the case neatly. I'm under a certain amount of time pressure from my Superintendent.'

'I'll help you, sir. I owe it to Amyas, and in a way to myself.'

Richard Lovelace fixed Posie with a haunted stare. 'I need to warn you about the level of danger you may be getting yourself into by agreeing to come on board in this investigation, Posie. The person or persons who killed Amyas Lyle have no boundaries. What we are up against here is pure evil. They are not like us, Posie. Are you sure you're still wanting to help?'

But before she could reply, Posie saw Sergeant Rainbird approaching from along the plush-carpeted corridor directly opposite Amyas Lyle's office. He looked flustered and excited, like *he'd* been the one drinking brandy, not providing it.

Rainbird was trailed by a man in a cheap-looking pinstripe; grey, fifty-ish, slightly built with watery blue eyes which roved quickly from Inspector Lovelace to Posie, and back again, as if sensing a trap. Presumably this was the Head Clerk, George. The most noticeable thing about George was a fob-watch which glimmered on a thick gold chain hanging from his pocket.

Both Rainbird and the Head Clerk came to an abrupt stop. Surprisingly, it was the Head Clerk who spoke first, jutting his chin out indignantly:

'Who's this, Chief Inspector? I thought you said we was keepin' people out. Is this the press? A *lady* journalist?' The outrage in his voice was barely concealed, and Posie knew him from that single look. She had met plenty of men like this before, men who felt women should be tied to the hearth and home, and Posie felt a flash of anger towards the man, meeting his affronted stare full-on.

Lovelace smiled. Posie knew this was just what he liked. A bit of non-conformity to shake things up a bit. 'Not the press, no. Miss Parker here is an associate of mine, George. Indispensable, as it happens.'

The rheumy eyes opened wider as they scanned Posie's less-than-immaculate appearance, but before the Head Clerk could speak again the Inspector cut in: 'What are *you* looking so happy about, Sergeant?'

Rainbird grinned. 'I've just taken a telephone call, sir, from the Deputy Head of these Chambers, a Mr Pickle, also a KC. He sounds very upset, sir. He's on his way back here from Eastbourne; he wants to help. Mr Pickle said he'll come in and see you later. In the meantime, he wanted to tell us about some thefts in these offices. Mr Lyle recently told all his staff that they should make their own arrangements for protecting their personal belongings: seems that even the main office safe was compromised. Mr Pickle told me that Mr Lyle commissioned a top carpenter to make a hidey-hole for him in a bookshelf in his office. He used the best marquetry man in London. Chances are high that the keys to Mr Lyle's flat and other personal items were placed in that secret bookshelf before he sat down and died.'

'Before he sat down and was *murdered* you mean, Sergeant. Get your statements correct, man. You'd be hauled up on that in Court, if you were giving evidence. As an *Inspector* I mean. If you ever *do* make Inspector, that is. Which is looking highly unlikely at present…'

Rainbird flushed an unbecoming shade of beetroot red. 'That's what I meant, sir.'

Lovelace raised an eyebrow. 'Well, this secret bookcase sounds interesting. Let's have a look, eh?' He indicated the Head Clerk should come too.

He put his arm out to stop Posie as she started to move. 'No. Not you, Posie. I don't want you in there. It's a bally mess. You've had enough fuel for nightmares to last you a lifetime already. I'm not going to add to that fire. Wait here.'

It was a command, not a polite request. So Posie stared at the honeycomb shelves again and waited in sullen silence.

* * * *

Two

Minutes later the four of them stood grouped on a tiny landing five flights up, as Rainbird noisily rattled and jangled the key in the door to Amyas Lyle's flat. Inspector Lovelace hopped from foot to foot, visibly impatient. He kept checking his wristwatch and tugging at his shirt collar which, when you paid attention, really did look impossibly white and tight, like it had been starched properly. For once.

'Good job we found *something* in that secret compartment downstairs, eh?' he muttered sarcastically to no-one in particular. 'These keys and a coin-purse! What a haul!'

At last the door swung open. Heat spilled out from the flat, and Inspector Lovelace shouldered his way in, beckoning the others to follow. The place was very small and stuffy and with four of them crushed into it Posie had the uncomfortable Alice-in-Wonderland sensation of having just entered a doll's house. Dust motes danced in the bright sunlight.

One long corridor ran on ahead of them, with windows all along one side looking out over Old Square.

Off this corridor to their right were five small, dimly-lit rooms in a row: a kitchen, a bathroom, a bedroom with an immaculate single bed, a dressing room and a study. There was no living room, and while heavy mahogany furniture was squeezed into all the rooms, the place felt bare regardless. There was not a single book or letter or framed photograph in sight. Nothing which spoke of Amyas Lyle himself, let alone the fact that he had a family, children, a life away from the law.

'Place feels like an hotel,' muttered the Inspector, opening up a window and taking deep gulps of the London air as if he were drinking ice-cold water after hours in a desert. 'Or a Club. It's not a permanent home.'

While Rainbird and Lovelace started to search the kitchen, opening drawers and cupboards, Posie turned to the Head Clerk who was hovering unsurely behind them all in the corridor.

'Did Mr Lyle spend much time up here in this flat, George? Or was it just somewhere to sleep on an occasional basis?'

The Head Clerk flashed unhappy eyes over at the Inspector who was coming out of the kitchen, begging *him* to place the questions, rather than Posie.

Lovelace clicked his tongue impatiently. 'Answer her question, man, if you please.'

The Head Clerk coughed. 'Mr Lyle had a family house at Eaton Square, Miss, with his wife and sons. In Chelsea. But if truth be told – and I'm sure you'll find out in the end – he never really spent time there. He was almost always here in Chambers.'

Posie looked about her with fresh eyes while a search of the bedroom was conducted.

'Nothing doing here,' declared Lovelace quickly. 'Let's try the study next, shall we?'

Amyas Lyle's desk dominated the small room, the green-glass reading lamp placed carefully on a leather-tooled writing blotter. A bottle of ink and a fountain-pen stood at the ready but there were no papers or letters or any documents to be seen anywhere. Lovelace sat down gingerly in the dead man's chair.

The Inspector rifled through the drawers. He looked up after a couple of minutes holding onto a small piece of paper. 'I haven't found a Will. But…'

He looked up at Sergeant Rainbird, thrusting the slip of paper towards him. 'This looks promising: it's a docket for legal work done, for *preparing* a Will. Undated. The firm is Pring and Proudfoot on Bedford Row. Can you telephone them and tell them to bring a copy of the murder victim's most recent Will to us?'

Posie stood and watched as Lovelace then pulled out scrap-books from the desk. 'And these look interesting.'

One scrap-book was about Amyas Lyle's legal successes, and a second contained newspaper stories from 1924, British and international in their coverage. Lovelace frowned unhappily at some of the news cuttings as he glanced at them but he slammed the book shut after just a couple of minutes, biting at his lip in a worried way.

'Nothing much here. Seems our murder victim hasn't left anything behind to tell us *who* he really was. I can't get a sense of the man.'

Posie agreed. She was staring around her at the study. It gave her the shivers. She found it a truly depressing place with its dark hues and solid, claustrophobic wood; the only light coming in from a small skylight overhead.

She scanned the walls, depressingly similar to those in Amyas' main study in the Chambers below: legal tomes in matching greens and golds lining the walls in row upon row of endless, unattainable chunks of wisdom and learning. All of these books were now useless to Amyas Lyle. Suddenly two ideas came to her, fully-formed. And Posie was at once certain of the truth of both of them.

Posie turned to face the Head Clerk, the gold of his watch gleaming dully in the dark room. He played with the thick chain in his fingers, feeling its weight over and over. Posie felt suddenly angry. What *exactly* was this man doing here, a party to the police investigation?

She appreciated that Inspector Lovelace and Sergeant Rainbird had seen a shocking thing this morning and were clearly a little out of sorts, but it seemed to her that they were giving the Head Clerk too much licence. She jumped right in:

'Would you say you got on well with Mr Lyle, George?'

George had clearly not been expecting any questions of the sort. The Inspector looked up suddenly, confusion playing on his face. George blustered:

'Of course, I'm very sorry about what has befallen the Master. Mighty sorry indeed. I never thought I'd see the day…'

'You didn't answer my question, George.' Posie shook her head. 'Even a tramp out on the street would be sorry about what has befallen Mr Lyle, but *you* had the experience of working with him, day in, day out. So tell me: did you two get on well?'

George swallowed and gripped his watch. 'I wouldn't say *well*, Miss. But I wouldn't say the Master got on particularly well with anyone, Miss.'

There was more here. Posie knew it, and George knew she knew it. And now she wouldn't let it go. 'There's something else though, isn't there, George?'

Rainbird and Lovelace were now staring over at her as if she had lost her mind.

'You'd had an altercation with Mr Lyle, hadn't you? An argument, recently?'

'How on earth would *you* know that?' George turned puce, and he was breathing in short, snippy little bursts. 'The devil take you, you wretched…'

'Now, none of that, man.' Lovelace was standing up, having closed all the drawers in the desk hurriedly. 'What argument are you talking about, Posie? George, was this some trifling work matter?'

George shook his head, purse-lipped, panic in his eyes. 'It was a mere misunderstanding, sir. A personal clash. It makes no difference to anything we're dealing with now. Believe me.'

Posie laughed in sheer disbelief, turning to address Lovelace. 'I have no proof, Chief Inspector. But I think that Mr Lyle may have sacked George as the Head Clerk. Probably very recently. I'm sure there was some paperwork terminating George's employment lying about and George, on discovering Mr Lyle's death early this morning, has now burnt it, thinking no-one will ever be any the wiser. With Mr Lyle out of the way and their argument literally gone up in smoke George probably thought he could continue to work as Head Clerk, for whoever comes in as a replacement for Amyas.'

Lovelace was gripping the edges of the desk, narrowing his eyes in displeasure. 'Is this true, man?'

The Head Clerk shook his head vigorously. 'Poppycock! I've worked with Mr Lyle ever since he was a mere nipper, when he came here straight from University as a pupil barrister. We've worked together the best part of fifteen years and our working relationship was fine. Why should Mr Lyle want me to *leave* now? As she says, this associate of yours has no proof of anything!'

'That's quite correct,' Posie said sweetly. 'But your time was up. Like it is now.'

She then motioned to the door, catching Lovelace's eye. 'I think that Sergeant Rainbird should escort George downstairs until you are finished here. I don't think George has anything more to add here, sir.'

'Agreed.'

After the two men had left, George indignantly protesting his innocence all the way down the corridor, Lovelace sat down heavily.

He leant back, twining his fingers behind his head, eyeing Posie keenly. 'Care to enlighten me? Because now you've mentioned it I'd say you're absolutely right. That man was guilty as hell about something…'

Posie shrugged. 'Call it a hunch. Something was being burnt in the grate downstairs in the Clerks' Room when I arrived, and George was behaving shiftily. *Something* was up with him. I put two and two together and made five. George was most probably the Chambers' thief.'

'A thief?'

'There had been stealing in the Chambers, hadn't there? People were beginning to hide their valuables, and even, in the case of Amyas, bringing in specialist carpenters to create secret safe places. My guess is that Amyas had realised that George was the thief, and had called him up on it. Maybe he caught him in the act? He probably sacked George, but got the man to continue working on through this holiday, as a punishment. Perhaps in return for Amyas *not* involving the police…'

'I say! But what put you on to it?'

Posie grimaced. 'That awful gold watch. Thieves are usually very good at displaying the fruits of their labours for everyone to see. But you don't need me to tell you that, sir, do you? I'll bet if your lads do a search of George's desk, or even his home, you'll find something there to incriminate him.'

The Inspector laughed knowingly. 'Well, we'll deal with our man George in due course. It's not urgent. I think he's a rogue but I don't think he's our killer, or even the author of these strange notes to Mr Lyle… *if* there are any other notes. If George wasn't lying about that.' Lovelace sighed, exasperated.

'But search me, I just haven't a clue as to where to look.'

'Oh, but *I* have, sir.' And this was the second idea which had come to her. 'Old dogs, sir. Old tricks.'

Posie went over to one of the study walls, where the books ran on in their green rows. She started at the top, tapping, listening for a hollow sound. Five rows down she stopped and turned:

'Here, sir. Doesn't it make sense that Amyas would get that skilful carpenter to come and build a secret compartment up here too? For storing away truly private things?'

The Inspector was on his feet now, bounding furiously across the room, all his senses alert, and within a few seconds of tentative clicking and pushing at the fifth row of books, they succeeded. A whole drawer with an artificial front of book-spines sprang out on new, freshly-oiled runners. It was exquisite work, and nobody – unless they had been forewarned and were looking very, very hard – would have been able to find the hidden drawer. It was large, perhaps two-foot-wide, and at least a foot deep, and it contained two black folders, each stuffed full of paperwork. Underneath them was a vivid red Christmas-edition Peek Frean's biscuit tin.

'By Gad!' exclaimed the Inspector, as he started to lift everything out. 'You've done it, Posie! It should be *you* entering for those Inspector's exams, not Rainbird! Now we might get some clue as to what our fella was really like, and why it is he's been murdered!'

They placed the scarlet Christmas biscuit tin on the desk top, and each took a black folder eagerly in their hands. But before she opened her folder, Posie blurted out a question she had been meaning to ask Lovelace all morning:

'Why *are* you so hard on Sergeant Rainbird, sir? You're constantly nagging at him at the moment. Is it because he isn't Binny?'

She was referring to the ever-capable Sergeant Binny, who had been a favourite of almost everyone, the Inspector included. Binny had died in the line of duty the previous year, and was sorely missed. But before Lovelace could answer, something had fluttered out from the black folder Posie was holding, falling to the floor. And as the Inspector bent to retrieve it, he stopped quite still, startled.

Posie looked over, intrigued, and saw that it was a photograph of a girl. From an age ago, maybe almost twenty years before, when women still dressed in white like romantic, floaty innocents, like princesses in castles who needed rescuing by gallant knights; before the Great War had come and stamped brutally across all those foolish, impractical ideals.

'Who's that? Is she important?'

'You tell me.' Lovelace thrust the image at Posie and she took in the pale, broad straw hat, a white high-necked blouse, froths of lace, a wide smile.

A schoolgirl.

The Inspector coughed delicately. 'I think she was the one our murder victim couldn't forget. Couldn't let go of.'

The photograph was at once familiar and yet horribly out of context. For Posie found her own face was smiling back up at her.

* * * *

Three

'You thought Amyas Lyle never gave you a second thought, didn't you? When you stood him up that time in Cambridge. But you thought wrong,' said the Inspector heavily, as if the weight of his words were almost painful to him. 'Doesn't it mean something that this is the *only* photograph in this flat so far?'

'I gave this to my brother Richard when he was in his final year at Public School. Beats me how Amyas got hold of it.'

Lovelace shrugged. 'He stole it? Paid for it? Who cares, does it matter now?' He was pointing at the same black folder the photograph had come from. 'Come on, then. Let's both of us look at this one together.'

And Posie turned the pages with a trembling hand, a growing sense of dread.

Inside, on page after page, carefully cut out and glued in, were magazine photos and newspaper clippings from the last few years, ever since Posie had become famous. Since she had founded her Detective Agency in Bloomsbury, the Grape Street Bureau.

There were at least a hundred cuttings. And every single one was about Posie.

Beside her, Lovelace whistled. 'By Jove.'

Posie swallowed nervously, remembering Amyas' words of the day before: '*I have followed you, too, Miss Parker.*'

She hadn't thought in a million years that he had meant it so literally. Had this simply been a lonely man's hobby? A harmless fancy? Or was this some kind of crazed obsession? For here were her professional successes, her triumphs, her best cases. The ones which had brought her publicity, and money.

But here too were her personal mistakes. A catalogue of bad choices of men on display, taunting her even now. Here she was photographed in the first year of her Detective Agency with her work partner, the easy-on-the-eye Len Irving, with whom she had enjoyed a few weeks of passion before he had chosen a girl elsewhere.

And then, page after excruciating page showed her photographed with her ex-fiancé, the ill-fated, handsome explorer Alaric Boynton-Dale. Posie felt a sudden piercing stab of futile sadness. Those last cuttings of Posie and Alaric together were from just before Christmas, from a case Posie had worked on in Venice eight months ago. A successful case, but a tragic one, too.

'Enough!'

Posie snapped the black folder shut decisively. She found herself looking hurriedly over at Lovelace, who now passed his hands over his eyes in an incredulous gesture.

'Why is it, old girl, that every time we work on an investigation together, we find the villain of the piece has developed some ungodly obsession with you? You can't keep them away, can you? Are you *sure* you've told me everything you know about Mr Lyle? Because he evidently felt he knew everything about you…'

Posie narrowed her eyes. Anger welled within her like a big, useless, surging bubble.

'What do you want, Richard Lovelace? An apology? Because you won't get one. How was I to know that Amyas followed my cases in this odd way? And what do you mean by calling him a "villain"? Surely you mean "victim"? Get your descriptions right: you were just upbraiding Rainbird for that very same thing downstairs.'

The Inspector grinned and just for a second he looked like a bashful boy, rapped over the knuckles for acting like a complete toe-rag in the classroom. 'You're right. I'm sorry, Posie. This murder seems to have set me right on edge. Of course Amyas Lyle wasn't a villain; he deserves justice, like every other man. But, oh, I don't know... these black folders, the secrecy. Something here doesn't feel right. It all gives me the creeps, to be honest.'

'I agree with you on that, at least, sir. Let's crack on, shall we? See if we can't find the handwritten notes George spoke of?'

'Fine. I'll take this second black folder and you take the Christmas biscuit tin.'

But before Posie had a chance so much as to remove the lid from the biscuit tin, Lovelace had groaned in disbelief. He was only a couple of pages through the second black folder.

'What is it?'

Lovelace didn't answer, but flicked on through all the pages, his mouth a grim line, and his hands tense. Posie couldn't bear it. She was waiting for the inevitable knuckle-cracking to start up again in earnest.

'Come on! What's wrong?'

Lovelace stood up hurriedly, leaving the open folder on the desk, and stalked out into the corridor as if he could no longer breathe the air in the study. He lit up, taking deep drags of his cigarette out of the window. When Posie snatched a look at the open folder he had left behind she could make out nothing more controversial than a formal bank statement on thick blue paper, several dates written down, and names and addresses listed over several sheets of paper. She marched out after Lovelace.

'So? Have you found a suspect for the murder?'

Lovelace shook his head. 'No, not a suspect. But maybe a *reason* for the murder.' He ground out the cigarette on the outside window-ledge. 'I had the feeling our chap wasn't a good 'un from the start. And now I know it for sure. In fact, I'm going to have to hand this particular black folder over to our friends in the Special Branch. Maybe the whole case, in fact…'

'Why?'

'Do you know anything at all about the British Fascist Party?'

'Yes, a bit.'

Posie swallowed, an increasing feeling of foreboding spreading over her. She remembered all too well her trip to Venice the previous November, when Mussolini's Black Shirts had been much in evidence, infiltrating most public positions, swaggering about as if they owned the place in their glittering medals, carrying guns. She shuddered at the memory of the fear they had seemed to instil in the general public in Venice. The fear they had instilled in *her*.

'They're moulding themselves on Mussolini's Italian party, aren't they, sir? But they're mixing up British so-called patriotism and a hatred of the Jews. They're a cursed bunch of idiots, the lot of them. Sinister fools.'

Lovelace rubbed at his eyes wearily. 'Many of the British Fascists' members believe they've simply joined a grown-up version of the Boy Scouts, a patriotic club. Their leader, that strange girl, Rotha Lintorn-Orman, seems to think she's running a scout pack. But you're right: it's sinister. They're no better than pond scum.'

'But what have *they* got to do with Amyas?'

Lovelace emitted a strangled laugh. 'Amyas was in it up to his eyeballs. I *thought* it was odd how much of the news scrap-book we found in his desk was focused on German news, on that lunatic Hitler's trial earlier this year in Munich. It obviously interested Amyas Lyle a great deal.'

'Sir?'

'You didn't follow it? The trial?' At Posie's slight shake of the head the Inspector continued:

'Hitler had been written off as a madman by most country leaders, but in February this year he was put on trial for treason in Germany, and the way he handled himself in the dock showed a mastermind at work. He managed to get all sorts of helpful publicity for his new Nazi party in just a few days. Fascist movements everywhere are now slavishly following Hitler's every move; he's got thousands of new followers, here in Britain especially. Our Special Branch are all a-jitter because of it and they're busy keeping an eye on the British Fascists. From what I've seen in this black folder it seems that Amyas Lyle was giving money to the movement. There are also dates of meetings and names of other members. We've been told by Special Branch to look out for members of the British Fascists in our daily work. And it looks like I've found one, albeit a dead one.'

'Well, you have no choice, sir, do you? You'll just have to hand the file in then, won't you?'

'Yes. I bally well will. When I get a minute.'

They turned back, defeated, into the study and Posie picked up the red enamel biscuit tin and shook it warily, fearful now of what it might contain. The truth about Amyas Lyle was just getting worse and worse.

The Inspector was impatient. 'Don't worry. It's not going to bite you, is it, old girl? Open it up, come on!'

And then he was punching the air jubilantly, and Posie was breathing a sigh of relief. 'The notes! Dash it all!'

The biscuit tin contained a small bundle of the things, all folded over, a pink legal ribbon holding them together.

'These are identical to the note we found with the body downstairs,' enthused Lovelace. 'Same paper, same handwriting. George *was* quite correct on that. Let's have a look at them, then.'

They unfolded the papers carefully. They had been stored by Amyas in chronological order. Each note contained a line, or a paragraph of black, clear handwriting. They had started up in February of this year.

Posie began to read them aloud.

1. *Some secrets last a lifetime.*

2. *Some tears never dry.*

3. *You will pay for what you have done.*

4. *Remember the beach where we used to play? The feel of saltwater on your skin? The sand giving way beneath our feet? The constant danger of slipping in the sea? That's how YOU should be feeling right now.*

Posie looked across at the Inspector, confused.

'These have been sent every month or so, sometimes more, since February. But they're not exactly terrible threats upon Amyas' life, are they? Apart from that third note – about paying for what he's done – they sound more like a trip down memory lane to me. Lyrical, almost…'

The Inspector chewed at his lip. 'Mnnn, I agree. It sounds as if the writer and our murder victim shared a past – a childhood past – or at least a shared reference to a past. It says "*Remember the beach where* we *used to play?*" Interesting. At any rate, it seems to rule out the fascist connection we've just discovered, eh? There's nothing so far accusing him of being a fascist…'

Posie reached for the other notes. She continued aloud:

5. *How can you live with yourself? Do you make anyone happy? Have you ever made anyone happy?*

6. *You will pay for what you have done.*

Posie looked up sharply. 'Same words were used in a note before, sir. Obviously, our writer felt it was a point worth hammering home.'

'Obviously.'

40

She read on:

7. *She never stopped thinking about you. You cold-hearted excuse for a man. You don't deserve to live. You won't live.*

8. *You'll be better off dead. Drowned like the rat you are, in a vat of tears.*

Posie felt chilled to the bone. She looked at the Inspector who was standing with his arms crossed, visibly shaken.

'Scrap what I said earlier,' Posie said in a solemn, humbled voice. 'These aren't friendly, lyrical little reminiscences. They had turned into full-on death threats by the end, especially that note: "*You don't deserve to live. You won't live.*" And I don't think there's any doubt at all that the writer of these is the same person who sent that note about saltwater yesterday, and who actually *caused* Amyas to be killed by using nitric acid.'

The Inspector agreed: 'I'd say no doubt at all. Although our handwriting expert and Forensics team will check, just to be sure. You're right that they aren't friendly by the end, but they *do* seem to be remembering a very personal past. There's even mention of a woman: "*She never stopped thinking about you.*"'

The Inspector started to pace up and down. 'I wonder *who* that woman was? A scorned lover? A wronged female client? Could these be from a man who loved the woman Amyas wronged in some way?'

Posie shrugged. 'Why are you assuming the writer – and the killer – is a man? It could very well be a woman. Aren't something like seventy per cent of poisoners found to be women, sir?'

Lovelace looked uncomfortable. 'Well, yes, as a matter of fact that's absolutely right. This just seems like a man's crime, somehow. That fish-box, the use of the Porter. The fizzing poison…'

'I don't think we can guess at this stage, sir. What I

find interesting is the reference the writer is making to what Amyas is meant to have done wrong. Is it *one* thing? There's reference to paying for "*what you have done*". Which implies it was one act.'

'True.'

For the first time that morning the familiar crackle of energy which usually accompanied their working relationship sparked again. It felt to Posie that finally she and Lovelace were standing looking at this appalling murder in the same way, as a team.

Posie picked up the red Peek Frean's biscuit tin again, to replace the notes inside it. 'Oh, hullo, what's this, then?'

Inside the lid, taped on with an adhesive plaster, was a black-and-white picture postcard. In their excitement they had missed it entirely.

The Inspector took the lid and narrowed his eyes, studying the postcard without removing it. 'Foreign-looking place, is it? Marrakesh? Israel, or Greece?'

Together they saw an impressive high dome-like structure on the postcard, bright white and exotic, with flags dotted all about it. But the bottom half of the structure was just a normal building, with a chain of cafés and shops set into it, facing a promenade, with a man standing nonchalantly in the foreground.

'No, it's not a foreign place,' Posie said softly. She had seen the tiny sign for an electric cinema, and the familiar triangular symbol of a Lyons Corner House. She knew the Inspector was short-sighted and that he was doing his best not to wear the spectacles he had been prescribed, a touching stab of vanity in a man who you would never have expected it from.

'It's here, in England. Sure as bread is bread.'

Posie's stomach fluttered with dread and she felt the trust they had just built up slipping suddenly away again, and there was nothing she could do about it. 'If you look at the small writing beneath the image you'll see it says "THE SPANISH CITY–WHITLEY BAY".'

Lovelace looked up, askance. 'Whitley Bay? Up in the north? Near Tyneside?'

'The very same.'

'Why on earth?'

'Whitley Bay is a popular seaside resort now, sir. The Spanish City is its crowning glory. It's got a ballroom and cafés and a cinema and a music-hall theatre all tucked away inside it. It was re-opened just a couple of years back, to give a bit of glamour to the north. It's quite the thing.'

The Inspector laughed bitterly. 'You don't say. We usually just stayed down in Kent for our holidays, Molly and me; did a bit of shrimping at Herne Bay. Nothing adventurous, nothing which was "quite the thing". Although Molly did once talk of wanting to go up to Scarborough…' He looked away, lost in another time and place, a time before last year, to when his wife had still been alive. He coughed in embarrassment and looked up at Posie slowly, making a connection.

'Hang on a minute. Weren't *you* about to go on holiday to Whitley Bay yourself?'

The flutter in the stomach again. 'Yep, that's right. Tomorrow, in fact. I told Amyas Lyle that exact same thing only yesterday. But there's no connection from my side. This image could just be a coincidence. I asked him yesterday if he knew Whitley Bay.'

'And?'

'He said he didn't. But I felt at the time he was acting oddly when he replied, lying perhaps.'

The Inspector stared at Posie a fraction of a second too long, then jemmied the postcard away from the lid with his fingernail. He flipped the postcard around. It was blank, save for a postmark showing 'WHITLEY BAY' and with a typed address for Amyas Lyle's offices in Lincoln's Inn.

'No message on it. No proof it's from the person who sent the notes. It's just an empty card, which means nothing,' said the Inspector with some disappointment. He squinted at the postmark. 'This was sent one month ago.'

Posie took the postcard and studied it again. 'Maybe the picture *itself* was a message to Amyas? Surely the fact he's stored it in the same place as the notes means *something*? Although I haven't a clue *what*. What are you doing now, sir?'

Lovelace was suddenly pulling something else from the tin lid, something which had been taped *underneath* the postcard; a tiny, barely bigger than a stamp-sized note, folded tight, over and over. 'This tin is like pass-the-parcel,' he muttered beneath his breath, but with a barely-supressed flicker of excitement. 'Now, what do we have here?'

It was another note. But on a different, lightweight paper. The writing was different from the saltwater notes. It was Amyas Lyle's crabbed black handwriting, familiar from his paperwork in the desk. It was headed 'SUSPECTS – THOSE WHO COULD HAVE SENT ME THE THREATS'.

'Oh, sir,' breathed Posie in rising excitement. 'This could be a break-through, of sorts. Don't you think? The dead man speaks, and all that guff?'

'Hold your horses, old girl. But yes, it could be just what we've been hoping for. I've felt like I've been bridled on this case so far. Can't even get a feel for the victim as a person properly. This could show us what Mr Lyle made of things himself. And whatever he was, he certainly wasn't stupid.'

He caught his breath, running ahead of himself. 'Now, let's have a look. Let's find out what our dead man says.'

* * * *

Four

Amyas Lyle's memo to himself was short, and surprising.

SUSPECTS - those who could have sent me the threats

1. Sawbones Bill

2. Antonia - because of FEVER STREET?

3. SELWYN

4. GEORGE - upbraided him, bears a grudge

5. Whitley Bay?

Posie looked up, having read the memo over a few times to herself. She saw that Lovelace was copying it into his own pad.

'Does any of this mean anything to you?' she said, frustrated. 'Apart from the reference to Whitley Bay, of course. So we were right about *that*, at least; the postcard had got him worried somehow.'

Lovelace was still scanning the list, as if reading it for the umpteenth time might produce something certain. He raked through his red hair. 'Nope. I can't add much. Other than "Antonia". The murder victim's wife is an Antonia, isn't she? Lady Antonia, formerly Roade.'

Posie's eyes opened wide in surprise. 'So Amyas suspected his own *wife* of this malarkey? These odd threats? That can't be right, sir!'

Lovelace almost grinned. 'Now, now. You were the one telling me to keep an open mind about a female murderer. And you know the statistics as well as I do, Posie. Ninety-five per cent of murderers are closely related to their victims, and a wife couldn't be a closer relation, could she? We'll have to ask the wife about Fever Street too,' he went on, eagerly, 'whatever *that* means.' He was noticeably happier than before, convincing himself of the slightly firmer ground they were now able to stand upon.

He started to put everything into a large brown 'EVIDENCE' bag.

'I wonder, sir,' said Posie thoughtfully, 'do you think the reference to a "George" could mean the Head Clerk downstairs?'

Lovelace looked startled. 'Perhaps. But George is a mighty common name, you know. It doesn't necessarily follow.'

Posie shrugged. 'Look at the language Amyas used in this note. He said he'd "upbraided" George. Not that he'd confronted him, or taken him to task. The use of "upbraided" to me seems to suggest someone of a lower class. A servant perhaps. Or his Head Clerk.'

Lovelace sealed the bag. 'Well, maybe you're right: maybe Amyas did think George was threatening him. But even if he *was*, I'd wager he's an unlikely murder suspect. It's a big jump, isn't it, from sending threats to actually killing someone in cold blood. We'll follow it up later, I promise. After we've grilled the wife. That's who *my* money's on.'

Just then the outside door to the flat banged open.

Sergeant Rainbird put his head around the study door. In his hands he held two bacon rolls. The smell wafted temptingly across at them.

'Two things, sir. I've had confirmation by telegram that the victim's wife will be returned home from France this afternoon. She's asked you to visit her at Eaton Terrace at four o'clock.'

Lovelace grinned. 'With pleasure.' Now that he had a real-life suspect and a real-life interview lined up he was like a nervy terrier with a hot scent to follow. 'And the second thing?'

'I've been speaking to the Deputy Head of Chambers again, that Mr Selwyn Pickle, sir. He's arrived at his London home and says he needs to freshen up and then he'll come to Scotland Yard to speak to you there. He suggested one o'clock.'

'Selwyn?' Lovelace looked at Posie. 'Well, well. That was one of the suspect's names on the list, wasn't it? Good. *They're* coming to us.'

He looked at his watch. It was eleven already. 'Perfect. Perhaps Mr Pickle can fill me in on the character of the deceased. And I'll show him a copy of that interesting list Mr Lyle had drawn up; see what he has to say for himself, and what he has to say about the others on the list. Rainbird, can you take this evidence bag over to the Yard, and give it to the Forensics lads? But make sure you take a copy of everything first. I don't want any of this stuff going walkies. It's more than your Inspector's exams are worth, my lad.'

'Will do, sir. I'll keep everything safe.'

Posie took both bacon rolls from the Sergeant and he took the evidence bag and scuttled off. Posie ate her roll in a trice, licking her fingers and trying not to drip bacon fat and butter down her silk dress which was already in quite a state. She would have handed the second roll over but the Inspector was opening and closing the desk drawers again, chattering as he worked:

'You'd better join me today, Posie. Come at one o'clock for the interview with this Selwyn Pickle fella. We can then go through any new leads, following which we can get a lift across to Chelsea to speak to Lady Antonia at four. Suit you?'

'Certainly. And I was thinking, sir, you keep saying you can't get a hold of what Amyas was really like as a person. Well, maybe Rufus could help us out? He knew Amyas at school and I daresay they were still in touch: they're probably the only boys from their class who survived the Great War. And I know for a fact that Rufus is in town, he's at the House of Lords all week. I'm sure he'd be willing to help us. I'll send him a telegram.'

'Yes, do.'

Lovelace was pleased, for the person Posie spoke of was worlds away from being a usual contact for a policeman to have on his books, and Posie was the useful entry into this world. Rufus was Rufus, Earl of Cardigeon, and Posie was often to be found in the company of Rufus' wife, Dolly. In fact, she had been dancing with her at the Ritz the night before. All night long.

What Posie *didn't* mention to Lovelace was that Rufus and Dolly's marriage appeared to be heading for troubled waters, and that Dolly was desperately unhappy at the man Rufus was becoming, both at home and in the House of Lords: a conceited, self-important, conservative, self-centred so-and-so, with not one iota of pity or understanding for those born less fortunate than himself. The kind of man Dolly would have run many, many miles from in the past.

Posie realised the Inspector was speaking to her now, and she dragged herself back to the present with an effort.

'Sorry?'

'I was saying you'd better get yourself smartened up, Posie. *I* don't mind if you look like you've been out on the razz all night, but it might not set the right tone with Lady Antonia. Or with the Earl of Cardigeon.'

Posie gaped. Lovelace had never spoken to her in such

patronizing tones before. *Who did he think he was?* Treating both her and Sergeant Rainbird like glorified skivvies... The cheek of it! She had come here as fast as she could, answering what had been described as an urgent call, and this was the thanks she got.

She bit into the second bacon roll savagely, and turned on her heel, grabbing up her carpet bag. She caught a brief impression of the Inspector's surprised face as she went. As Posie marched along the corridor with its big windows and stuffy heat, she heard him call out behind her:

'See you at one o'clock, Posie. And maybe you can tell me then just why it is that you're off to Whitley Bay. You know I'm not one for believing in coincidences!'

But she didn't bother to reply.

* * * *

Five

Posie stood on the small blue-carpeted landing outside her office on Grape Street, three floors up, steeling herself to go in. She'd come back from Lincoln's Inn at a brisk trot, hoping to walk off her anger in the ten minutes it took her, but all she'd done was work up an unattractive sweat. Not wanting to waste time by going home, she'd dunked her face under the cold tap in the tiny office bathroom on the landing and hoped for the best.

In days which seemed long gone she'd not have cared two hoots who saw her in last night's clothes, but the new Posie felt sadder, wiser. Definitely older.

'Thirty-three this coming birthday,' she muttered to herself with some distaste. 'Oh, just grow up!'

She pushed at the office door with its frosted glass window but, to her surprise, found it locked. Relieved, she dug around for her keys and passed through the empty client waiting room, making for her own private office at the back.

The air here, as everywhere, was hot and stuffy. A blue glass vase of past-their-best roses, bought off a barrow last week, added a pungent note. Posie hoisted up the double sash windows behind her desk, sending a group of pigeons who had been taking advantage of the shade of the window-ledge soaring skywards.

The view from Posie's office window was nothing special. In fact, it was dull as ditch-water, with its vista of three sides of tall grey office-backs, fire-escapes and sooty chimneys; ringed around a scrubby courtyard where office workers huddled together on coffee breaks, smoking and laughing, calling out to each other or sometimes singing snatches of music-hall songs. When Posie had first come to London from Norfolk, in 1921, using up the tiny amount of money her dead father had left her to establish the Grape Street Bureau, this office had seemed a paradise. A refuge, a haven. And a way forwards.

The grey urban view from this window, so different from the open sky, rolling green fields and golden shores which Posie had seen out of the Norfolk Rectory windows almost her whole life, represented a complete change, and a welcome one at that. Even now, three years on, with the Detective Agency a force to be reckoned with, not to mention money and a successful reputation under her belt, Posie still felt a thrill of appreciation when she looked out of this window.

London, all before her, in all its guises. London, which stood for opportunities, for luck and for changes; for independence, and for a future beyond that dreadful war they had all had to go through.

Posie sighed. She felt hot and cross and sad.

London held no future now for Amyas Lyle. No more luck, or change, or opportunities for *him*. Someone had taken it upon themselves to snuff out all the talent, all the fame, all the complexity -both good and bad- that had been Amyas Lyle.

Posie was on her hands and knees now, grimly determined, pulling out the contents of a small cupboard under her desk. Here she kept a few changes of clothes for different occasions, and a bag with a bit of make-up and hair pomade. In the past, when he'd first known her, Len Irving, her now-partner in the Detective Agency, had referred to Posie keeping a 'glamour-attack' in here, as she'd normally kept a set of stunning evening clothes on hand, just in case she was asked out, or had to work over dinner.

Things were different now. Quite the reverse, in fact. And Posie sighed wistfully as she slipped out of her dirty silk sheath dress and stepped into a beautifully-cut but plain emerald silk shirt-dress, a row of smart gold buttons down the front the only decoration. She thrust her feet into matching dark jade t-bar shoes and huffed as she clipped on green paste earrings, which pinched atrociously.

'Smart enough now for you, Richard Lovelace?'

Bright red lipstick followed, and exaggerated eye-black. Attacking her very short dark hair with a steel comb, she patted wax onto the shingled curls. She finished off with a large squirt of Parma Violet: no other jewellery, not one ring. Outside in the main office she heard the door swing open.

'Posie? That you?'

Len Irving tapped lightly at her door, then stuck his head in. 'I just nipped out for cakes. But what with it being the holidays and all, Lyons only had a small selection. Come and join me. Prudence is in the kitchen putting the kettle on.'

Posie made a moue of discontent; she didn't really have time to be sitting around eating cakes. But then she made up her mind. The day when she didn't have time to eat cakes with her office colleagues and employees was a very grim one.

'Just coming.'

The area they used as a client waiting room consisted of two settees and two armchairs, all grouped around a low coffee table which held a selection of popular magazines and at least one newspaper. The fireplace behind them was used all through winter, but now someone – probably Prudence – had put a large woven basket containing dried flowers in the empty grate.

Posie sank down on one of the sofas just as Prudence Smythe, their office secretary, entered with the tea-things. Len had opened all the windows in pursuit of air and then thrown himself down opposite Posie on the other sofa. He tore open the striped blue Lyons paper bag in silence, and cleared a space on the table for Prudence to put down the teapot and cups.

'There!' Len grinned, a mischievous energy playing over his devilishly handsome tanned face, his light green eyes alight with happiness. He shook out his purchases as Prudence perched on an armchair and silently poured out the teas. Two fancy iced biscuits featuring a red Eiffel Tower and two iced biscuits with the Olympic symbol of five interlinked multi-coloured rings clattered onto the big shared dinner-plate.

'If we can't be in Paris at the Olympics, let's go for the next best thing, eh, and celebrate anyway?'

He then shook out a few more iced biscuits in the shape of bright yellow gold medals.

'See? I was saving the best for last. These are to celebrate good ol' Harold Abrahams winning the gold medal last night for Britain! Talk about a wonder – the under-dog beating all the favourites, especially the Yanks – in the 100 metres dash! Wish I'd been there to see it. I was listening on the radio, though. My Aggie couldn't tear me away from our wireless set, even for my supper. I felt like I was running along *with* Abrahams, and I was that excited and exhausted by his victory I couldn't manage more than a few mouthfuls of my shepherd's pie when I eventually did sit down to eat!'

Posie laughed despite herself and crunched down on a gold medal. Len was sports mad, but even if you weren't, news of the summer Olympics being held in Paris was splashed all over central London; on news-stands and in newspapers. There were boys shouting on street corners about it. You couldn't avoid it, even if you tried. The newspaper on their own coffee table, *The Times*, carried only news about the winning of the gold medal. The attempts by the runners Harold Abrahams and the Scot, Eric Liddell, to win a medal at the Olympics were being followed avidly by the nation. In particular, Eric Liddell's strictly religious stance which had led him to refuse to run on a Sunday, had become the tea-room chatter up and down the country.

Len slurped his tea: 'By Jove, what I wouldn't have given for a ticket last night. But I'll be listening in again on Friday evening, when Liddell is running in the 400 metres. Maybe God really does have a plan for him: needed him to rest up good and proper last Sunday, eh? So he could save his energy for Friday's races…'

At Prudence's rather scandalised look, he changed the subject quickly and looked pointedly at his business partner. 'You look jolly nice, Posie. Someone lucky taking you out for lunch, are they?'

Posie finished off her tea and shook her head. 'No. *This* will be my lunch, and a dashed good one too. I'm off to meet the Inspector at the Yard, on a rather horrible new murder case. Not that *he's* in my best books just now.'

'What's the problem? The Inspector and you are normally thick as thieves.'

'Let's just say he's not in the most favourable of moods today: biting heads off left, right and centre. He ought to be careful; he'll have no-one left working for him at this rate. I don't know what's the matter.'

'Poor man,' muttered Prudence, half to herself and half to Posie. She rose, rather self-righteously, brushing crumbs off her unfashionably long black skirt, which looked hot for a summer's day. 'It's barely been seven months since the loss of his wife, Molly. Who knows what's the matter with him? Maybe it's an important day today. His wife's birthday? Or a wedding anniversary? You'd do as well to remember that, Miss Parker. I do realise we have all lost people important to us recently, but *some* of us seem to cope better than others, don't we?'

And Prudence turned quickly on her heel, crashing out and slamming the office door loudly behind her. She could be heard lumbering heavily down the stairs.

Len got to his feet, unsure whether to follow Prudence or not, but stayed rooted to the spot. He exhaled, slowly:

'What the deuce was that all about? So, yes, we all know that poor old Lovelace lost his wife in that bally house fire.' He coughed self-consciously. 'And you lost Alaric, but who on earth has Prudence lost? And why's she so narky with *you* all of a sudden, Posie?'

Posie chewed at her lip, dismayed. 'I suppose she means she's lost Sergeant Binny. Don't you think?'

Prudence had never been much fun, but in the last year Posie and Len had seen a sweeping change come over the prim, efficient secretary: a sadness which couldn't be shaken off; a snappishness at work and a shortness with clients and the young, enthusiastic office boy, Sidney. In the busyness of their own lives – and their own problems – they hadn't addressed the problem of Prudence, letting it simmer on.

Posie nodded now, certain of her ground. 'There was a photograph of Binny on her desk for a while. About a year ago. I never questioned her about it. It vanished after his death last July.'

There had been the glimmer of a plain gold ring, too. Worn for just a couple of weeks on Prudence's wedding ring finger. And that had been about a year ago, too. Posie had seen it at the time, but not commented on it, conscious of Prudence's very private personality; waiting for her secretary to share her good news at the right time. But that right time had never come.

'I think they may have been briefly engaged. Do you remember how Prudence was acting at Binny's funeral, Len? Like she could barely support herself? They hadn't announced it yet, I'm guessing, and she didn't feel she could speak of it when he died. Perhaps she felt people wouldn't believe her? Sergeant Binny was rather a dashing lad, wasn't he? And Prudence is just, well, *Prudence*.'

'Poor old sausage.' Len grimaced. 'She's only got her old mama, hasn't she? And *she's* an invalid. Old Binny must have been the answer to all her dreams. And then he was snatched away so cruelly. It accounts for the awful black clothes she wears, day-in, day-out. And have you noticed she seems to have lost a lot of weight, too? Those widows' weeds positively hang off her...'

Posie sniffed pointedly. The subject of weight – weight loss in particular – was an uncomfortable one to her. As each year crept by, she seemed to have grown ever more voluptuous, and her twice-yearly visits to her dressmakers seemed to involve ever more instances of lettings-out of the seams of her existing clothes and slightly larger, more forgiving choices of patterns and materials for her new clothes.

Seeing his error, Len rushed on: 'At the end of the day, it's a shame. But these sad things happen. We all have our lonelinesses, don't we? Doesn't explain why she's so mad at *you*, does it?'

Posie shrugged. 'I suppose Prudence thinks I don't mourn Alaric enough, that I'm not clad often enough in black for him, maybe? I know she idolised him, had a bit of a pash on him. She loved that whole fame thing. Whenever she came across a picture or an article about Alaric in a newspaper, she cut it out for one of her dashed scrap-books.'

For a fleeting yet vivid moment Posie thought about Amyas Lyle, and *his* scrap-book about her, which had made her feel so uncomfortable. That too had also contained pictures of Alaric.

'Prudence always blushed like crazy whenever she answered the telephone and the Operator announced his name, or when Alaric called here… but it's not as if I killed him, for goodness' sake. Or that it was even my fault. And it's not as if I don't mourn Alaric. In my way.'

Len placed an arm on Posie's sleeve. 'Let it go, old thing. In truth she shouldn't have spoken to you like that. You're her employer, after all. And we should haul her over the coals for it. But we'll let it pass: give Prudence the benefit of the doubt. Let's see where we are at the end of the year, eh? If she's still not happy working here we can get another gal.'

Posie looked doubtful but Len carried on: 'I've a client coming in, in twenty minutes,' he grinned wolfishly, 'and I need to tell him his wife is definitely doing the dirty on him, with a work colleague, no less! I've got the photographs to prove it. But before he comes, do tell me about this horrible new murder case of yours.'

And so Posie found herself telling Len all about her morning, and Len exhaled in disbelief as Posie dug around in her carpet bag, bringing out her silver notebook, flicking through to the page where she had copied down Amyas Lyle's own list of suspects. She thrust it at Len who read it quickly.

Posie sighed. 'We really need a break-through with this list. At the moment it could be written in Russian for all I understand of it!'

She was just putting the notebook away when Len grabbed her by the hand. 'Hang on a minute.'

He looked excited. 'Show me that list again.'

Posie obediently dug out her copy of Amyas' list. Len stabbed at it vigorously. 'Fever Street,' he said, nodding with certainty to himself.

'You know it?' Posie had never heard of it before. She watched as Len ran to his own office, and came back clutching at a worn and grubby map of central London, held together along its waxy seams with an assortment of tapes and sticking-plasters.

'I'll say I know it!' Len was a shadower, responsible for photographing and documenting evidence of adultery for divorce cases so that they could proceed to Court. Lucrative work, if immoral and slightly grubby. But work which had kept the Grape Street Bureau going through several lean patches, and work which Len obviously relished.

He stabbed at a tiny street on his map.

'It was your mention of things *Russian*, which did it for me! It's more of a courtyard, really. A set of mews houses all facing each other. Fever Street! There it is! SW1! It's off a little hidden lane, just opposite Hyde Park, near Hyde Park Tube Station. It's dashed convenient, handy for the city and yet very discreet. I've been there a few times on a job, but not for a while now.'

Posie raised her eyebrows quizzically.

Len nodded. 'Time was, and for some still *is*, that every self-respecting gentleman in London of a certain means and status kept a mistress there.'

'A mistress?'

'Yep. A Russian mistress, actually. Fever Street is part of a very chic Russian enclave, and it's well known that Russian mistresses are the most beautiful and the most in demand in London. Not to say the most loyal and faithful, in their way: strictly loyal to the man who keeps them, and keeps them in style. Oh, yes, *I* know Fever Street. And so did your Amyas Lyle, by the sounds of it.'

Posie tried not to look too shocked. 'And so too did his wife, if this list is anything to go by. It sounds as if maybe Lady Antonia had found out about the mistress he kept there?'

Len clicked his tongue triumphantly. '*That's* a real motive for murder, isn't it? Jealousy. The old green-eyed monster. Pure and simple.'

But Posie shook her head as she watched Len begin to clear away the tea-things. '*Nothing* about this case is pure or simple. Unfortunately.'

And now there was someone else to consider, someone else who probably didn't yet know that Amyas Lyle was dead. Someone who might, even now, be waiting for him on Fever Street. Relying on him…

Back in her office, and collecting her carpet bag and her raincoat and umbrella, Posie took a final moment to stare out of the window, before she re-entered the hustle and bustle of the outside, everyday world. She heard the gravelly rumble of Len's client's voice, just arrived, in his office next door. She thought about the bad news Len would be imparting in just a matter of minutes, and the end result: another lonely, single person in London, wondering where it had all gone wrong, and why. She rubbed at her eyes wearily.

What was it that Len had said? '*We all have our lonelinesses, don't we?*'

Well, that was true enough. Perhaps even Len, apparently happily married and with two small children in tow, felt the odd moment of doubt and disbelief and yes, loneliness. Prudence obviously felt lonesome, as did Dolly Cardigeon, a woman who seemingly had it all: untold wealth and a title and husband and children.

And Posie too. She was all alone. Alone with the shadows of men dead and gone.

She had come to London, rather like Dick Whittington, with just a cat for company, but now that cat – a relic of her past with her father at the Norfolk Rectory – was gone, too.

Mr Minks, the haughty and completely spoiled Siamese – who had refused to lodge with Posie at her flat in Museum Chambers, and had lived a life of glorious isolation in the office – had vanished at Easter time. He had been a very elderly cat, not prone to adventures out of windows and doors, but nonetheless, Posie, Len, Prudence and Sidney had searched the vicinity of Bloomsbury for days looking for him. Fly posters advertising a small reward for finding

Mr Minks, or for news of him, had been pasted about by a woeful Sidney, but there had been no news and no answers.

A few weeks after the disappearance of the cat, late one afternoon as Posie was packing up to go home, Sid had hung behind, bashfully leaning on the doorframe to her office.

'What is it, Sidney? Anything wrong? Len treating you quite all right, is he?'

'Oh, yes.' The boy had turned his tweed cap over and over in his hands in a way which had made Posie quite unaccountably irritated.

'So what is it?'

'It's about the cat, Miss. I jus' wanted to tell yer somethin'.'

A horrible pregnant pause. 'Oh, yes?'

'I know you is sad, Miss. What with losin' your fiancé, and now the cat. It mus' seem an unlucky patch for yer, Miss.'

'Well…'

'I heard it said, Miss, that when a cat is ready to die, it jus' takes itself off, Miss. Doesn't want to bother anyone. It's had its time. So don't be sad. It was probably jus' time. Everything has its time, innit? You gotta be kind to yourself now, Miss.'

And with this pearl of wisdom dutifully delivered, the teenage Sidney had hurried off.

Posie smiled now to remember this. *Out of the mouths of babes*, she had thought at the time, and she thought it again now.

The cat never came back: Mr Minks had had his time.

And all those others who had been lost had had their time, too, by the same reckoning. Posie willed herself to be kinder now, not only to herself but to everyone. To be nice to Prudence when she saw her next; to ask her about Sergeant Binny – and give Prudence's mourning some sort of outlet. She willed herself to be kind to Inspector Lovelace, too, even if he was acting oddly.

Posie pulled herself together: she had a telegram to send and a public library to visit *en route* to Scotland Yard, and she'd not let herself down again in the Inspector's eyes.

She had to be a first-class professional, through and through.

* * * *

Six

Perhaps it was because of his comic-sounding name, but Posie had expected Mr Pickle to be a funny sort of fellow, a larger-than-life Englishman. But she couldn't have been further from the truth.

Mr Selwyn Pickle, KC, was an oily-looking gingery man, short and troll-like, with a big, bald head which seemed to crane forwards on a reed-thin neck. He wore gold-rimmed spectacles on his shiny nose and he was immaculate in off-duty linen. He had an edgy, nervy manner, and Posie had to keep reminding herself that here was one of the very best legal minds in the country.

She'd looked him up in the *Who's Who* in the public library on the Theobalds Road on her way here: it made sense to know who you were dealing with in advance.

Pickle was apparently fifty years old, had attended Westminster School and then Oxford. He was married with two grown-up sons. He had been a barrister for the best part of thirty years, becoming a King's Counsel three years previously; the same year Amyas Lyle had also been given the honour. Pickle was from a family of barristers; had been destined for the job. He practised criminal law – as did all of the lawyers at 20 Old Square – but clever, up-market criminal law: mainly defending very rich men accused of hiding money in clever places, like Amyas had done. Pickle had obviously done very well for himself, both professionally and financially.

But not as well as all that, perhaps? Selwyn Pickle was a good fifteen years older than Amyas Lyle had been. Had it galled him to see the much younger, more brilliant man rise to the top and become famous, running the Chambers he was the mere Deputy of?

Now they were all sitting at a round, polished table with a vase of shop-bought flowers and a box of expensive cigarettes placed at its centre, in a room reserved for meetings of Scotland Yard's most exalted guests. It was a clever touch on Inspector Lovelace's part, Posie thought to herself: it felt like a meeting of equals, not an interview at all.

Posie sat next to Selwyn Pickle, and on Pickle's other side sat Detective Constable Fox, a lean, blonde wolf-hound of a young man, all aquiver for his next promotion; his police notepad and pen held pristine and at the ready. It was his job to make the official transcript of the meeting.

Chief Inspector Lovelace sat almost opposite them, and next to him sat Inspector Oats, a man Posie hated with a passion, although she knew the feeling was mutual and Oats was eyeing her with a look of barely-concealed contempt. Posie presumed that given the seniority of their guest, two police Inspectors were called for to attend. She couldn't explain Oats' noxious presence otherwise.

Posie had simply been introduced as an undercover associate of the police, and Pickle had seemed to accept this, although not without giving Posie a slightly incredulous stare from the keen eyes which sparkled behind his round glasses.

'Forgive me for the delay.' Lovelace smiled, shuffling papers, but indicating he was ready to begin. 'It's a pretty dreadful business, all of this.'

'Absolutely, I can't quite believe it,' said Pickle. His voice was surprisingly rich and smooth for such a small man, like melting chocolate. He hadn't asked permission to smoke, but had helped himself to a cigarette from the box on the table. And now coils of thick grey smoke were wreathing upwards in the hot little room.

'As I said to your Sergeant,' and here he looked over at Constable Fox, who looked pleased as punch at the mistake, 'on the telephone this morning, I'll do anything in my power to aid you. I came up to London straight away. I couldn't have stayed on in Eastbourne, not after what's happened to poor Amyas. Your Sergeant told me about the manner of the murder, too. Absolutely dreadful.'

He shook his head in bewilderment. 'What a way to go! It beggars belief. The audacity of the thing. I was telling my youngest son, Robin – he's in his final year of Chemistry at Oxford – about it. Actually, we have a small working chemistry laboratory at our house here in London. It's a sort of hobby and we often conduct experiments, as a way of spending time together, really. We were just saying on the way up here that anyone could make up a batch of nitric acid, but only a madman or a devil would try and use the end result on a living human being!'

Pickle blew a surprisingly perfect smoke ring. 'I have to go to 20 Old Square after this, get things in order, you understand. I'm now *acting* Head of Chambers, but I'll need to call an extraordinary meeting and try and get all our barristers to return from holiday and vote on whether to swear me in permanently, so to speak…'

Ah, thought Posie. *So here was the real reason Pickle had been so anxious to return to town. Professional ambition, not a duty to help the police find Amyas' killer, after all.*

He wants to be sworn in permanently…

But was naked ambition enough to want a man dead? Was Selwyn Pickle, as Amyas Lyle had jotted down in his biscuit tin list, really now a full-blown suspect in a murder investigation?

'Of course.' Lovelace smiled reassuringly. 'We hope we won't keep you that long, sir. Thank you for your help so far. We would have been simply *forever* looking for Amyas' personal belongings and keys if you hadn't told us about the hidden bookshelf in his office.'

Pickle inclined his head silently in acknowledgement.

The Chief Inspector rushed on: 'Bally strange business, what? All very cloak and dagger. You mentioned in your telephone call that there had been thefts at 20 Old Square recently?'

'That's right. It had been going on since the start of the year, actually. It was money mainly, cash here and there. And costly items too: a fob-watch, an expensive set of jewelled cufflinks, a solid silver photo-frame...' And here the barrister suddenly swivelled around and stared for a second at Posie before turning back again, looking slightly confused.

Lovelace smiled. 'I see. And has the spate of thefts finished now? Did your personal security measures work?'

Pickle looked caught off guard for perhaps the first time so far. 'I can't think what a spate of petty thefts has got to do with the abominable murder of a famous barrister, Chief Inspector. Why are we wasting time talking about this? Unless...you don't think they're connected, do you? The thefts and the murder? That's surely quite impossible.'

Inspector Lovelace shrugged. 'Anything is possible at this early stage, sir. You didn't answer my question: so *have* the thefts now stopped?'

Posie was conscious of Constable Fox's scratchy writing coming to an abrupt halt, sensed his pen at the ready. She felt Pickle exhale the last of his cigarette beside her and grind it out on the ash-tray provided. A quick decision was being made.

'The thefts *have* stopped, yes. The situation has been dealt with. It was felt that we —eminently reasonable men — could deal with the situation at 20 Old Square between ourselves. We felt there was no need to call you good gentlemen in.'

Into the full silence of the hot room an uneasiness crept in. The two police Inspectors stared at Pickle, who stared back unashamedly.

Posie turned demurely, raised her perfectly-kohled eyebrow: 'So what you mean is that Amyas found out that George, your Head Clerk, was the thief. Isn't that correct? Amyas probably sacked him, too, and shared the knowledge with you, as his Deputy. I'm guessing you've already lined up George's successor, a new Head Clerk, who will begin work with you at the start of the new term. Although George may not know that yet. Or even know that you and Amyas spoke about him being the culprit. Am I right?'

Pickle raised his glasses for a second, stared at Posie intently before snapping them back down. When he spoke his voice betrayed neither anger nor surprise. 'Miss Parker, isn't it? You are right, as it happens, although Amyas and I wanted to keep it very close to our chests. Doesn't do us many favours if people get to hear a man we've trusted, and employed, has been doing the dirty on us, does it?'

Inspector Oats was looking at Posie in his usual half-vengeful, half-disbelieving way, and Lovelace hurried things along.

'I'm afraid, Mr Pickle, that when it comes to a murder investigation, *nothing* can be kept close to any chests. Is there anything else which was out of the ordinary – or strange – in Chambers recently which you wish to let us know about? Or in relation to Amyas himself?'

Selwyn Pickle shrugged casually. 'Those odd little notes to Amyas, I suppose. You *do* know about those? Handwritten and hand-delivered.'

Lovelace dipped into his box-file and shook one in Pickle's direction.

The man nodded. 'Amyas showed one or two to me,

as he did to several other colleagues. Laughed them off, but I sensed he was uneasy about them. I told him not to worry: probably just some "victim" with too much time on their hands. Someone who felt Amyas had helped keep a criminal from going to prison.'

Posie turned to the barrister. 'Had Amyas received other threatening mail in the past?'

A sharp bark of laughter. 'Good gracious, yes. You show me a criminal barrister in London who *hasn't* received threats in his career, and I'll eat my hat. We all get them from time to time; usually just some crack-pot wanting to let off steam. Or a dissatisfied client. It comes with the job.'

Posie, who had been making her own notes, looked up again: 'But have they ever resulted in real physical violence for any other barrister at 20 Old Square before, sir?'

'Of course not, Miss Parker.'

Pickle swivelled around to face the police Inspectors again. 'Am I to understand from this very forward woman that this is a serious line of enquiry? That Amyas Lyle may have been murdered by a disgruntled client, or someone on the opposite side of him in the Courtroom? Is this an ongoing danger to other barristers? Including myself? Should I warn my colleagues?'

Inspector Oats puffed. 'Absolutely not, your honour. You don't need to worry. This 'ere murder stinks of the personal touch. Our murderer had a very personal account to settle.'

Posie and Lovelace shot each other a warning look. *Oats is annoying but don't contradict him now: let the silence speak for itself.*

Pickle watched as Lovelace got up and opened the one high-up long window in the room, letting in a blast of air: salt from the River Thames, the perfume of cut-grass from a communal garden, a mix of tar and dirt from the busy Embankment outside. A frying scent was rising from a nearby hot-barrel stall on the pavement far below. Bacon, probably. Or sausages. Posie heard her stomach rumble.

Lovelace stood underneath the high window, resting his back and a foot up against the wall, the picture of ease. Pickle took another cigarette for himself.

'What I'm finding hard to piece together, sir,' said Lovelace conversationally, 'is just what type of a man Amyas Lyle really was. He seems elusive to me. Can you add some colour? As a *friend*?'

Selwyn Pickle's face grew watchful. After a few long seconds he put down his smouldering cigarette. 'I think you mistake me, Chief Inspector. Amyas Lyle and I were work colleagues. No more: no less.'

More pen scratching from Fox's side of the table.

Pickle carried on: 'But if you want colour, I'll give you some. I knew Amyas Lyle for around the last fifteen years, which is the length of time he's been at 20 Old Square. An *uninterrupted* time of fifteen years: he didn't serve in the Great War, for what I always understood were medical reasons, although he never divulged exactly what those were. Amyas Lyle had come from not very much, and both his parents were dead. He was an only child. So far, so unremarkable. But he was the most ambitious man I've ever met; ultra-talented, well-connected and with an ear to the ground on most things. He always seemed to be watching you; was always one step ahead of you, somehow. Spooky, really: as if he could have given you the answers to what was wrong with your own life. It goes without saying that he had no friends in Chambers; everyone feared him. We drank champagne recently to celebrate the news that he had been appointed as a High Court Judge, but people only stayed for the one drink, out of courtesy and fear. And that was the crux of it: Amyas Lyle was feared because he was a man with nothing left to lose. In short, Amyas Lyle had sold his soul.'

'How had he sold his soul?' Lovelace returned to his chair.

'His marriage. My guess is that he only married Lady

Antonia because she's the daughter of "End of the Road" Lord Justice Roade. A marriage made on the understanding that Roade would help Amyas to become a fellow Judge. You see, Amyas may not have come from an impeccable legal background, but he married into one. He probably thought it was all worth it to advance his career, and to hell with the weird problems which were part and parcel of the marriage.'

'Sorry?'

'Lady Antonia may be stinking rich in her own right, but she's as barmy as they come. They were living entirely separate lives: I think Amyas only saw her and the boys at the family home on Sundays. It's an open secret she's snorting her fortune up her nose. And "End of the Road, Roade"; well, I'm sure you'll find out if you dig deep enough, he's a nasty piece of work, personally and professionally. He's part of this dreadful new British Fascist Party, as is the daughter.'

Lovelace interrupted, interest heightened: 'And Amyas? Was *he* part of it, too?'

Pickle balled his fists up angrily. 'He was definitely attending their monthly meetings with Lord Justice Roade. Paying Roade lip-service I expect, rather than actually believing any of it. But I *do* know he had that odd-looking girl, Rotha Lintorn-Orman, their leader, in our offices back in the spring. Can you believe it? She was taking tea in his office, just as pally as can be. Amyas was laughing and writing things down which she was telling him. I blanked him for several days after that, but Amyas probably didn't even notice. Ambition can lead you into strange places; places from which there is no return.'

It seemed to Posie as if the meeting was winding up, and Selwyn Pickle was starting to check his watch, but then, out of the blue, Lovelace pushed a neat, cream piece of paper across the table, like a magician brandishing a rabbit from a hat in his final, most exciting act.

'Before we all go, I wonder if you, Mr Pickle, could cast your eyes over this list, sir. It's a bit of a puzzle to us, I'll admit. We found it among the murder victim's things.'

Everyone looked at the typewritten words. And Posie saw it was a typewritten copy of Amyas' own list of suspects, although the accusatory title had now been carefully omitted.

1. Sawbones Bill

2. Antonia - because of FEVER STREET?

3. SELWYN

4. GEORGE - upbraided him, bears a grudge

5. Whitley Bay?

Posie watched as the barrister with his clear, logical lawyer's mind and his clever skills of deducing salient information read and re-read the typewritten list.

Inspector Lovelace tapped his pen on the table. 'Can you shed any light on any of the people named there?'

A reluctant nod.

'Sawbones Bill, the first person on the list. Well, that's William Dawney. *Dr* William Dawney. He's a surgeon, specialises in bones. He's probably the only real friend Amyas had. They suited each other well. Ambitious men, both. I think they were school chums together.'

Posie frowned at this new name, wondering if William Dawney might have been friends with her brother Richard, too, at school. The year had not been a big one and Richard had been a popular boy, but the name meant nothing to her, less than nothing. Which was strange.

Pickle flicked a finger at the next item, shaking his head doubtfully. '"Antonia"…well, this is a reference to the wonderful Lady Antonia, Amyas' wife. But I have no idea what "Fever Street" might refer to.'

The lawyer looked up, and sensing encouragement, moved on. '"Selwyn"…this next reference is obviously to *me*, isn't it? To the best of my knowledge I don't think Amyas knew anyone else by the same name.'

He turned to Posie. 'This fourth name, "George", is obviously our Head Clerk. Is this how *you* knew about him stealing? You'd seen this odd note ahead of me? It says here he was "upbraided". That's about right. Amyas took him to task about it all before the summer recess.'

Receiving no reply, he moved on. '"Whitley Bay?" No idea.' He made as if to pass the paper back towards Lovelace, but then stopped.

'Hang on a minute. Isn't that the place with that famous dance-hall, the Spanish City? In the north? Well, if it *is*, then Amyas knew someone who lived up there.'

Posie stared. 'How do you know this?'

Pickle almost blushed. 'I'm not a spy, or a snitch, but there are times when a fella happens to be in the post room when George or another clerk spread the post all over a desk in order to arrange it alphabetically for the pigeon-holes. I saw postcards arrive for Amyas. I'd say he got a postcard every couple of weeks. Going back to the start of this year I suppose. Yes: January is when they started up.'

'January, sir? Are you certain of that?'

'Positive. It was just after New Year. I must have seen at least twenty of the wretched things. Always the same card.'

'Every couple of weeks? Are you sure?' Posie watched as the Inspector knitted his eyebrows together, also puzzled. They had found only *one* postcard, not twenty, and it had been fairly recent. So where were the others? Or was this man lying? And if so, why?

'Of course I'm sure. I have a first-class memory. I have to, in my job.'

'And who were these postcards from?'

'Haven't got a clue. The postcards had nothing written on them. Blank, the lot of them.'

Selwyn Pickle huffed, embarrassed. 'And yes: I turned them over. Human nosiness, I suppose.'

The Inspector nodded, satisfied. The description of the Whitley Bay postcards matched the one postcard they had already retrieved. The lawyer was standing up now.

'Now, if that's everything, I really must go and organise this meeting. I want to tell my colleagues the news about the murder myself, rather than their having to read about it in the newspapers. I'm guessing the story about Amyas hasn't broken yet?'

Lovelace shook his head. 'Not so far. But I can't promise to hold the press off for long. I'm sure it will be all over the place tomorrow. It *is* silly season, after all.'

Selwyn Pickle suddenly looked down at Posie. 'I must say, Madam, I feel I may have met you previously. Or seen you in the newspapers? I usually have a very good eye for faces.'

But before Posie could mutter an answer about having a very familiar-looking face, or some such tosh, Inspector Lovelace, still sitting calmly, came to her rescue. 'Could I just ask you to confirm, sir, for my records, that you were definitely in Eastbourne *all day long* yesterday? Nowhere near London at around two o'clock? The time of the murder?'

The small ugly man bristled. 'I say! Are you treating me as a bally suspect? Of course I was in Eastbourne all day, on the beach in fact. There are any number of witnesses: my wife, and my son, Robin, for starters. Might I remind you that *I* volunteered to come and help *you* in an enquiry in which you seem to know precious little? The usual police incompetence! What on earth makes you think *I* am a suspect?'

Lovelace calmly drew the typewritten note back towards him and took from his box-file the exact same note, the original, in Amyas' own writing. He put them side-by-side, and then held them up for Pickle to see.

'See, sir? The list you have been perusing is a *copy* of Mr Lyle's own list. He had compiled a list of people he considered "suspects". See the title? Albeit they are suspects for sending strange and threatening mail to Mr Lyle, not murdering him. *That* is why I have to ask, sir.'

Selwyn Pickle seemed on the verge of losing his temper. But instead he picked up his panama hat and stepped towards the door without looking back.

'Constable Fox, can you escort Mr Pickle out of the building, please?'

And in the flurry of the lean policeman leaving and the door opening and closing, Posie thought that Pickle had finally gone. Indeed, Inspector Lovelace was blowing out his cheeks in relief and snapping his box-file closed.

But then the door opened again. The enormous, out-of-proportion head emerged, the golden spectacles glittering. There was a jab of a finger in Posie's direction.

'You!'

Posie could see Constable Fox bobbing about uselessly in the dark-wood corridor behind.

'I *knew* I had seen you before!'

Posie's heart sank. During her time with the famous explorer Alaric Boynton-Dale she had been in the newspapers and magazines a fair deal. And sometimes in her own right, as a Private Detective. But not recently. Had Pickle suddenly and inconveniently remembered one of these articles? Well, there was no crime involved. She hadn't lied about who she was. Just hadn't advertised it very clearly. That was all.

'Amyas Lyle didn't keep a photograph of his wife or twin sons anywhere. Not on his desk, nor up in that horrible little hole of a flat upstairs.' For just a second Pickle paused, and swallowed, perhaps realising that the horrible little hole might very well become *his* now, as a perk of the job, and that maybe, after all, it wasn't quite so bad.

'But he *did* keep one picture. On his desk, for all the

world to see. All the years I knew him. In an expensive silver photo-frame. It was *you*, I'm sure of it. Younger, for certain. With plaits. A schoolgirl, I'd warrant. Oh, years younger! But it was *you*. I remember it especially because his silver frame and photograph was one of the items stolen. Amyas was incandescent with rage about it. Eventually, he got the photograph back, but not the frame. George had sold it, apparently.'

Posie gulped, her face burning, her heart racing. All eyes in the room were on her. So the photograph they had found upstairs had until recently been out on display. For years.

'I asked him once who it was in the frame and he basically told me to mind my own business, but the gist of it was that the girl in the frame was dead. "*Long gone, and mourned*," he said. I assumed it was a sister. But oh! How wrong I was! And here you are now. Alive and kicking.'

Pickle wagged a finger at the Inspectors. 'Maybe that's a mystery you need to solve, too, my good sirs? And maybe you should add Miss Parker here to the list of so-called suspects!'

And with that he slammed out of the room for a final time.

* * * *

Seven

'Pah!' Inspector Oats broke the silence, simultaneously shoving his brown homburg hat on his head and angrily rising from his seat. His stance was of a man in interrupted flight.

'Oh, do get it off your chest, Bill,' said Lovelace wearily, still sitting.

'Well, I will then, *Chief* Inspector,' Oats snarled. The fact that Richard Lovelace had made Chief Inspector first, despite their both starting at the Yard at the same time, was something that obviously still rankled with Oats. His pale blue cod-like eyes roved suspiciously from Posie to Lovelace and back again. He wagged his finger in Lovelace's direction.

'I've told you before, Richard, and I'll tell you again: involving Miss Parker here in proper police work always results in a catastrophe. The girl's like mildew on my nice cabbages at my Peckham church allotment. You think you've got rid of it but it's there all the time, right at the heart of the matter. What the blazes is this "*long gone, and mourned*" business?'

Oats shook his head in disbelief, and continued: 'See what I mean? She's right at the heart of it, again! Romantically involved with the murder victim! You asked me in here as the Superintendent wanted another Inspector to write up the report – to make sure things were done properly for our esteemed guest – and I'll do so now, but I'll not mention this romantic business. It's an embarrassment. As is *she*.' He pointed an accusatory finger at Posie, who sat very still, staring back, trying to make the red flush in her face go away.

Lovelace sighed heavily. 'Thank you, Bill. Always a pleasure.'

Slightly wrong-footed, Oats shrugged himself into his greasy trench-coat, ubiquitous, despite the heat.

Lovelace continued: 'And based on what you heard here, what would be *your* professional opinion on the case, Bill?'

Posie had the distinct impression that Inspector Oats was secretly very pleased to be asked. He made a show of chewing the end of his straggly brown moustache, leaning heavily against the door-jamb. 'Well...' he consulted his notebook, 'I'd normally say the wife – nine times out of ten it's the spouse – but we know she was in Paris. Can't kill someone in England if you're in France, can you?'

'She could have paid someone else to do it, though, couldn't she? Stayed in France while it was carried out according to her instructions? A professional hit-man with a degree in poisons?' interjected Posie sarcastically, but Oats ignored her as he steamrolled on.

'My next best bet is this Head Clerk.' He stabbed a finger in his own pad. 'George, wasn't it? The one who's stolen all the treasure? Including the frame with Miss Parker in it?' He paused, as if going to make another nasty comment and then obviously thought better of it.

'So I'd say *him*. The usual choice of motives: if it's not love, or jealousy, it's money. George 'discovered' the body yesterday, didn't he? All this story about a Billingsgate Porter could just be a fancy fabrication. George could have done the whole thing himself, arranged the box of poison himself and had it there ready for when Mr Lyle got back from lunch. Nothing easier.'

'Where would he have got that particular chemical mix from, Bill?'

'Anything can be got when you're paying enough for it in London, Richard, as you and I both know.'

'True enough, but it seems a bit fanciful for a simple clerk, and what about the threatening mail arriving since February? Did George write all that, too?'

'Perhaps. Maybe the fella's screwy in the head? Or he was trying to create a smokescreen on the side, away from his thieving activities? He must have been making a fair packet out of those rich lawyers. And we heard, he was selling it all for gain.'

Lovelace looked appreciative. 'Well, thank you for your opinion, Bill. I look forward to your report. And enjoy your holiday.'

Inspector Oats harrumphed and looked slightly more down in the mouth than usual. If that were possible. He loitered at the doorway.

Posie smiled sweetly. 'Not looking forward to your holiday much then, Inspector Oats?'

Oats ignored her, speaking over her head to his colleague. 'We normally go to Ramsgate; *Margate* at a push if we're feeling flush. But my Tilly's got some fanciful notion in her head this year to have a *glamorous* spell away; she's been reading all about it in one of these fancy women's magazines. So, we're off to this Whitley Bay for two weeks, can you believe it? The very place in the postcards your murdered fella was receiving! All the way up north! Five hours on the train tomorrow evening and it will be all the same as just an hour down south would be: sand, wind and fish-and-chip suppers. But Tilly wants to see the Spanish City. I ask you!'

He rolled his eyes as if he were talking about a trek to the North Pole. 'So, no: I'm not looking forward to it, but thank you for asking.'

'Brave man!' Lovelace smiled encouragingly. 'Enjoy.' He picked up the veneer cigarette box and proffered it Oats' way. 'Do help yourself, Bill.'

'Don't mind if I do.'

Once Oats had gone, his trench-coat pockets suitably stuffed, Lovelace went to stand by the still-open window, lighting up his own cigarette.

'You're very pally-pally, all of a sudden,' said Posie curiously, aware that she sounded more than a little childish.

'With Oats, you mean?' The Inspector's eyes twinkled. 'Well, as you heard him say, the Superintendent wanted another Inspector to be present. The only Inspector I could find wandering the corridors was Oats; it *is* summer holiday season after all. Besides, it sounds as if it's *you*, rather than me, who might have to be pally-pally with him. Two weeks in Whitley Bay, eh? I'm sure you'll see each other along the promenade, on the beach…' He laughed wickedly. 'When are you leaving exactly?'

'Tomorrow. If I'm not wanted here. But I'm only going for five days. I'll be returning next Monday.'

Lovelace ground out his smoke and snapped the window shut. 'Go. Go by all means. Although you might not be having much of a holiday up there. I might want you to do some specific digging if it seems that the Whitley Bay connection is a real lead.' He returned to the round table and fixed Posie with a searching look. 'I must say, I never thought I'd agree with Bill Oats on *anything*, but I think he's right this time.'

Posie was dumbfounded. '*What?* You too think George the Head Clerk is behind all of this? How, sir? He's just a chancer, a silly little man who's got in too deep.'

Lovelace shook his head. 'Not about that. I agree with Oats about not mentioning the fact that Amyas Lyle had a picture of *you* on his desk for a decade. Things are complicated enough. I need your help here, Posie. I don't want you being asked to step down by my Superintendent.'

'Oh, I see.' She breathed an audible sigh of relief, as the Inspector carried on: 'But as to George the Head Clerk, of course Bill is wrong. There's more to this murder than meets the eye, somehow. Something complicated is going on. What did you make of the ever-helpful Selwyn Pickle KC?'

Posie looked down at her silver notebook, then closed it again and threw it on the table top like a piece of useless rubbish. 'You know me, sir. I usually go with my gut instinct. And I would say he's not our man.'

'But? I sense there is a "but" coming?'

'Yes. He *could* have done it, certainly. Selwyn Pickle was obviously jealous of Amyas Lyle in many respects and right now he's thrilled he's stepping into Amyas' role as Head of Chambers. Pickle has a motive, sir: naked ambition. It was ugly to watch. And he was only in Eastbourne yesterday, it's not a million miles away from London. He could have easily come up in the morning – it takes two hours by train – and then got back again for tea-time and no-one would be any the wiser.'

'Mnnn. Or Mr Pickle could have hired your aforementioned hitman with the degree in poisons? The one you thought Lady Antonia could be employing?'

Posie grinned for what felt like the first time in ages. 'Exactly, sir. But better still, he could have made the batch of chemicals up himself. Pickle told us he has a laboratory at his London house. I think these are important points, sir. Although I can't for the life of me understand the background to the threatening notes in relation to Pickle. Can you? There doesn't seem to have been a shared history between the men, especially given the vast differences in their ages.'

'True enough,' said Lovelace. 'And at least we've found out now from Pickle who "Sawbones Bill" is. He was our last unexplained person on the list of suspects. I'll go and telephone to the Royal College now, ask if we can speak to Dr Dawney later. Then maybe I can tempt you to a spot of luncheon? Actually, Posie, there's something I need to talk to you about.'

But just then Sergeant Rainbird hurried importantly into the room, sheaves of paper wedged under his arms, a pencil clamped tightly in his mouth.

'Sergeant,' muttered Lovelace darkly. 'Where on earth have you been all this time? We've finished here. I thought you were going to be sitting in on our meeting with the KC, and instead I had to rely on that green lad, Constable Fox, to take notes. Well?'

Rainbird sat, nodding briefly to Posie, huffing and puffing slightly as he spread out his papers in an urgent fashion. 'I'm truly sorry, sir, but I got caught up with the Forensics boys, and the evidence team, sir. And I had several of our lads researching Selwyn Pickle's background in detail, in advance of the meeting with him.'

'Bit late now, isn't it, Sergeant? That particular bird has been and gone.'

'I'm sorry, sir. It took longer than anticipated. But two useful points have emerged which may make you look a little closer at Selwyn Pickle KC.' Sensing no encouragement, Rainbird rolled on. 'His youngest son, Robin Pickle, is a Chemistry student at Oxford. He could have made up the lethal concoction, couldn't he?'

Looking all about him and seeing that this was not new news, he carried on regardless: 'And also, and I'm sure he didn't share *this* gem with you, Selwyn Pickle has a second son, Charlie, who's something of a black sheep in the family. They've fallen out time and again and now they don't speak. The lad's been thrown out of every educational establishment Selwyn Pickle has ever paid for him to attend: a case of Pickle by name and pickle by nature, eh? Well, guess what Charlie Pickle is working as right now, *this summer?*'

Lovelace rolled his eyes heavenwards. 'No idea.'

'He's a Porter! Been at it two months or so. At Billingsgate Fish Market!'

Both Posie and Lovelace sat up ramrod straight. Posie felt inordinately glad that poor Rainbird seemed to have done something vaguely right at last. And the Billingsgate connection was an interesting one, although she didn't know exactly where it led them right now. Although not in Selwyn Pickle's favour, undoubtedly.

When Constable Fox knocked and announced that the Earl of Cardigeon – or Rufus, as Posie knew him – had just this minute telephoned in response to her telegram, and that he was awaiting their visit in the restaurant at the House of Lords, Posie felt an unusual sense of relief at the thought of meeting her old pal again, a familiar face she had known since childhood. Even if he wasn't in her best books just at the moment, for being such a dreadful husband to wonderful, beautiful, quirky Dolly. But at least he was familiar, in this awful sea of uncertainty. Posie stood up, hoping the Inspector would follow suit.

'There's something you should know, Miss.' Constable Fox looked decidedly awkward, hanging back somewhat.

'Oh?'

'When I spoke to his Lordship just now, he seemed somewhat *irregular* in his manner, Miss, if you take my meaning.'

'I'm not sure that I do, Constable. Be clear, will you?'

'Well, I didn't want to be too specific, but let's just say that perhaps the Earl of Cardigeon has had a wee drink or two. Or five. Or ten.'

And Posie's heart sank.

* * * *

Eight

The walk to the House of Lords was anything but enjoyable. Posie cursed under her breath as she went. Inspector Lovelace had tried initially to offer a consoling remark: 'Don't be too judgemental. Maybe there's an explanation?'

To which he had received an angry retort: 'There's *never* an explanation!'

And so they walked in silence among the crush of black-suited office workers, the many omnibuses beeping and honking past them. Thoughts of a spot of lunch were long gone. Parliament Square, looming on their right, was a cacophony of noise; the traffic worse than Trafalgar Square with masses of banked motor-taxis, and horses and carts rearing this way and that.

Posie fumed. Rufus had been the Earl of Cardigeon for almost a year now, since his father had died the previous November, but Posie had known him since she was a child, since her brother Richard had brought Rufus – a thin, snotty boy, albeit a real-life Lord – home to Norfolk for a Christmas holiday. She had felt actively responsible for him since the end of the Great War, six years before, when Rufus' life had gone spectacularly off the rails in a wild frenzy of chronic alcoholism and depression and wild partying, all stemming from a terrible guilt he had felt at simply having survived the trenches, when most of his men had not.

But since 1921 Rufus had been married to Dolly, a woman Posie and Rufus had met when they happened to be involved in the same case. Posie was of the firm opinion that Dolly was by far the best thing that had ever happened to Rufus. He had been at his lowest ebb before meeting Dolly, barely caring if he lived or died. And he had been lucky to get her, which he knew. When he had married Dolly, Rufus had sworn off alcohol for good. For ever.

Apparently.

The dry spell had lasted three years. And now it seemed it was over.

Posie rolled her eyes unsympathetically. But she remembered her vow to be *kind* today as she and Lovelace entered the huge oak doors of the House of Lords.

Perhaps it wasn't so surprising, after all, that Rufus had started drinking again. Rufus was often at the House of Lords these days, taking an active role in government, and it would be fairly standard to be among other men who drank, in the well-stocked bar and restaurant of the house, where policy and the lobbying of votes often took place over a drink or two. Or several, by the sounds of it.

Having given their names to three different Porters, Posie and Lovelace started to walk through the vast, cool, black-and-white tiled halls of the House of Lords, the dizzying heights of the boss-encrusted ceilings causing their footsteps to echo loudly. Posie was almost marching along, her heels angrily sharp on the floor.

'Calm down, old girl,' Lovelace muttered, realising yet another Porter was on their tail. 'Walk a little slower, can't you? We're attracting all sorts of the wrong attention here.' And a flash of his police identity card sufficed in getting rid of the vigilant Porter.

The House of Lords was deserted, like everywhere else in town, and Posie started to feel less charitable about Rufus spending his time here. What on earth was keeping him in town when no-one else was about to vote on anything, anyway? Why not take Dolly and the three children away to the sea? The Riviera? Or return to the fresh air and good fishing on his own estates at Rebburn Abbey near York?

They came across Rufus on the spectacular balcony of the House of Lords' restaurant, sitting in the far left-hand corner at a wrought-iron table, facing the river that sparkled in the strong sunlight.

Rufus was bareheaded, and very red and shiny in the face, possibly sunburnt. A silver teapot sat on the table, as did a half-empty bottle of a first-class single-malt whisky. The balcony was empty except for him, as was the rest of the cool, dark restaurant inside.

Posie smoothed down her emerald silk skirt and sat herself down on a spare chair without waiting to be asked, pulling out another chair for Lovelace.

'Ah! Nosey Parker.' Rufus fixed his gaze upon Posie, none too clearly. 'To what do I owe the pleasure?'

Posie noted how his waistcoat buttons were straining and how his collar, although starched and pristine, seemed much too tight about his throat. Rufus was getting fatter, and soon he'd start to look like his father had done, froggy and puffy about the face. The spare, coltish good looks of his youth were almost gone, his thick mop of blondish hair now sparse and greasily fine, with large gaps where shiny sun-burned skin now showed through.

'Where's your hat, Rufus?' Posie said snappishly, pulling down the brim of her own straw boater to shield her face from the sun's angry glare, and also taking up the teapot, which was mercifully still full, and hot as you like. She poured out two teas.

'My *hat*?' Rufus boggled.

He was leaning back with an arm outstretched along the top of his chair, his jacket off, a lit cigar smouldering on the table. 'Is that what you've come here to tell a fellow?

Is *that* what was urgent, in the telegram you sent? By Jove, and you've got good old Lovelace in tow as well? Has it come to that? Scotland Yard's finest attending me because I'm not wearing a bally hat?'

'Of course I'm not here because of your hat. That's by the by.'

Rufus shook his head and picked up his lit cigar, teasing away the excess ash. He took a forlorn drag. 'So why are you here? I thought you'd come here because of last night.' He half-sighed. 'To tell me all about it.'

'What happened last night, your Lordship?' asked the Chief Inspector, puzzled. Although he knew Rufus, and had indeed stayed at Rebburn Hall once before as a guest, he could never convince himself it was right not to use Rufus' proper title in conversation.

Rufus jabbed his cigar roughly in Posie's direction, smiling blearily. 'Nosey here is leading my wife astray.'

'Come again, your Lordship?'

'They were out all night. Dancing, apparently. Stayed overnight at the Ritz in a suite: cost me a small fortune, I expect. When the Countess *did* finally turn up this morning, and I asked her where she'd been, she said it was none of my bally business. I only found out where she was because she'd left her handbag behind at the Rivoli Bar and the Manager of the Ritz himself came across in a taxi to return it while she was soaking in her bath! He told me the Countess and Nosey here had been having a high old time of it all night.'

'And why shouldn't we?' cut in Posie, cross now that Lovelace knew exactly where and with whom she had been the previous night. A little mystery is no bad thing for a girl.

'Touché, touché, old thing,' said Rufus. His gaze seemed suddenly clearer, an urgent flash of appeal directed straight at her. 'So anything to tell me, Nosey? Anything at all?'

Posie narrowed her eyes, realising that Rufus must

understand at least part of Dolly's unhappiness at the current state of their marriage. Did he really expect her to spill the beans? To trot out Dolly's confidences here as if they meant nothing at all?

'There's nothing to report.'

Lovelace looked from one to the other, raised his eyebrows incredulously and attempted desperately to impose some sort of order into the unruly tangle of misunderstandings so far. 'Your Lordship, I think you may be mistaken, or unaware, but we are here on official police business.'

There was a sudden visible panic on Rufus' part, a hasty sobering-up, eased by a casual wave of reassurance from Lovelace. 'Your own family are all safe and well, to the best of my knowledge, your Lordship. No worries there.'

'Oh?' Rufus took another drag on the cigar, relaxing again. 'Well, that's a relief. And please don't mind my joshing with Nosey here about her dancing around town with my wife. All to the good, what? As if I really give two hoots! So, tell me. What's happened?'

'Amyas Lyle, your Lordship. Do you know him at all?'

Posie watched Rufus' face intently. His was usually a face you could read clearly, the emotions played out there for all to see. And now Rufus looked from one to the other of them, confusion giving way to a resigned acceptance, a raise of an aristocratic eyebrow.

'Yes, I know him. Or *knew* him.' He ground out his cigar. 'He's dead, isn't he?'

'Yes.'

Rufus exhaled but didn't look surprised. 'And I'll warrant in bally strange circumstances, eh?'

Posie cut in: 'Why do you say that?'

'Because Amyas Lyle was a strange man. Once, I thought he'd make a good spy, because he was such a lone wolf, with nothing to lose. But I daresay he wasn't honourable enough. He was a bad apple. You know we used to call him "the Vampire"?'

'Yes. I knew that.'

Rufus splayed his hands. 'Boys, eh? They can be mean. But accurate: they can scent out strangeness like a dog can. And Amyas Lyle *was* strange.'

'In what way, Rufus?'

'I'll give you an example. Once, when we were about eleven, I lingered at the doorway of our Headmaster's Office. I'd been sent on an errand by another teacher to bring the Headmaster something, but I saw he was busy; there was another lad inside. It was Amyas. He was being told off for repeatedly talking out loud -apparently to himself- in a corridor which was an official "silent zone". When he was asked to apologize, Amyas said absolutely not: he had been talking to his imaginary friend, and he wasn't sorry for it. In fact, he said it was quite necessary; the friend being always with him. Well, you should have seen the Headmaster's face as he flexed his cane! Quite the picture. He must have thought the boy was possessed! And Amyas, standing his ground, convinced he was in the right, even then. You can imagine I shared that little morsel around with the other lads! We all had a good laugh.'

The Inspector cut in: 'Seems a harmless enough fancy for a lad of ten or eleven, your Lordship, if you don't mind my saying so. Are you sure you weren't being a little harsh? No love lost between you two then as boys?'

Rufus shrugged. 'No, not really. There was no love lost between Amyas and *any* of the boys...' Rufus looked across the Thames, his eyes not on the water or the heavy barges puttering along, but on other dreadful sights and times, six years past.

'All those boys... I can see them now. You know, there were fifty boys in our year at school? All except four of them were dead by 1918. The survivors were me, Amyas, William Dawney, and one other – Teddy Whishaw – but he would have been better off dead. Poor Teddy, he's in a clinic in Suffolk with the worst case of shell-shock you're ever likely to see.'

'I'm sorry to hear that, your Lordship. That was a very low survival rate, to be sure.'

Rufus smiled ruefully at Lovelace, who he liked and admired a good deal. 'Don't be sorry, old boy. You were there too, Richard, in those ruddy trenches; you know what it was like. Which is more than can be said of Amyas Lyle, who didn't bother to serve his King or Country. The weakling!'

Lovelace was consulting his policeman's notebook. 'We've heard from another source that Mr Lyle didn't serve in the war due to medical grounds?'

Rufus laughed scornfully. 'That's right. There was some vague rumour of a bad heart, even in our schooldays. I remember he never played sport. But I expect when it came to the Great War he paid someone to sign him off with a dodgy doctor's certificate.' He sounded angry. 'Seems the sort of thing he'd do to save his own skin. He didn't have to actually fight, did he? He could have volunteered for a hundred other non-physical things. As I said, a weakling. And add to that he was a bone-idle coward, who didn't want to serve his country. No morals, no values. I'd not go as far as call him a traitor, but, well… you get my meaning.'

Posie suddenly thought of Rufus and Dolly's only son, Lord Raymond Cardigeon, a baby of not yet one. Born very premature, the current Lord Cardigeon was a very delicate baby, prone to all manner of illnesses and generally 'sickly'. Posie privately hoped against hope that Rufus would never decide to call Lord Raymond any of the names he had just been calling Amyas, and that he might be a little more understanding of the medical conditions of his own son. But who knew Rufus anymore? Not even his own wife, it seemed. Perhaps poor Teddy Whishaw in Suffolk wasn't the only one still feeling the after-effects of the war.

But what was it, Posie asked herself, which she was hearing, over and over again, about Amyas, which never seemed to have an adequate explanation?

Morals.

That was it. When she was eighteen her brother had warned her off Amyas due to his having no moral compass, and holding lives very cheaply. And she had blindly accepted his opinion. And here was Rufus, years and years later, in wildly different circumstances, saying the same thing over again. But why? On what she had heard so far about the murder victim, it didn't add up.

Inspector Lovelace had wanted 'colour', had wanted to understand Amyas Lyle as a person, and yet so far the lack of sympathy for Amyas was a puzzle. Like that nickname, 'the Vampire'. It didn't really make any sense. Posie went on the attack.

'Rufus, I know there was jealousy between my brother and Amyas, and I know he was an arrogant, competitive boy. And I quite see that you thought he was peculiar, wittering on about an imaginary friend, but there's a level of loathing I sense, and I remember Richard being the same, which can't be explained by these things alone. What on earth did Amyas do to you boys to earn that dreadful nickname? Tell me. I know there's something you're not saying.'

Rufus stared at Posie, squinted in the sun, but said nothing.

'Go on, Rufey. If you tell me, I won't go on about that wretched bottle of whisky on the table between us. Although I really *should*.'

A pause. 'You won't tell Dolly? Not any of it?'

Posie bit her lip, and felt her foot being shoved under the table by Lovelace. *We need some sort of break here. Do this. Tell him anything. Swear black is white with your fingers crossed behind your back, but just do it.*

Keep him talking.

'Fine. I won't tell Dolly.'

Rufus poured another two-fingers' worth of whisky into his tumbler. He didn't water it down or call for ice, just

89

drank it back quickly, too quick to enjoy it properly or feel the peaty burn at his throat. It was the act of a desperate man. He sniffed and looked out at the river again.

'You're right, Nosey. You always are. Amyas Lyle was an excessively clever boy who didn't have two groats to rub together. That was how it was when he first came to the school. But then, over the years, he got harder, greedier. I'm not sure if you know this, but Amyas Lyle was into betting, big-time. He was a first-class gambler; he won at everything. He'd bet you at anything: cards, what the weather would be like tomorrow, heads or tails on a coin spinning, which horse would win on any given race. It was all fairly innocent stuff to start out with. Amyas would play poker for silly trophies: a packet of milk chocolate or a book,' he darted a look at Posie, 'or even a photograph, if that was all you had.'

He sighed. 'But then, when Amyas was about sixteen, it started to get serious. He had a runner – a junior gardener, I think – who took real betting slips down to a proper betting shop in the local town. Amyas got other boys hooked, too. Twice a week Amyas and a friend would go around collecting slips in the dormitories, and the boys' money. Then the runner would take it all to town. It became like a drug, an addiction for some.'

Rufus' hand trembled as he picked up the whisky bottle again. Then put it down.

'Amyas was making money on all of this of course, as was the junior gardener, and Amyas' friend. Amyas started to act as a sort of banker for some of the boys who had got themselves into debt with him; he'd cover their losses at ridiculous rates of interest. It was all highly illegal of course. Immoral. But he and his pal managed to get away with it for about a year.'

'And then?' Lovelace crossed and re-crossed his legs on the uncomfortable metal chair, impatient.

'Amyas was preparing for the Cambridge University

exams, to read Law, as you know, when the story broke. One of the more junior boys, a little lad, about fourteen, a choirboy, his name was Harold Robertsbridge, had got himself into a bad way with this whole set-up. He'd lost and lost and lost and couldn't seem to quit betting. And it turned out he'd borrowed money from Amyas to fund yet more betting, and had lost time and again. He'd got himself into trouble with Amyas and couldn't afford to repay him whatever crazily small sum it was. Amyas wouldn't let the matter rest and hounded him for the money constantly, with his friend. They thought it was some sort of sport.'

'What happened?' breathed Posie, but in her heart she knew. All at once she seemed to remember shadows of this story; half-heard snatches of conversation from outside the door of her father's study, when her brother had come home for the holidays. A newsletter which had come home, telling only half the story. Her father's strained voice inside his study, sad and surprised: '*A tragedy, Richard. Thank goodness you weren't involved. Reprehensible. Who could be at the heart of such a tragedy? No moral compass…*'

'This lad, Harold, he couldn't face the shame of it, or the bullying from Amyas: I don't know which. Whatever the case, he hung himself just before the Christmas holidays, and left a note instructing his father to settle his outstanding account with Amyas. Said how sorry he was to have brought shame and disrepute upon the family.'

Rufus shook his head dismally. 'It was all hushed up, of course. And Amyas was presumably dealt with by the school authorities, but by then he had got into Cambridge and he didn't have long left at the school. But we all hated him and his friend for what had happened to Harold. We avoided Amyas like the plague; called him names behind his back. Names which stuck.'

Inspector Lovelace had been scribbling in his notepad, but now he whistled. 'Quite a story, your Lordship. It does add a certain something to the mix. Could even give us a new edge? A new suspect?'

Posie was puzzled. '*Who*, sir?'

'Well, anyone connected with this poor lad who hanged himself, Harold Robertsbridge? Someone after a spot of revenge?'

But Rufus was shaking his head.

'You're hiking up the wrong path there, old chap. Robertsbridge was one of three boys. His two brothers were later killed in the Great War, and his father, a widower, committed suicide on Christmas Day 1918, after the Armistice. Couldn't cope with the loneliness and heartbreak, I expect. A first-class tragedy. I remember my father reading me the story from one of his newspapers, in a vain attempt to jolly me along, I suppose, when I was in hospital. And I remember thinking at the time that the name was unusual, it must have been the very same family. So if Amyas *has* been murdered, which you still haven't told me officially, there is no-one left to avenge poor Harold's death. No-one at all.'

'Besides,' said Posie. 'That all happened so long ago now. Awful though it was. Why wait until *now* to seek revenge? Can I ask a further two things, Rufey?'

Rufus shrugged. 'Be my guest.'

'Point one,' she tapped her index finger, 'was William Dawney the friend who helped Amyas with the gambling racket at school?'

Rufus laughed bitterly. 'That's right. Yes. He thought he was God's gift to everyone, even then.'

Posie frowned. 'I don't remember Richard ever mentioning a boy called William Dawney. I've racked my brains but I'm drawing a blank. It's strange.'

Rufus half-laughed. 'Nothing strange about it. I'm not surprised Richard never mentioned Dawney to you; he hated him with a passion.'

'But why?'

'I think Dawney may have put Richard in his place. I can't say more I'm afraid. I don't know more. Richard never told me the exact nature of his grudge.'

'I see.' *Although she didn't*. Posie tapped her second outstretched finger. 'Second point: do you know if Amyas Lyle carried on gambling? Carried on in adulthood?'

'Of course he did,' said Rufus darkly. Lovelace was writing hurriedly again. 'I'm surprised you haven't found evidence of it so far. Gamblers don't stop, do they? They *can't*. Maybe what they gamble on changes, but not the desire to.' He shook the whisky bottle again. 'Desire like *this*. It doesn't go, even if you pretend it does. Even after three years.'

'But do you have proof of his gambling activities, your Lordship? Or is this just your opinion?'

Rufus got up at last, walked over to the balustrade. Posie watched him carefully.

He turned after what seemed like ages and when he spoke there was no blurriness, no alcohol-haze. He was deadly serious. 'I *do* have proof of his activities, Richard. Because a few months after I got back to London from the trenches – it must have been early 1919 – I had the bad luck to run into Amyas Lyle again, at my club on St James's. I wasn't quite in my right mind, as you may know. It seemed Amyas was a regular there; knew all the gambling men, seemed to know their movements and habits better than they knew themselves. We met a few times, all with bad results for me. I got myself into a spot of bother, much like Harold Robertsbridge had, all those years before. The bother being Baccarat, this time. I kept losing. I couldn't stop. I lost a fantastic sum. The difference was, I was in a position to pay. But Lyle didn't want any old payment, did he?'

'What did he want, Rufey?'

'Amyas wanted something of mine, precious to me. Something which had cost me a small fortune. I'm a very rich man, as you know, and at the time Amyas wasn't. *He* would never have been able to afford this in a million years. It was a prize which would make him forget all about that drab porcelain-doll of a wife.'

'Drugs, your Lordship?'

Rufus laughed. A hollow sound. 'Hardly. Her name was Olga. She was Russian, and she was my mistress. She'd been married before and my father would never have sanctioned my marrying her, so she would have stayed my mistress forever, I suppose, nothing more. Amyas had seen me about the town with her: she was stunningly beautiful, a real treat on the old eye. In fact, she looked a good deal like you, Posie. Anyhow, she meant a good deal to me. In fact, I adored her. I'd bought her a place to live in, as it happened.'

Posie took a sharp intake of breath. 'On Fever Street?'

Rufus stared. 'How the devil? No. Don't answer me that. But for goodness' sake don't tell Dolly. This was all before her time.'

He groaned at the memory. 'I'd bought a house for Olga to live in in the mews at Fever Street. Amyas wanted both. And that's what he got. I think he kept them both, too. I don't know. I never spoke to either Amyas or Olga ever again.'

****

Nine

They climbed into the waiting police car as Big Ben was striking half-past three. Sergeant Rainbird sat up front, next to the driver.

Parliament Square was in chaos. The four roads of mixed traffic moved jerkily around the central square, where a few black-hatted ladies stood half-heartedly in the summer sunshine holding placards about women's rights. Nearby, a traffic policeman was having an argument with the driver of a horse-drawn cart carrying empty milk bottles, and a long queue of traffic, mainly motor-omnibuses, was building up behind. Beeps and horns sounded out.

Suddenly, and out of nowhere, a flock of dirty-looking long-haired sheep belted out into the main grassy section of the square, some streaming across the street itself. Posie looked in vain for anyone herding the sheep, but the animals seemed to be on their own.

'The deuce!' muttered Inspector Lovelace irritably, suddenly jumping up. 'Wretched sheep! Whoever passed these new laws about sheep eating grass in the city ought to be hanged!'

He had bounded out of the police car before she knew it and was off having irate words with the beleaguered traffic policeman, both of them searching around in vain for a shepherd.

Posie banged at the glass partition until Rainbird turned around. He grinned at her and slid back the window.

'All right, Miss?'

'*I* am. But dash it all, what's wrong with the Chief Inspector? He's not himself today at all. He seems very cross.'

The Sergeant looked at his boss in the distance. 'He's always like this – distracted, and snappy – when he's got a big decision to make.'

'A big decision?'

'That's right. I'm surprised he hasn't told you. That's why this Lyle murder case – high-profile as it is – needs to be investigated to the letter, absolutely properly. No cutting of corners. He needs to make a good impression. Although you'd think he'd be more amenable to sheep than he seems to be…'

'Sheep? Sorry, I don't follow you, Sergeant.'

But before he could answer, Lovelace had wrenched open the car door and climbed in. He picked up his notepad and scrawled something, thrusting the paper at Rainbird.

'These are the leads so far, bits we've gathered from Selwyn Pickle and the Earl of Cardigeon. Not much, admittedly. But all sorts is coming out of the woodwork and we'd better make a show of following it up. Now you get back to the Yard, Sergeant.'

Lovelace jabbed at the paper. 'Check out this name, "Robertsbridge". See what you can dig up about a tragedy: death of a fourteen-year-old schoolboy in about 1905. See if there are any living relatives. And while you're at it, check out the estranged son of Selwyn Pickle you found out about, the one who works at Billingsgate. If there's any suspicion of *anything* untoward, bring him in and await my return before questioning him.'

Rainbird got out of the car dejectedly. Posie wasn't surprised at his ill humour: this was surely work which was more in the line of a Constable?

He stooped at the window. 'I made contact with the Royal College of Surgeons, sir, after you two raced off to see the Earl. Dr Dawney is giving a lecture there tonight, in Lincoln's Inn Fields. His secretary said he would speak with you afterwards. Around seven?'

'Fine.' Lovelace knocked on the partition, to the driver. 'Chelsea, fast as you can.'

The car moved off, the thin rubber tyres bumping off along the cobbles.

Posie pressed her hands to her head, massaging her temples. She had the startings of a headache. The blur of London going past was much like the facts she seemed to have assimilated today about Amyas Lyle; too much, too unbelievable, too out of place.

'Just when I think we don't have enough on the man,' muttered the Inspector, mirroring her own thoughts, 'we suddenly have *too much*. I don't think I've ever disliked a murder victim so much before. It's unbelievable! Meet Amyas Lyle: fascist, philanderer, gambler of the worst kind; the sort of character who thinks nothing of bullying a young lad to death.'

Posie shook her head. 'We don't know that for certain, sir. We only have Rufus' spin on things, although I admit the business about the boy who hanged himself does sound terrible. But this all happened a long time ago. People change. Maybe Amyas felt sorry about it, maybe tried to make amends later on in life, in his own way?'

Lovelace laughed incredulously. 'Hah! How? Amyas Lyle was a wrong 'un, through and through. Your pal Rufus thought so, didn't he? No wonder people talked about him having no morals. And now we have to go and meet his wife and tell her how sorry we are about the fact he's died, as if he was the best sort of fella! And she'll have no clue what he was really like, of course. I hate my job sometimes.'

'Isn't it highly likely his wife knew exactly what sort of character he was, sir? We've been told they were living separate lives. Maybe we don't need to pretend too much. After all, we know from Amyas' list in the red biscuit tin lid that she probably knew about Olga, the mistress. That she wasn't pleased about it.'

Posie stared out of the open window, unseeing, as the streets of St James's turned into Victoria, then Pimlico, then Chelsea.

'I can't quite believe it,' she muttered.

'Believe what?'

'The mistress!' Posie hissed and shook her head in disbelief.

Lovelace looked up at her, a half-smile playing over his face. 'I'm glad we had that little chat with his Lordship back there. *Most* illuminating.'

Posie shook her head, her face black as thunder.

'What is it which has got your goat?' asked Lovelace, the grin now cracking his freckly face from ear to ear. 'Is it the fact Amyas had a mistress, and had it all handed to him on a plate so easily? Or is it because Rufus had a mistress in the first place?'

'Why, Rufus, of course! And the fact that this poor Olga creature was transferred like so much rubbish between the two men, like a chattel, with probably no say in the matter at all.'

Lovelace laughed, folding away his pad. 'Ah, Posie. Sometimes your innocence touches me; it really does. I think if a man such as Rufus *hadn't* got a mistress squirrelled away somewhere in this great city of ours it would be more of a surprise to me...'

Posie gasped. 'What, even *now*? Married to Dolly?'

Lovelace coughed and tugged at his immaculate collar, ignoring her. 'Oh, look,' he said brightly as the car slowed, 'here we are, Eaton Terrace. Now, by Gad, Posie, don't set the cat among the pigeons by hinting to the grieving widow that you meant more to her dead husband than life itself, eh? Got that?'

"Course,' she said defiantly, quickly re-applying her scarlet lipstick. A huge white-stuccoed townhouse reared up before them, part of a line of perhaps twenty identical homes. Posie followed Lovelace to the front door, but as they were waiting for the door-bell to be answered she felt a familiar pin-prickly sensation at the back of her neck which sent shivers down her spine. Normally it meant that someone was watching her.

Turning quickly, she saw that opposite the houses, across the road, was a long oblong-shaped communal garden, smartly hedged-in by laurels and a freshly-painted black wrought-iron fence. It concealed immaculate gardens of roses and gardenias, and a tennis court, from which came the sounds of soft shouting and laughter, and the reassuring swishing noises of racquets hitting balls. For a second Posie thought she saw a person loitering among the hedges, watching her, but on a second glance, shielding her eyes against the bright sun, there was no-one there. It was very hot. Maybe she was seeing things?

'Everything fine, Posie?'

'Absolutely, sir.'

Feeling foolish, she watched as Lovelace straightened his tie, and slicked back his unruly hair. Every one of his movements seemed to say: '*This one's important. Don't mess this up.*'

But there it was again.

Posie turned around again suddenly, on an instinct, and there, sure enough, a man was watching them.

He was standing right outside the black wrought-iron fence. Posie scrunched her eyes up against the sun. He was tall and dark, with film-star good looks. He was dressed casually, in blue flannels and a striped white shirt, holding a newspaper, with a raincoat in the crook of his arm. And then she gasped.

Could it be?

She grabbed at Lovelace's jacket sleeve, flailing, not taking her eyes off the man. 'Sir, sir…'

'Posie, what the deuce? I say, are you hallucinating? Is it this wretched heat?'

'Sir, look! Turn around! You won't believe it, sir!'

The Inspector did as instructed, following her pointing finger. But there was no-one there. Nobody standing on the hot dusty pavement at all.

Posie read consternation in the glittery fire of Richard Lovelace's grey-green eyes as they searched her face for an explanation. She felt a fool, but...

'Sir, are we *sure* Amyas Lyle is dead?'

'Come again, Posie?'

Ringing footsteps could be heard approaching on the other side of the stained-glass paned front door. Professional footsteps. Posie found she was still clinging to Richard Lovelace's arm. She blurted everything out in a mad rush:

'Oh, I know there was a corpse this morning in his study at 20 Old Square, but are you definitely *sure* it was Amyas Lyle? Wasn't the corpse terribly disfigured?'

'What the blazes are you talking about?'

'I'm sure I've just seen him, sir. Amyas Lyle. Standing right across from us. Watching this house. Staring at us. Just now. Alive as alive can be.'

Wide-eyed, the Inspector looked back over his shoulder again, but seeing no-one there, he shook his head in disbelief.

'There's no way, Posie. It was Lyle, dead as a doornail this morning. We'll have the dental evidence and post-mortem results later, but everything so far points to it being Lyle. Almost no doubt. Now, you're definitely not the ticket, are you? When we get inside I'll ask if you can have a glass of ice-cold lemonade. Or tea. Yes: sugary tea. That will be the best thing. You'll be right as rain again in just a minute.'

And he smiled pleasantly at the Butler who peered out, and then led them inside.

* * * *

Ten

Inside the hallway, they side-stepped over a giant mountain of suitcases, hat-boxes and trunks, all monogrammed in gold with 'ROADE' visible on every surface.

'Do forgive the mess,' muttered the Butler. On closer inspection he was quite a young man, nervous, with a violent shake of the hands which spoke of serious war-damage.

'We are quite at sixes and sevens here, you know. Not expecting the Mistress or young gentlemen back for another few weeks. But it seems they have been recalled quite suddenly from their holidays. Goodness knows why... The Mistress has only been at home for the last twenty minutes or so. And now we've had word that Lord Justice Roade is to call, too. Dear, dear. This way please...'

So the staff did not yet know about Amyas Lyle's death.

Or perhaps they suspected something was amiss, as a bickering row could be heard echoing down from the top of the stairs, as two black-liveried maids quarrelled with each other openly, hardly bothering to lower their voices as the Butler announced Posie and Inspector Lovelace into the Drawing Room.

Lady Antonia sat among a vast pile of richly embroidered silk cushions in the middle of an oriental-style settee. So vibrant was the room, that both the Inspector and Posie felt they had to adjust their eyes somewhat to actually locate the Mistress of the House, who was small and fragile-looking in the midst of all the colour.

Antonia Lyle had translucent milky skin and almost colourless grey eyes, her strange beauty enhanced by her very short hair which had been dyed a shocking blue. Th overall effect was of a small ghost who had been let loose in a fancy-dress cupboard.

'Please do sit. Forgive me if I don't get up, won't you? I've been travelling all day and it's been *such* an effort.'

The voice, unlike the woman, was rich and authoritative, and they found themselves sitting on low foot-stools, like supplicants, in front of her. Posie noticed how the pupils in her eyes were simply enormous, the blackness fully dilated, almost filling the whole iris.

Just what had she taken to get into this state? Posie wondered, as the Inspector trotted out all the standard niceties.

'Thank you for agreeing to meet us, Lady Antonia, and may we offer you our deepest condolences?'

'How kind of you to come. A Scotland Yard Inspector, no less, and the famous lady detective we read about so often.'

It was impossible to tell if Amyas Lyle's wife was being ironic or not. Either way, if she had been crying, she had wiped any tears dry. A compact mirror with a small mound of white powder – probably cocaine – and a child's striped paper straw sat at her side on a mirrored oriental table, in full view of both of them. The lack of any attempt to hide the drugs spoke of the devil-may-care attitude of the serious addict. Perhaps it was the proximity of the drugs, but Lovelace seemed unnerved by the woman, much to Posie's annoyance.

Antonia Lyle didn't move an inch, but indicated towards another small low table, this one set with tea-things and a shop-bought Madeira cake, still in its package. Posie took the hint and poured tea for all three of them, although by now she felt simply awash with the stuff. She made a go of cutting the cake, however, and then sat back and tried not to look wrong-footed.

But try as she might, Posie couldn't help staring around herself. The room was a bit of a shock, given the blank austerity of the expensive exterior of the house, and given what they had seen of Amyas Lyle's plain office and dull flat.

This Drawing Room was a riot of colour: reds, golds, silver. Silks and maps covered entire walls, and the dividing wall was given over to a show of stuffed animal heads: monkeys; hyenas; tiny, fragile-looking deer. In one corner, near the enormous bay window with its view out over the road, a full-sized tiger head and pelt was nailed to the wall. All around it was a collection of perhaps fifty dancing, leering, white-faced puppets with oversized heads; all wearing red pyjamas and playing miniature pan-pipes. They looked like little gods. The variety and exoticness of the things on display was simply dazzling, and Posie tried to focus her gaze back on Amyas' wife.

One thing was certain: if this world was Lady Antonia's, Amyas, or his presence, was not to be found anywhere here.

'I see you like my Indian Drawing Room, Miss Parker. Have you been to India? Is that why you seem so peculiarly riveted? Or has the tiger got your tongue?'

Posie put her untasted tea down, resisted the urge to lick at her lipstick, and smiled coolly. 'I have never been to India, Lady Antonia. But I should like to go one day. Very much.'

The woman narrowed her eyes. '*I've* never been, either. I don't think the climate would like me much. This is all my grandparents' stuff. They were running the show out in India for a while, out in Shimla. All this came back with them, and was inherited by my mother who put it straight into storage, afraid of offending my father. And then later, when my mother died, my father was going to throw it all out, so I took it. My father is *very* Church of England; he's from a long line of strict Protestant lawyers. There are also very prominent churchmen, Bishops and Archbishops, in the Roade family, dating way back. So there's no way my father wanted all these Indian gods taking up space in his own house; nothing remotely "pagan" as he would term it. So I took it all and fixed it up here. Suits the place a treat, don't you think? You see, I'm a woman with a past. A historical past, which I want to acknowledge. Which is something my husband didn't have. Could *never* have had.'

'What do you mean, Lady Antonia? When you say your husband didn't have a past?' Lovelace checked his notebook quickly. 'You mean his parents are dead? We know that already.'

'No: I mean because my husband came from nothing, into nothing. He was adopted as a baby. So who knows where he came from? Or who he was before he became Amyas Lyle? Quite literally, he was a man without a past.'

This was news to Posie.

She cut in: 'Did Amyas *know* he was adopted? Or did he find out just recently?' She shot a meaningful look at Inspector Lovelace: here perhaps was another lead, a motive for murder?

But Antonia Lyle was dismissive. 'Oh, Amyas always knew he was adopted. His adoptive parents didn't hide anything from him. They said they would help him connect with his birth family if that was what he wanted. But he wasn't interested. He wasn't one for stories, or historical baggage.'

So he hated this room, thought Posie to herself. *And probably you, too. With your weight of history bearing down upon you…*

Posie suddenly felt like stirring things up: they were getting precisely nowhere here. Why was the Inspector being so nice? Why was he treating Antonia Lyle with kid gloves when he'd previously said she'd be his number one suspect for the murder of her husband?

'So are you *at all* upset at your husband's death, Lady Antonia? Or are you just hiding it very, very well?'

Beside her she heard the Inspector draw in his breath tightly, but he didn't fill the silence which followed with empty, ridiculous words of appeasement or apology. *He* wanted to know too.

Mrs Lyle had cocked her bright blue head on one side.

'I'd normally have your guts for garters, my girl. But seeing as the Inspector here seems to rate you as highly as he does, I'll answer you. No, I am not upset. Angry, yes. Angry and bewildered. But not upset. Amyas and I, well, our marriage was part of a deal, a plan. But I gave him everything I had.'

'Meaning?'

'My money, the chance to use this house, which is mine. I gave him children, too. All of these helped make Amyas Lyle – the man who came from nothing – into the man he was, the man he was *becoming*. A King's Counsel, a High Court Judge... And you wonder why I'm angry? Because the plan was all for nothing! It got interrupted.'

'By his death?'

'Exactly.'

Posie stared at the woman, at the two bright red spots which seemed to burn feverishly on the cheekbones of that beautiful, terribly pale face. How cold, how remote was it possible to be? Perhaps she and Amyas had suited each other perfectly, in fact.

'And if Amyas got so much out of your deal together, what was in it for *you*? Hadn't you had enough of living in the shadow of big, important men with a career in the Law Courts to last you a lifetime?'

At this Lady Antonia pointed a finger out of the bay window, to the invisible tennis courts beyond. 'There!' she said, softly, almost to herself. 'I got my twin boys.'

At Posie's frown she smiled defiantly, dangerously. 'I was very young, and Amyas was just starting out as a pupil barrister when I met him at some legal party. Well, when I told him later that I was in the *family way* he did the right thing, the honourable thing. We got married very quickly and he saved my honour. One good deed deserved another, surely. We owed each other *that*.'

Lovelace, perhaps feeling himself privy to a women's conversation, made a deal of coughing and harrumphing, changing the subject entirely.

'Was your husband a gambler, to the best of your knowledge, my Lady?'

Antonia Lyle's kohl-enhanced eyes narrowed menacingly and she clamped her mouth shut, a hard line in the beautiful, dreadful face.

Lovelace pressed on: 'Please answer the question. Was he a gambler? Did you know your husband had a reputation for gambling as a lad, at school? Please be honest with us: it could be important.'

'Very well.' Amyas Lyle's wife crossed and re-crossed her arms. 'You seem to have done some research already, I'll give you that. Yes: my husband was a gambler. He'd put money on anything, as it happens. He won most of the time. But that all stopped in 1914.'

'Oh, yes?' The Inspector was leaning forwards, hands on his knees, hardly bothering to conceal his interest, brows knitted together. 'What happened in 1914?'

'We got married. I told you: our marriage was a trade, a deal. My father and I knew Amyas had a problem, so part of the bargain in marrying me was that he gave up the gambling. It wouldn't have looked good, would it? My Protestant father's son-in-law, a betting man?'

Posie dared the briefest glance at Lovelace, to see if he was doing the calculations too, had seen the problem, but he was just nodding.

Lady Antonia was carrying on in a rush: 'It was all written up in a marriage contract. In it, Amyas agreed to give up the gambling and live honourably, *loyally*; supporting me and my father as the occasion demanded. And in return my father would support Amyas, as the occasion demanded. You can see the contract if you wish. It will be with our lawyers, Pring and Proudfoot, on Bedford Row. With our Wills. The Wills are identical to each other, by the way; Amyas and I leave everything to each other.'

Posie dashed on quickly: 'But that timing – 1914 – is not quite right, is it, Lady Antonia?'

'I beg your pardon?'

A flash of a warning glare from Lovelace, which Posie ignored. 'We have it on very good authority that your husband was still gambling in 1919. Only five years ago, but five years *after* you're telling us he'd stopped. And the stakes he won were big, too.'

Antonia Lyle, perhaps the palest woman Posie thought she had ever met, seemed to go even whiter. 'You will have to take my word for it, Miss Parker, but I believe he had stopped. He had to kow-tow not just to me, but to my father, and my father wouldn't have tolerated *that*.'

Posie didn't dare look at Lovelace. The woman's responses seemed genuine enough, and yet they knew from Amyas Lyle's own list that he considered his wife might be a suspect in sending him threatening mail, and that she had known about his mistress.

'So how do you account for the house on Fever Street, then? For the woman there?' *There, she had said it.*

And as soon as she had, Posie realised she had released some inner banshee in the woman opposite her.

Lady Antonia almost whispered her response, but slowly, deliberately, enunciating each syllable, like a cat about to pounce. 'How do I *account* for it? I don't. It wasn't my job to account, or understand. When I found out about *that* arrangement, I simply put up with it. What else could I do? *That* was Amyas' business. If he wanted to keep a cheap woman in secret, he was welcome to her.'

There was boiling anger here, lava erupting, barely contained, and a strange hurt, despite all the protestations of having a marriage of convenience. A refuge had been sought by Amyas, but not *here*, not here at the 'home' provided for him. Was this why his wife was ragingly angry at him?

And she obviously didn't know that Olga had been won as part of the spoils of a bet.

Posie's head was spinning at the strangeness of the situation, but she pressed on regardless:

'So how did you find out about her, then? The mistress? And we *know* you did. Your husband left written evidence more or less stating that you were livid with him because of it.'

A gulp of an acknowledgement. 'I'm frankly surprised he took that on board.' And then, suddenly, Lady Antonia seemed to make a snap decision. 'Come, follow me.'

She stood and then sashayed out of the Drawing Room and down the main hallway, where the strains of the housemaids' row on the landing upstairs could still be heard, and they followed her to a small darkened room off the end of the corridor, at the very back of the house. A quick pull at a blind flooded the room with a watered-out daylight, and Posie saw that they were looking out over the miniscule walled garden with its twisting trees. There wasn't much to see in the room itself: a small, expensive-looking desk and matching chair; a shelf with a framed print of King George V on it and a couple of gilt-embossed leather legal tomes for decoration; a fireplace which had obviously not seen a real flame in years.

Lovelace was looking about with genuine interest.

'This was my husband's study.' Suddenly Lady Antonia was wrenching out a drawer in the desk, pulling out papers, her hands shaking, her whole body jittery. 'I set it up for him here when we first married. He never used it once in all that time.'

Posie felt a surprising stab of pity for the woman in front of her, and she had a horrible flash-back to the life she had briefly created with Alaric; the room she had made so nice for him in her beautiful apartment at Museum Chambers in Bloomsbury, the way he hadn't seemed to notice or appreciate her efforts, although he *had* actually used it, to be fair.

Suddenly Antonia Lyle looked up, guilty for a second. 'Look, you should know, I had someone with their ears to the ground and their eyes wide open working for me at 20 Old Square. Keeping a look out for me there, telling me what Amyas was getting up to.'

'You had a spy at his work? A paid spy?' Posie asked incredulously.

'Call it what you will. In January this year my husband's behaviour really changed. Amyas stopped coming here almost completely, he stopped seeing the boys as much. He only came here on Sundays. I wondered if there was another woman, so I paid someone to check up on him at work, to gather evidence from January onwards. That's how I knew later on about the threats he was receiving: he certainly wouldn't have told me. And it's how I found out about *her*, too. Olga Karloff…'

Lady Antonia passed across wads of thin, tissue-fine pages of notepaper. All of which had been crumpled badly. There were probably a hundred pages in total. Lovelace and Posie took a few each, and started reading. There were rows of inked figures, the numbers penned in clearly, with annotated descriptions for each row.

'Household accounts,' muttered Lovelace. Here was the hum-drum of everyday life dating back over the last six months. Bills for grocers and coal-men, bills for a metre of sapphire-coloured velvet, bills for blue paint, bills for a painter to re-varnish the front door of 57 Fever Street. Here was what they *hadn't* found in Amyas' room; evidence of the mistress and her life, paid for by him. Each page had been annotated by the initials 'OK'.

'Amyas paid these, didn't he?' said Posie. 'But then routinely threw them away. He'd been doing that for years, until your spy found these particular bills in Amyas' bins earlier this year, and gave them to you. How *lovely*.'

Amyas' wife shrugged. 'I'm not proud of it. But needs must.'

The Inspector waved the papers in the air. 'Keep them, can I? So did you go to Fever Street yourself and confront your husband's mistress?'

A slightly too-high laugh. 'Oh, no. That would never do. I went there, of course. Lots of times. In my car. I sat in the back and watched the place out of tortured curiosity. Recently as it happens. Just before we went to France. But I never confronted anyone. Certainly not Madame Karloff. She wasn't in a state to have any confrontation levied at her, not from anybody.'

Lovelace frowned. 'Olga Karloff? Why, what was wrong with her?'

'It's not my place to say, is it? You'll have to meet her yourself.'

Posie handed her portion of the household bills to Lovelace, who packaged them up, but Posie kept her eyes riveted on the desk. 'Lady Antonia, what else did George, the Head Clerk, obtain for you – for it was *him*, wasn't it? Indispensable, faithful George…'

She watched as the woman kept very still, eventually nodding.

'I'm sure George must have found other useful things in the bin. What else do you have there?'

'Nothing very interesting. Just some picture postcards which George picked up. Apparently they came so frequently that Amyas always threw them into the bin without further thought. *I* was going to throw them away, too. They, unlike these bills, mean nothing to me. Told me nothing. Gave me nothing new.' She was rummaging again, pulling out cards haphazardly, lots of cards. Postcards.

Lovelace almost snatched at them. 'So he was right,' he muttered, counting through them. 'Twenty-two of the things. Starting right at the beginning of January.'

He passed them over to Posie. Here were the postcards Selwyn Pickle had seen arriving; all of them identical to the one they had found taped to the top of the biscuit tin. All of them showing the fashionable Spanish City at Whitley Bay. They were all postmarked locally.

Posie looked up, genuinely puzzled. 'Did your husband have any connection to Whitley Bay? Or to the north? Did he ever go there? Maybe with work?'

'No, I don't recall him ever mentioning the place. And I certainly don't think he ever went there. Not while I knew him.'

Ah, but you didn't know him, did you?

Inspector Lovelace placed the postcards in the same envelope and then looked over at the picture of the King high on the bookshelf. At last he broke the silence. 'There is no delicate way of putting this, my Lady. But it seems your husband may have been a supporter of the new fascist movement which is growing in London. Can I ask, is it a surprise to you to hear such a thing?'

Lady Antonia smirked knowingly. 'Gracious, no. My father is practically bank-rolling the whole thing. And don't look so shocked. It's little more than an extension of a London club. I told you already: Amyas when he married me had to sign a contract – he had to support my father whenever my father requested support.'

'And that included supporting his politics?'

'Oh, yes. Definitely.'

Lovelace tried not to look sickened. 'I only have one thing left to ask, my Lady. And that's to ask if you know how your husband was getting on lately with a Dr William Dawney. Had they fallen out?'

Lady Antonia almost threw her head back and laughed. 'William? Fall out with Amyas? Gracious, no. They were friends. Those two knew each other at school. They wouldn't throw that away. They respected each other. Helped each other...' She began to pull the blind down again, and then opened the study door out into the corridor.

'In what way did they help each other?' Posie was curious.

'In the last couple of years poor William has endured terrible losses. *Personal* losses, not professional ones, mind. Both his parents died within a year of each other, and then his lovely young wife, Kate, died earlier this year. Most unexpectedly. She withered away within a couple of weeks. Such a shock. William's was a very Catholic family, you know, but he was the only child. He had no-one to turn to in his hour of need, except us here, and Amyas. William would come here and see Amyas on a Sunday; they'd both spend time with the twins. William seemed to be getting better, brighter; like he had energy returning to him after Kate's death. William told me a while back how good Amyas had been to him; how he was returning the favour by helping him with a new project. But don't ask me what it was; I don't know.'

They were out in the corridor now. The shaky Butler had reappeared as if by magic with coats and hats.

'This has all been most helpful, my Lady,' said Lovelace, putting on his homburg.

The woman nodded, her white silk clothes fluttering. She was trembling violently now. *Whatever she takes*, thought Posie, *she needs it again soon.*

'I say,' said Posie brightly, 'I do know you are only just back, but have you seen a man – a tall, dark, good-looking man – hanging around outside Eaton Terrace at all, watching your house?'

Lovelace coughed in disbelief, but Lady Antonia tittered brightly. 'Oh, Miss Parker, how funny you are! Are you one of those women who see ghosts everywhere? Shades lingering in dark places...'

The Mistress of the house shot a brief, guilty glance at her Butler before focusing on Posie again. 'Was it the war which shook you up so? Amyas didn't go, you know; he had a bad heart, some genetic problem. But he might as well have gone: he seemed to spend forever at his Chambers during those war years. Busiest he ever was, I think. Goodness knows what he was up to.'

Lady Antonia seemed to have trouble focusing now, pulling herself back to her subject with an effort. 'But it seems every Tom, Dick and Harry has a good ghost story from the Great War worth recounting, don't they? Albert our Butler here is always seeing things, aren't you? Where was it you served, Albert? When you got sent home for good, trembling like a leaf all over?'

'Ypres, my Lady.' Albert bent his head in shame. 'Lots of ghosts there now, I'll warrant.'

The man's hands jerked wildly, then smoothed down his black jacket, again and again. Posie spoke softly: 'I was there too, you know, Albert. On the Western Front. I was an ambulance driver. I won't ever forget the sights I saw. Or the noise. I still dream of all the noise.'

Antonia Lyle tittered as if Posie had made a good joke: 'Oh! How interesting you are, Miss Parker, a real all-rounder!'

It wasn't obvious if this was praise or irony, and before Posie could decide, the woman had whipped around to her Butler again, frowning, her black pupils somehow nightmarish in their size, in their intensity.

'But seriously, Albert. *Have* you seen any tall, dark, good-looking men spying in on us here? Like Miss Parker describes?'

'I can't say I've noticed any, my Lady.'

But Posie saw how he couldn't quite meet his Mistress' eye. Or hers, for that matter, as they swung out of the door.

* * * *

Eleven

For some reason they automatically turned right in unison and hurried together in the direction of Victoria, although Sloane Square would have been nearer for the Underground. Their police car was long gone. It was still very hot and the smell rising from the dusty street was strong: grit and tar and festering horse dung.

'*That* was interesting,' said Lovelace. 'Not what I was expecting.'

'You mean you behaved yourself, sir, because you thought she was stunningly beautiful, *and* well-connected, despite the fact she's a fully-paid-up drug addict?' Posie laughed in disbelief. 'So *is* she a suspect in the murder of her husband, sir? Earlier you thought she'd be the prime candidate. You certainly weren't throwing accusations at her, were you?'

The Chief Inspector opened his mouth and then closed it again. Posie grinned. 'Yep, I know. You were just being gentlemanly. And I agree, anyhow. Lady Antonia doesn't seem to be on the ball enough to organise anything, let alone a cold-blooded murder.'

A hot, light rain was starting up and Posie grabbed at her umbrella from Thomas Brigg. It was a rich, bright yellow, which didn't match anything, but it made her feel cheerful and she put it up now anyhow.

'You look like a giant buttercup, old girl.'

'At least I'll be dry. Unlike you.'

'Mnnn. So you reckon she didn't kill Lyle, then? Or arrange to have him murdered?'

Posie shrugged. 'I'd find it unlikely. We know she was in France for sure yesterday, but I doubt she paid a hit-man to do it in her absence. It's as she says: the death has messed up her plans.'

Lovelace adjusted his hat as the rain slanted down. '*Something's* not right there, though, is it? Something wasn't being said.'

'You felt that too, sir? I agree. Something didn't make sense in her story. But I can't quite put my finger on it…'

'Well, let me know when you do.'

'We found out something else which we didn't know before, didn't we, sir? About Amyas being adopted. I didn't know that.' Posie shrugged. 'And I don't think my brother Richard knew, otherwise he would have said something. Do you think it might be relevant to the murder?'

Richard Lovelace shook his head. 'I doubt it. This is a murder based on something *now*; a current grievance, not something based on an historical adoption of thirty-five years ago!'

He checked his wristwatch. 'Almost five o'clock. Do you feel up to pursuing the mistress, Olga Karloff? Alone? You'll most likely have to break the news to the poor woman.'

'Fine.'

'Thank you. We know the address now: 57 Fever Street. Ask her all the usual questions. But turn tail and come back to the Royal College of Surgeons for seven o'clock. I want your impression of Bill Sawbones, the man with the murky schoolboy past and the tragic present. It's important we see everyone on that list *today*, while the tragedy is still fresh in their minds.'

Posie exhaled noisily. 'What a day! It's busier than most, that's for sure. Where are you going?'

'Oh, I've got a big internal meeting at the Yard. Procedures. Appointments. Nothing very exciting.'

'It sounds scintillating, sir. Oh, I say! Who's this? What's all this carry-on?'

They turned around hastily. From the direction they had just walked, from Eaton Terrace, a booming, authoritative voice was making itself heard through the rain, calling out Lovelace's name.

'Is that Antonia's father, sir? Lord Justice Roade?'

Inspector Lovelace narrowed his eyes to focus on the figure coming into their immediate vicinity and then he straightened his hat. He stood a little taller in the rain. 'Yes. I think it must be.'

Quite suddenly a very, very small, very finely-boned man in his late fifties was upon them. He looked very much like his daughter. He was fragile-looking and very fair, but with a gigantic walrus-moustache, stained yellow from tobacco, a hang-over from the Edwardian period he had so obviously grown up in, his glory days. The man looked almost comic: he wore rumpled cricket whites and a canvas umpire's hat, and around his neck was a silver whistle. He was half-drenched with rain. That this man could inspire terror into the heart of criminals in the dock on trial, and cause endless column inches to be written about him in the newspapers, was quite frankly unbelievable. That this was the deadly 'End of the Road, Roade', the hanging Judge, was almost laughable.

Posie wouldn't have believed it except for the voice. It was piercing and commanding. You didn't mess with the holder of a voice like that. So what on earth did *he* want, running up to them in such an undignified fashion?

'Chief Inspector? What-ho? Chief Inspector Lovelace, isn't it?'

'That's right, your Honour.'

'I've only just arrived at my daughter's house. Forgive the rig. I've been playing cricket with some of my old school chums down at the Oval, while its empty for the summer holidays. I was there all day yesterday too, as it happens, before you ask me for my whereabouts.' He gave Lovelace a piercing look, laden with meaning. 'I know your Superintendent actually. He came down himself to give me the bad news about Amyas this afternoon.'

'Oh, yes, your Honour?'

'Jolly fine man, your Superintendent.'

'Mnnn.'

'And he tells me that you're investigating the death of my son-in-law, eh, Lovelace? *Personally?*'

'That's right, your Honour. A terrible business. May I extend my condolences to you.'

'Yes, yes. A shock, really.' So far the Judge hadn't spoken to Posie, or looked at her for even a second underneath her yellow umbrella. He continued, speaking only to Lovelace, a confidential tone suddenly replacing the previous booming commands:

'I mean, Amyas Lyle wasn't the husband I'd have chosen for my only child, gracious, no: but then, as you've seen, Antonia is hardly the child I'd have chosen for myself, either. She's an addict, a scatter-brained fool, with no sense at all, but plenty of money; all coming from her wretched mother's side, and all disappearing into the hands of some good-for-nothing drug dealer.'

The small man looked as if he might burst with anger, Rumpelstiltskin-like. 'What I'd give to get my hands upon that drug peddler, but Antonia won't give away the identity of her dealer if it's the last thing she does! Good job the house here on Eaton Terrace is in a trust for her, rather than actually belonging to her outright. It means Antonia can't sell the place from underneath herself and shove the proceeds up her nostrils ...'

'Ah, er, I see.' Lovelace shuffled awkwardly.

'No use being polite about it, Chief Inspector. You'll have seen the mess the girl's got herself into, eh? And the drugs themselves, out on display for all to see. By Jove! Good job those twin boys of hers are made of sterner stuff. They're worth ten of her, and I don't mind admitting it: they're the apples of my eye. But Antonia's the reason why I've come rushing out here in the rain like a mad fool; to clear her from your suspicions. You've seen the state she's in, and the house too, eh? Antonia can barely run a house, let alone know how to kill a man. She'd be completely unable to do that.'

Posie coughed demurely, cutting in quickly: 'You said you wouldn't have chosen Amyas Lyle as a son-in-law, your Honour. Why was that?'

Lord Justice Roade's colourless grey eyes swivelled towards her and bore into Posie. Roade turned quickly back to the Inspector. 'This your wife, Lovelace? She's jolly fresh if you don't mind my saying so. Your work has obviously rubbed off on her, what?'

Lovelace smiled. 'No, your Honour, this isn't my wife. She's my associate. Miss Posie Parker. Unorthodox perhaps, but we work well together. Get good results.'

In the empty beat of a pause which followed, Posie held her nerve, desperately trying not to laugh, or to flush with embarrassment. The rain had stopped but she held the carved black wooden stick of the umbrella up anyhow, focused on her own dignity.

'I see,' the Judge said at last. He swallowed uneasily, swivelling around to Posie. 'Well then, Miss Parker, I was proud to tell people Amyas was my daughter's husband, especially as he was about to become a High Court Judge. I was happy to have helped bring him on. But that was the *professional* man. Underneath it all I couldn't help but feel glad that he and my daughter and their children lived separate lives.'

'Why was that, your Honour?'

The small man drew himself up as tall as he could. 'I'm ashamed to admit it, Miss Parker, but I'm not surprised he was murdered. Amyas Lyle was a frightening vacuum of an individual. He lacked any sense of right or wrong. Do you know, he didn't do any war work at all? Isn't that despicable?'

'Hardly grounds for being murdered though, are they, your Honour?' Posie smiled sweetly, slowly folding down her umbrella, taking her time. 'And didn't Amyas have a serious heart condition which excused him? Hopefully the boys haven't inherited it…'

Posie watched a flush of anger darken the Judge's face, but she went on, unafraid of this trumped-up little man. 'Amyas must have seemed biddable enough to you, though? Handy, when you needed support. Following your political lead into *questionable* places.'

Posie heard the Inspector almost choke beside her, and she watched as the Judge's eyes bulged in outrage.

But she was just getting going: 'I'd say you didn't like Amyas mainly since you found out he was keeping a mistress. Isn't that right, sir? You probably found out in January of this year, when your daughter told you so herself. After everything you did to help him, he hurt Antonia, didn't he? He had embarrassed her. And it put you in a tight spot: you'd already advanced Amyas well along the road to becoming a High Court Judge, so you couldn't turn back. You couldn't even demand that Amyas and your daughter divorce. Admittedly, you're not a Catholic, but your family *are* upstanding Anglicans. Divorce would have sullied the family name in a very public way. So you were stuck with the mess, weren't you?'

Posie bit at her tongue: she had been about to say that Amyas' death had no doubt suited Lord Justice Roade; had come at a very *convenient* time for him. But that was tantamount to accusing the man of murder, and not even Posie had the courage to go that far…

Lord Roade had gone very still. He stared from Posie back to Lovelace. When he spoke again it was very quietly:

'Good job you're not married to her, eh, Lovelace? You'd be scolded all day long. Although I'll give her this: she's got nearly as first-class a brain on her as my dead son-in-law. She's quite right.' He nodded. 'Amyas made a first-class mess for Antonia. Funny, really, eh? How things work out.'

He turned to go, but then seemed to think better of it and swung back. 'I hear from your Superintendent that you've got a big decision to make, Lovelace. Can't be that difficult, old chap, eh? Seems fairly black-and-white to me. But it's a good reason to solve this case quickly, and with a good, satisfying outcome. You'll want a high note, eh?'

And then he was gone.

Posie scowled. 'Good riddance! Poisonous little man, wasn't he? I'd love for you to stick him right at the top of your suspect list, but I know you won't. And what on earth was all *that* about, sir?'

She sensed panic in her own voice, a rising wail which she tried to halt. 'What high note? What big decision was he talking about?'

For a second her heart -and her world- seemed to spin on a dizzying axis and she thought she might fall over there and then in the street. *What was Richard Lovelace, one of the most steadfast and reliable people she knew, doing which required a big decision?* Surely he hadn't decided to leave the city? Move out of London? She frowned: she couldn't imagine London without him in it, somehow. Or her life without him in it, either.

'Oh, it's nothing.' Lovelace grunted dismissively. 'It's just a managerial thing, a promotion of kinds. Now, this case, have you noticed how everything – Amyas' behaviour changing, Lady Antonia spying on her husband and finding out about Olga, the strange postcards and notes arriving – began around the same time? At the start of this year?'

Posie agreed. 'The key *must* be the mistress. I'll go there now. Find out what she has to say.'

'If anything,' muttered the Inspector darkly, before rushing away into the crowds of Victoria, swallowed up among hundreds of others. And Posie watched him go, wondering why it seemed like he only had half his mind on the job.

Or why she even cared.

* * * *

Twelve

Len had been right: the little enclave of Fever Street was a secret world. As the motor-taxi bumped into the cobbled street of neat black-and-white mews houses the driver pulled up and gave Posie a cold, hard stare from the front mirror.

'I'll not wait for you, Miss.' He sniffed. 'This isn't the sort of place I'd like to get a reputation for hanging around in. And it's not the sort of place I'd expect a lady like *yourself* to be finding herself in, either.'

Posie snatched up her bag and stood outside the open front passenger window, paying the cabbie. 'I'll ask you to hold your tongue, and reserve your judgement on ladies like me, thank you very much.'

She walked away without looking back, the pin-prickly feeling at the nape of her neck intense, knowing that many pairs of eyes were looking at her from behind immaculate lace curtains which seemed to be fitted in all the houses in the horseshoe-shaped enclave. There was a heavy sense of foreboding hanging about Fever Street. As evening approached, the sun dipped below the roof-level of the line of houses, and the whole place was suddenly pitched into shadow. Posie located number 57 at the very end, an immaculate white house with black painted windows and shutters, and a blue-varnished stable-door in two halves with a polished knocker in the shape of a dolphin. The epitome of good taste.

She rapped on the door and stood back, imagining what Olga Karloff, the mysterious mistress of both her old friend Rufus *and* Amyas Lyle, would be like. After a little while footsteps on hall tiles could be heard inside, approaching the front door, and there was a drawing back of a bolt, followed by the top half of the stable-door swinging inwards.

Frightened eyes met Posie's. Blue eyes, vivid blue like sapphires, but they were set in a face tight with worry lines, and the woman with the lovely blue eyes wore no make-up or fancy clothes, just plain black linen. Mourning dress. Posie remembered suddenly that Rufus had said Olga had been married before, but Posie had not been expecting her to be so old.

'Madame Karloff? Are you Olga?'

The frightened eyes narrowed and the woman shook her head before quickly looking out into the street, this way and that, like a frightened cat. Posie got out her silver card case and presented one of her business cards to the woman – a Housekeeper? – who read it slowly.

'I'm Miss Parker,' Posie said slowly, motioning to herself, sure now that the woman was not English. 'I'm working with the police, and I need to ask Olga Karloff some questions. If she isn't here could you tell me when I can come back again? Later? When will be a good time?'

To Posie's horror, the woman rubbed at her face where tears were now coursing down her cheeks. The woman drew back the bolt on the lower half of the door and stood back, motioning Posie in.

'There no good time to come back, Miss,' the woman said in a heavily-accented Russian voice, every word a terrible tremble: 'My Mistress, Olga Karloff, she dead.'

****

Posie found herself taking her umpteenth cup of tea of the day, the silver tea-things and the fussy lace doily which accompanied a plate of sweet, foreign biscuits placed carefully on a table in a Drawing Room which was the very opposite of Lady Antonia's.

The pale cream painted walls and light blue chairs and blue linen curtains spoke of elegant, simple taste. Nothing was over-the-top here, it was an oasis of calm. Posie sipped at the tea, made with boiled cream and cinnamon, like in the Orient, and tried not to wince at the unbearable sweetness of it. Masha, the Housekeeper, sat opposite Posie on a stool. They were in front of a fireplace, and above the mantel was a large painting of a serious-looking young woman with similar blue eyes to Posie, with the same dark hair, but wearing the white floating chiffony clothes of at least fifteen years before. Olga Karloff, presiding over the room, even in death. Posie stared.

It felt surreal but she did indeed find an echo of herself in the woman who had been painted so beautifully in this portrait. As Rufus had said, they had been similar types. Amyas Lyle's type, evidently.

Masha was wringing her fingers in despair. 'But why you here, Miss? I no understand. No-one knows yet about Olga. I try, and I try to contact the Master, but he no come.' Masha twisted at a lace handkerchief in her lap, panic and uncertainty washing over her face.

Posie blew out her cheeks, paused for a second, tried to summon her gentlest manner. 'Do you mean Amyas?' she asked quietly. 'Mr Amyas Lyle? The famous barrister?'

Masha was nodding now, thankful for someone with some common knowledge in a world full of secrets. 'That's right. Mr Lyle.'

Posie told the woman as quickly as possible what had

happened, and how Amyas had been murdered the day before. She cut the worst bits out.

The revelation led to more weeping; to anguished cries which Posie suddenly realised was the greatest show of grief she had heard so far in the whole sorry mess of investigating Amyas Lyle's death. Genuine sorrow. Masha's tears went on and on, and Posie's thoughts ran ahead of herself.

Olga Karloff was dead too? But how was her death linked to Amyas' death? A murder followed by a suicide? A double murder? Posie's mind boggled as she poured the Housekeeper a cup of the sugary tea and passed it across in the only gesture of comfort she could find.

'We're investigating Mr Lyle's death, you see. That's why I'm here. I wanted to speak to Olga. But now you tell me she's dead too. What happened? Why is it so hush-hush?'

To her surprise Masha the Housekeeper laughed mirthlessly. 'Why "hush-hush"? Why you think, Miss? My Mistress, she the finest of women, but she has the reputation. Like all the women in this place. Kept women, women with no will of their own. Trying to manage on alone here after fleeing from the Revolution back home, when we are all made paupers overnight, or worse. So everything is – as you call it – hush-hush. Even Olga's death, the way she dies…'

Posie watched, trying to conceal her impatience as Masha left the room, before returning with a pale orange piece of paper. Posie knew straightaway what it was, had dealt with these documents on numerous occasions before: death certificates, issued by hospitals.

'I say!' She took the certificate from Masha, scanning the orange sheet quickly. Her heart seemed to constrict within her chest, to beat too fast for a second. Oh, the complications of this wretched case. The ironies. The sadness of it all.

There was no suicide here, no murder. Just terrible, terrible timing.

This accounted for Antonia Lyle's vicious hatred of Olga, growing over the last few months as she had come and spied on her, sitting in the car. It accounted for Lady Roade saying that she hadn't spoken to Olga because she 'wasn't in a state to have any confrontation levied at her'.

'Olga died in childbirth very early this morning,' Posie muttered.

'Yes: at the Royal Waterloo Hospital. A tragedy. I am by her side. I cannot believe it. When Olga she go into labour yesterday lunchtime, I send word to the Master's Chambers, at 20 Old Square.'

But by lunchtime yesterday Amyas Lyle was dead, and in no position to help anyone. Not his mistress. Not even himself.

'I try again today. Telephoning, and sending a telegram. But he no come. Now I know why. I can't believe it! And that poor little girl! The baby!'

Posie looked up, aghast. Of course, the child! 'She lived? The baby lived?'

Masha smiled rapturously. 'Oh, yes! Ekaterina. They agree the name between them if it is a girl. Katia for short. She's a poor little thing – little darling! Too small. Much too small. My little *dorogoya*! She's in the special hospital for children, with a room to keep her warm. Funny cots with heating inside them.'

'At Great Ormond Street?'

'That's right.'

But in all this barrage of news, Posie focused on something seemingly random she had just heard:

'You said Amyas and Olga spoke about the baby's name? I wonder… Please don't think me rude, but was the baby something they were looking forward to? Something of a joy?'

Masha was twisting the handkerchief again. 'Oh, yes. I no know if it was planned. But it is certainly a beautiful joy to both of them. You should see the nursery they make upstairs! Master Amyas himself was choosing the toys and linens at the Army & Navy Store. What will happen now? What will happen to poor little Ekaterina?'

Posie's mind was racing, unsure of what to say, what to promise. She placed her hand on the woman's arm, held it there.

'I don't know, Masha. But I'll do my very best to help you, I promise. In fact, I'll check and see if Amyas made any provision for Olga in his Will. And if he didn't…'

If he didn't this whole secret existence here will stop overnight: brought to a halt by the jealousy and anger of Lady Antonia, thought Posie.

The child might end up in the workhouse, or…

'I also know Rufus, the Earl of Cardigeon. He was Olga's – friend – before Amyas. Did you know him too, Masha? This was a few years ago now.'

The woman's face cleared, seemed to find some light. 'Oh, oh, yes! I know him. A lovely man, a truly lovely man, for all he suffer in that dreadful war.'

'He'll help. He has a lot of money. He'll see it as a duty.'

Masha was slightly comforted. 'We thought it a disaster when Mr Rufus he tell us he will abandon us – we no understand it at all – but it turned out good. Mr Lyle and Olga were perfect together. So very much in love during these last five years.'

Posie raised an eyebrow. From what she had heard she wasn't sure if Amyas Lyle was the sort of person who could be in love with anything or anyone except himself. She thought about timings. *Five years.* A long time. Five years since the wager which had led to Amyas owning this house, and 'owning' Olga. But things had only started to get tricky these last six months. Since Amyas had distanced himself even further from his wife, since he stopped visiting his sons, stopped going to Eaton Terrace, except on a Sunday.

'Masha, can you tell me, did anything happen in January this year? Think hard, please. It could help me find out what happened to Amyas.'

The woman had a little colour in her cheeks now. 'I no need to think hard. In January this year Master Amyas he move in here. He lived here permanently.'

Posie almost gasped. 'He *lived* here?' She thought of the family house at Eaton Terrace which was not his, where he had not belonged, and then the tiny claustrophobic flat above his work which was horrible, lacking in any personality. So *this* had become a refuge. A home. Perhaps understandably.

'It was – how you say?- *unconventional*, I suppose. Not quite right,' the Housekeeper said. 'My Mistress she was married before, and Mr Lyle says he is in a trap – that's what he call it – which he can't get out of just yet. But he move in here anyway. I think he wasn't living with his wife before, but from January onwards we see her here a lot: all the Russian ladies see her, sitting outside in the courtyard with her funny blue hair in the back of her big black car; the chauffeur reading the newspaper for hours and hours, and she – well, she just stares. Stares at this house. It is uncomfortable. Master Amyas he went out once to tell her go away. I shouldn't be listening but I do. He say to his wife that people all have secrets, but some are better hidden than others, and that she should go away, because he was happy here.'

'I see.'

Posie counted on her hands.

'In January Olga was about three months pregnant, wasn't she? That's about the usual time when a pregnancy is deemed "safe" and you can tell people about it, isn't it?'

'Yes. Olga tell Master Amyas as soon as she is certain of the baby, and he move in almost the next day. So happy he is. Happy every day since. Would you like to see nice nursery upstairs? Or the bedroom he use? Or his dressing room? Everything is here, his clothes, his shoes…'

But Posie shook her head sadly and stood, barely able to meet the eyes of the woman in the painting above the fireplace. Olga Karloff had been failed repeatedly. And Posie had seen enough, and heard enough. She believed that Amyas had found some sort of peace here. Unexpected peace.

But none of that was any good in catching his killer.

* * * *

Thirteen

As she emerged from the tram station on the Kingsway and zig-zagged her way through the small, dark paths around the Holborn Empire and Chichester Rents, Posie realised she was shivering.

A harsh, salty wind was now blowing up from the river, bringing the promise of yet more rain, and the summer evening had turned dark and chilly. Dry leaves and a horrible cocktail of greasy rags and bits of newspapers swirled around the dirty cobblestones, and it felt decidedly like autumn.

Posie thought briefly of her summer holiday which she was embarking on the next day, so nervously anticipated.

She thought of the things she would need to pack in her holdall later tonight. She thought too of her hopes for the short holiday: a change of scene; the sea; a chance of romance. But what if this strange weather was set to stay? And wasn't she now supposed to be conducting some sort of investigation into the source of the postcards from Whitley Bay which had been sent over the past six months to Amyas Lyle? How exactly was she supposed to do *that*? Talk about a needle in a haystack!

A mare's nest. And as for the romance...

Might she be disappointed?

As she crossed through the park in Lincoln's Inn Fields it seemed as if an eternity had passed since she had sat here so cheerfully in the café – was it really only yesterday? – when she had seen Amyas Lyle striding past, gloweringly handsome despite the passage of years. Perhaps even *more* handsome, and just as enigmatic. How could either of them have known what the next few hours would bring? The ancient, huge plane trees seemed to shake mournfully now, sending more leaves cascading down, blowing in ghostly dances across the paths and scattering across the empty bandstand. The park-keeper was hovering by the café, jangling a large bunch of keys, his beady eyes assessing how many people he would have to shoo out in ten minutes.

Through the plane trees and the iron fence ahead, Posie saw the Royal College of Surgeons loom menacingly. It took up almost a full side of the square, all white classical splendour and full, juddering columns rising from an imposing set of steps. It looked like a castle, an impenetrable fortress. A row of real torches had been lit above the portico and you could smell the petrol which had been used to ignite them from here, across the road. Men in black gowns were flitting in and out of the rotating glass doorway, some hovering on the steps, smoking. Lights blazed in all the ground-floor windows.

She stepped through a gate just opposite the Royal College, and almost tripped headlong over Sergeant Rainbird, who was loitering on the pavement under the dense overhang of a bush, standing well back in the shadows.

'Sergeant! You startled me!'

'Likewise, Miss.'

Posie felt a first-class fool as she now realised Rainbird was simply having a smoke, and that a shiny black police car was parked right in front of him, the lights off, the driver in the front seat squinting at a newspaper in the already-failing light.

Rainbird ground out his smoke quickly as Inspector Lovelace came into view, walking briskly through the brick archway of Lincoln's Inn on the left, giving them an easy wave.

'You still don't know, do you?' Rainbird said suddenly, the words coming all in a rush. He motioned at the Inspector who was now crossing towards them, but before Posie could answer, the promise of rain was suddenly fulfilled and sharp stinging sheets of the stuff came pouring down, lashing at them through the trees.

'Quick! In here!'

Rainbird was wrenching open the door of the police car, and Posie was half-stepping, half-bundled up into the back seat, closely followed by the Sergeant. All in a mad dash Lovelace had climbed into the car as well, and the three of them sat tightly squashed together, uncomfortable and tense and relieved all at once, the scent of damp, wet wool and leather enveloping them in an all-embracing fug.

'By Jove!' said Lovelace, taking his hat off and shaking it out the window. 'What rain! They say it's here to stay. Good for my garden I suppose, less so for your holiday, Posie.' He rubbed his hands together briskly. 'This is perfect. A proper mobile meeting room! Let's catch up quickly before we see the good doctor. We have five minutes. Now, Posie, what did Olga Karloff have to tell you?'

And Posie recounted the whole sorry tale, ending with a shake of her head. There was a stunned silence in the car. Lovelace cradled his head in his hands and emitted a low groan.

'Well, I'm blowed! Poor little mite! What did you say her name was?'

'The baby? Ekaterina. Katia, I think, for short.'

He shook his head, perhaps thinking of his own daughter, Phyllis, little more than a baby herself, whose mother's death the year before had robbed them of a normal family life forever. 'So poor little Katia is born too small, or ill for some reason, and on the same day both her parents die in terrible but differing circumstances, leaving her quite alone. It quite beggars belief.'

Into the silence Rainbird spoke up: 'It *is* dreadful, sir. But I think the baby's birth and the mother's death must stand apart from the father's murder investigation for the moment, don't you? The coincidence is great but it's just that – a coincidence.'

'I agree with the Sergeant, sir,' said Posie. 'There's nothing we can do for Katia at the moment except pray, and help catch her father's murderer. That, and try and work out how she will be provided for in the future. Keep her from the workhouse.'

Lovelace nodded aggressively. 'Quite right. Speaking of which, maybe Amyas made provision for Olga and the child in his Will. Have you got a copy of it yet, Rainbird?'

'No,' Rainbird said with a glum shake of the head. 'Pring and Proudfoot will have it to us first thing tomorrow morning. They're sending a lawyer over with it to explain things.'

'Fine. Anything else to report, Sergeant? Any other updates?'

Rainbird turned the pages in his police notebook, squinting in the dim light. 'Well, we're still waiting on the post-mortem results, and the Forensics chaps haven't said a thing yet, but we *do* have confirmation from the dentist that the body we found in 20 Old Square *was* definitely Amyas Lyle. No doubt about it. A perfect match.'

Posie felt a cold shiver pass over her like a clammy hand. Was she just like Lady Antonia's Butler, fragile, imagining people where no person should be? The shadowy man she had seen outside the communal gardens earlier at Eaton Terrace had definitely *not* been Amyas, then. A simple trick of the light. A man with a fleeting passing resemblance. Her own mind playing tricks on her.

Get a grip.

Rainbird carried on: 'You asked me to check on the story of the school lad who killed himself as a result of Amyas' gambling racket? As background?'

'And?'

'It definitely happened, sir. I went through the old police reports. A sorry little story but nothing could be proved as to the guilt of anyone specifically. There was no proof that Amyas Lyle was putting the screws on Harold, although there *was* definitely money owing to Amyas Lyle at the date of the death, and the suicide note *did* mention him by name. But there was evidence that Harold was of a depressive nature anyway. "Morose", apparently. He could have got upset about anything, and then topped himself, according to his teachers. It was inconclusive all-round, and recorded in our files as a non-suspicious death. And before you ask, no: there's definitely no family left. Each and every single one of the Robertsbridges are dead and buried.'

'Good work, Rainbird,' said the Inspector. 'It's as well to rule these things out.'

It was the first praise Posie had heard him give his Sergeant that day. 'Now, do you have any information on Dr Dawney which might be useful before Posie and I go and meet him?'

Rainbird flicked to another page. 'Nothing criminal to report, sir. By all accounts Dr Dawney is a model gent, a model doctor, and a model citizen. He has no family, his wife having died earlier this year, and they had no children. Parents dead, and he was an only child. Religious by all accounts, he attends the Brompton Oratory in Knightsbridge every Sunday without fail.'

The Sergeant worked down his list of points. 'He served for almost the whole of the Great War, mainly as a junior doctor assisting in the field hospitals on the front-line. Learnt his craft there, and now he's the best trauma surgeon in London. Fixes bones, that's his thing. He's got all sorts of accolades and prizes. Now he's the Chief Surgeon at the French Hospital, over in Shaftesbury Avenue: you know, that place which admits foreigners, and has little French nuns in white habits as nurses?'

Posie cut in: 'Wasn't the French Hospital the main receiving hospital in London in the Great War? Took in soldiers?'

'Yep,' confirmed Rainbird. 'It had the best operating theatre and laboratory in London; it was newly fitted out, which is why it was chosen. So Dawney works there. And tonight he's giving a lecture, and it's well attended, despite most people being on holiday: the surgery students from the French Hospital and other doctors from around town made sure they stayed in town to hear Dawney speak. He's tipped to become the next President here at the Royal College. Oh, and incidentally he picked up the nickname "Sawbones Bill" in the trenches.'

'Golly!' said Posie, with a raise of the eyebrow. 'He must have seen some grim sights in that time. I don't envy him those experiences.'

For a second, Posie thought of other doctors she had known. She thought back to another case she had worked on, a couple of years back, another doctor who had worked in the trenches, a Dr Winter. A man who had disappeared without a trace. And she thought too of a doctor who had worked on the other side of the enemy lines: Max, a German. A man who hadn't wanted to be part of the war, a man who had later reinvented himself into someone quite different. Max was currently up in the north of England, and she would be reunited with him again very soon. For a very short while, at least.

She dragged herself back to the present and the information about Dr Dawney, a man who, unlike the other doctors she was recalling to mind, had resolutely carried on throughout the war.

'Mnnn,' muttered Lovelace, jamming his damp hat back

on his head, and holding at the door handle impatiently. 'So he's some sort of doctor-war-hero, then, is he? But let's not forget he was once one of the lovely duo who made a poor wee lad feel so dreadful that the only option left to him was to kill himself.'

'*Perhaps*,' cautioned Posie, licking her finger and attempting to smooth her hair down. 'And that was a long time ago now, sir. People can change, can't they? Or maybe he still feels guilty. Hence going to church so much?'

The Inspector clicked his tongue. 'Poppycock. You know as well as I do that people don't change, Posie.'

Posie was just thinking that actually people *did* change, for better or for worse, for example Rufus Cardigeon himself, when she realised that Lovelace had already made up his mind against the man they were about to meet.

'Sir, why are we speaking to Dr Dawney, anyway? Is he a suspect?'

'Amyas Lyle had him on his list of suspects, didn't he? It's not a massive jump of the imagination to think he might have killed his old pal. And he's a medical man, isn't he? A vat of nitric acid would be child's play to him, wouldn't it? In fact, isn't there a laboratory here, inside the Royal College? And at the French Hospital you spoke about?'

Rainbird looked awkward. 'You might want to hold your horses, sir, if you're throwing accusations around. The last week has seen Dr Dawney up in Scotland. A whole day or night by train travel, sir. He's only just back today into London.'

Lovelace's face fell, but he got out of the car into the pouring rain with a spring in his step, professional as ever.

And Posie followed with a heavy, sinking heart, feeling the mournful gaze of Rainbird upon their backs.

* * * *

Fourteen

The office was dark and claustrophobic, lit by low electric desk lamps with green glass covers. No windows.

There were shelves everywhere, filled with gruesome specimens, pickled, it looked like, perhaps a million years ago. Posie tried not to stare too much. There was a strange chemical smell overlying everything, presumably formaldehyde. Footsteps circled behind them.

'Oh, don't mind this chamber of horrors, will you? It's not mine. I'm just borrowing it for our little chat. You'll have some tea?'

Two blue enamel mugs of very milky, stewed-looking tea were banged down unceremoniously on the desk at which Posie and Lovelace were sitting, interview-style, side-by-side. They had placed their business cards at the ready, for inspection. Dr William Dawney lurched around the desk and sat down opposite them, cradling his own identical mug.

'I'm William Dawney.' He gave the business cards the merest flicker of attention. 'Pleased to meet you, although obviously not in these circumstances.'

He was a thin, fair man in a black gown, blessed in life with the sort of handsome face you usually only encountered in the world of artworks. Posie saw at once that his slightly impatient, rakish air belied a forceful nature which was not used to being questioned, let alone disobeyed.

'Oh, hang this tea,' Dawney muttered, fumbling in an inside pocket. 'I need something stronger and there's no whisky here.' He brought out a case of Turkish cigarettes, offered it around.

'No? Don't mind me, then, will you?' He lit up and took a deep drag, eyes closed, head tilted to the ceiling. Posie saw that he still wore a plain gold wedding ring on his left-hand ring finger.

'Amyas, eh?' he said at last. 'Murder. Poor devil. The show is finally over, then. I'll miss him. A terrible thing. What a waste.'

'Indeed,' agreed Lovelace. 'Did you hear about his murder from anyone *before* my Sergeant got hold of you this afternoon, doctor?'

Dawney shook his head, and exhaled quickly out of the corner of his mouth. 'I've been working all day up at the French Hospital. I didn't break at all, not even for luncheon. I first heard the news when Sheila, my secretary, came in at the usual time with all my other messages. I can't quite believe it. By Gad!'

Posie cut in: 'Do you know about the *manner* of Amyas Lyle's death, sir? Have you been told?'

Dawney turned wide, dark brown eyes on Posie, and blinked in surprise. He flicked off the excess ash of his cigarette on what looked like some sort of fossil. 'No,' he replied. 'I was just told it was suspicious. Most likely a murder, committed yesterday. That's all. Are you going to enlighten me or just feed me titbits, Miss Parker?'

Lovelace seemed to sit higher in his chair. 'We'll let you know in due course, doctor. Tests are still being run on the chemicals used. Everything is up for debate.'

'*Chemicals?*' Dawney's eyes grew wider still and ranged from one to the other, and Posie felt rather than heard Lovelace curse wholeheartedly at letting the cat out of the bag. '*Now* you've foxed me. Chemicals, you say, eh? Well, we do have a lab here. But I'm afraid *I* was a good four hundred miles away from it, and from Amyas, when he died. I've got patients and doctors and medical students up in Edinburgh several times over who will swear it to you. Been up there this last week on a teaching course. I only got back this morning, stepped into King's Cross off the overnight sleeper. So you can jolly well rule me out as a suspect.'

'Very good, doctor. We're not here to accuse you: far from it. We're here for information, really. As a friend, someone who knew the deceased. We *have* already spoken to Lady Antonia, but, well…'

Dawney rolled his eyes heavenwards. 'You're quite right, of course. Antonia and Amyas didn't know each other at all. That marriage began and ended on a piece of paper. You've heard about their marriage contract, of course?'

Both nodded.

Dawney laughed grimly. 'It was sad. Amyas spoke of getting divorced once, a few months back. As if he'd only just realised it could be done. But, well… *that* never happened, did it?'

The doctor finished his cigarette. 'Amyas and I were boys together at school, then we moved in the same circles when we were both here in London just before the Great War; he was starting out as a lawyer and I was in training at Guy's Hospital. Same rounds of parties, don't you know. This year he's helped me take my mind off things following the death of my wife.' He twisted at the wedding band on his finger.

'I heard. My condolences, doctor.'

'Thank you.'

'Where did you and Amyas usually meet up, doctor?'

'Usually? Lately just at Eaton Terrace, if I called around on a Sunday, after church.'

Posie had the sudden feeling that things had changed

here too for Amyas, in *this* friendship. Had he been cutting free of Dawney, too? Not meeting him as often as before? Or in a different place? She clicked her pencil against her teeth:

'And before? Where did you *used* to meet each other, sir? I'll warrant not just at home…'

'How observant of you, Miss Parker. Yes: we used to go to a club or two in the wee small hours, Pall Mall and the like. Having fun.'

'Gambling, was it, sir?' Posie held the doctor's gaze and saw how he didn't flush with embarrassment or deny it.

'That's right. Betting buddies. We've won a helluva lot over the years. Money *and* other things. Amyas must have been quite a rich man when he died yesterday, rich in his own right.'

Posie was curious. 'Did you know that Antonia, his wife, thinks he stopped gambling when he signed their marriage contract in 1914?'

Dawney shrugged. 'As I said, they didn't know each other at all. And anyway, if I'm honest I think Amyas *had* given up gambling. But only fairly recently. He didn't come out so much anymore. We'd had years of betting on everything together and then he swore off it almost overnight. I didn't notice it at the time: my wife Kate died about then – January, it was – and I was hardly in the mood to notice anything much.'

The Inspector was writing quickly. 'Did you know about the notes Amyas had been receiving, or the postcards? The postcards started up in January; the notes a month later.'

Dawney laughed. 'Yes. I told him I thought there was no harm in it, to forget it. Probably just a simpleton's way of having some fun, of passing the time. Or someone he had caused injury to through his work.'

'You think so, sir?' Posie smiled back across the desk. 'You didn't think someone from your collective shadowy pasts – maybe a school chum you had caused injury to through your gambling racket – might have been sending the threats? Or someone connected to Harold Robertsbridge, for example?'

Dawney folded his arms under the gown and smiled back. 'Very good, Miss Parker. I see you have left no stone unturned.' He splayed his hands out quasi-apologetically, long fingers upturned, those clever fingers which had done so much good. 'What can I say? We were so young. On the road to learning who we were. On that road you make mistakes, sometimes.'

He stared into the distance briefly, past the specimen jars and the darkness above the glass lamps. 'But in answer to your question: no, I didn't think of a school connection. Nor of Harold Robertsbridge, little worm that he was. Neither did Amyas. We never spoke of the boy, not in recent years. Despite the fact that the school and his family tried to pin the blame for his death squarely on our shoulders, almost scuppering our university futures.' He knitted his fine eyebrows together. 'Tell me: do you think the person who sent the notes killed Amyas?'

'We don't know at present, doctor.' Lovelace rapped his pencil impatiently on his notepad. 'His wife told us you were helping Amyas with a new project. What exactly was that?'

Dawney checked his fob-watch. 'Amyas was adopted. I expect you know that? He hadn't ever shown any desire to trace his real family. That changed early this year: he was beginning to show the stirrings of an interest. It was very bad timing, as his adoptive parents are both dead and there was no paperwork to be found anywhere about where he had come from. I told him I would help him.'

'How could *you* have helped?' asked Inspector Lovelace, frowning. 'The whole adoption topic in this country is an ungodly mess, isn't it? Like unpicking tangled wool. Especially if you look back around thirty years ago to when Amyas was adopted? It was an unregulated hell of sinister women replying to adverts for unwanted children: all those awful stories of baby farming. Thank the Lord there will be some rules in place before long, and that adoption will have to follow proper legal processes at last! Protecting the poor innocent children involved.'

Posie turned for a second in a state of almost-shock to look at Lovelace. She had never heard him speak so passionately before on a subject. His daughter, Phyllis again, she supposed. *He's wondering what would become of her if something happens to him.*

I'm the girl's godmother. I should reassure him I would look after her, take her in.

Dawney laughed. 'I seem to have hit a raw nerve, Chief Inspector.' But he became serious again. 'You're absolutely right. It's a complete mess. If truth be told, I had a lead; an idea. I thought I would pursue it and then pass the findings over to Amyas. Let him decide what to do about it.'

Posie moved to the edge of her seat. 'And? What happened?'

'I'm afraid to say the lead ran cold. It got me precisely nowhere. To my annoyance.'

Just at that moment a soft knock came at the door and a woman entered, late thirties, dark and efficient-looking with a blunt black bob. She almost bowed down low before Dawney. 'Sorry to interrupt, Bill.'

'What is it, Sheila? Can't you see I'm busy here?'

'One of the visiting Professors wants to speak to you, Bill. Says it's important. He's waiting in the entrance hall for you now, along with a bunch of your usual hangers-on.'

'Fine. I'll be right along.'

As Sheila closed the door Dawney fixed his gaze back on Posie and Lovelace. 'Is there anything else I can help you with?'

There were several things, actually. But Posie found herself blurting out: 'The lead you had, about the adoption. What was it?'

Dawney sighed, as if the question was an irrelevance. 'I wondered if Amyas' original family were up in the north, if you must know. It was those wretched postcards which gave me the idea – you know, the Spanish City, Whitley Bay? He received the first card in January. I wondered if it might be a clumsy attempt by the birth family to get in touch? So I went there in late January, on the way back from a conference I was attending. I had time on my hands, anyway, after Kate had died. I spent a weekend there – dreadful place, so much wind and rain, felt like it was the edge of the world – and I did some digging around. I asked in the tea-shops, and in the hotels and even in the local nursing home where women go to give birth. I'm a thorough sort of chap, but there was nothing doing. Turns out Whitley Bay isn't such a small place, and no-one answered any of the adverts I put in the local newspapers, or on the local shop noticeboards, even for a rather hefty financial reward. Of course, it didn't help that I didn't know Amyas' true name, or his original surname. All I could give was his rough date of birth and information about the people who had ended up adopting him, the Lyles. It was a complete waste of time.'

'Did you think the sender of the postcards and the strange notes which followed might have been the same person, sir?'

'No. Two completely different matters.'

Posie was about to push further on this but Lovelace was racing ahead. 'I appreciate you are short of time, doctor, but could you tell me your thoughts about Amyas Lyle and the British Fascist Party?'

Dawney raised his eyebrows incredulously. 'Amyas was no more a fascist than I'm a Frenchman.' He picked up the two business cards and put them into his inner jacket pocket, smoothing it down. 'He went along with everything his father-in-law told him to do, even if he found it distasteful. But he told me he'd had enough. He'd got what he wanted – the High Court Judgeship – and he was getting out.'

'Getting out? Was this when he spoke of a divorce, sir?' asked Posie, intrigued.

'Yes. It was admirably devious really. He wanted to distance himself from the lot of them, apparently. But I don't know if he could really have cut free of the Roade family; your guess is as good as mine.'

The doctor rose, and they followed his lead.

'One last thing, doctor.' Lovelace closed his notebook and put it away. 'What can you tell us about Olga Karloff?'

For a split-second something like a flicker of distaste seemed to cross the man's handsome face. He stopped at the door. There was a second of crackling silence.

'The Russian woman? I've actually never met her, not even after all these years. Amyas kept her very much to himself, the spoils of war and all that, perhaps.'

He groaned. 'Oh, Lord. I had hoped this wouldn't come out as public knowledge.'

He ran his hands through his thick, blonde hair. 'I think it will rip Antonia – or what's left of her now the drugs have done their worst – apart with shock. The marriage was a sham but Antonia took it seriously, for the boys' sake.' He shook his head sadly. 'She's a tragedy already – you should have seen her in the good old days, a magnificent creature – this will send her over the edge. You can't think that Olga Karloff had anything to do with Amyas' death, can you?'

Lovelace shook his head. 'No. But it's as well to check.'

Dawney seemed to consider this. 'I *do* know that Amyas was going to change his Will, in Olga's favour, to include a small legacy for her. He told me so recently. He had to tell me, I'm one of the Executors, you see. I tried to discourage him, naturally. After all, the woman was just his mistress – nothing more – but it was the deuce of a thing: he seemed keen to give Olga something.'

Posie's heart sank at the thought of the 'small legacy'.

It sounded as if it wouldn't go far in keeping Masha and baby Katia going. She would have to check the contents of the Will, and otherwise start ringing around, practically begging, if she had to.

'And *did* he alter the Will?' asked Posie.

Dawney shrugged. 'Your guess is as good as mine, Miss Parker. Why are you asking? For motives? You mean maybe he'd told Olga he was leaving her a fortune and she arranged to bump him off in the mistaken hope of gaining wealth? I don't know if that's what's happened. Can't you speak to *her* about all of this?'

At their silence he opened the door. The gleaming walnut-and-cream marble tiles of the corridor stretched on ahead. They walked back to the reception area with its crystal chandelier and smell of furniture polish, empty now save for Sheila, clutching at folders, and an older, bespectacled black-gowned man who was looking at skeletons in the long glass cabinets which lined the room. Trays of half-finished glasses of champagne were dotted about the place on low tables. A small crowd of men in their mid- to late twenties had joined the older man and were pointing excitedly, their eyes glassy and luminous in the reflected glass of the cabinets, glasses of champagne held precariously in nervous hands, their drunken talk getting louder and louder, almost raucous.

Dawney raised his voice and it threw across the echoey room, a command, but a command with a smile in it: 'Cut it out, lads, eh? Some of us are still working, can't you see?'

Instantly the other men were quiet, awkwardly milling about.

'Look,' Dawney said, extending his hand for a final time. 'You can see I'm a pretty busy man. But if you think I can help you, contact me again. I want you to catch Amyas' killer, I really do. In many ways Amyas was a lost soul: always proving himself, as if he was lacking something he once had, maybe, or seeking an audience. Whoever killed

145

him has done a terrible thing. You know, I'd say that for the first time in his life Amyas was actually *happy*.'

They turned to go, but Dawney's voice rang out again:

'I know who you are, by the way, Miss Parker,' he called. 'Twenty years and a good deal of money and a few extra pounds don't alter the girl you once were. *Richard Parker's little sister...* Well, well, well. You know, Richard came and betted with us once? Even though he made no secret of the fact he hated both Amyas and myself and what we were up to. He was a hypocrite, and he couldn't pay his bill, either. So Amyas took the only thing Richard had: his photograph of you. Amyas kept it too, like a kind of trophy. I remember your brother was most unhappy about it: threatened to fight Amyas for the photo. But naturally, it was me who stepped up and fought your brother, because Amyas had a bad heart. I won, too: of course. Your brother was a weakling. Still, we mustn't speak ill of the dead ...'

Richard.

Now Posie saw how William Dawney's name had been like so much mud to Richard, why he had never uttered it to Posie. *Dawney had simply beaten Richard at a fight.*

Silly male pride had been wounded in a silly long-ago fight. What did that all matter now, anyhow? Except William Dawney obviously remembered it: he couldn't let that victory go, and he had to taunt Posie with it, even now.

Posie's heart was beating wildly and she felt her face burning in the glittering light of the entrance hall. She didn't turn around and bother to reply, not quite trusting herself, but she walked on, feeling a burst of fury and solidarity in Lovelace, beside her. She put her hand on his arm, squeezed it tight.

It's fine.

Although of course it wasn't.

* * * *

Fifteen

Outside, the rain was heavier than before and the evening seemed impossibly dark. Posie shivered as they sheltered under the huge stone portico, but she refused the Inspector's jacket as he began to shrug it off for her. She was still angry about Dawney and his comment about the *few extra pounds*. And for the fight with her brother.

Lovelace lit a cigarette.

'What did you make of all *that*?' he asked, inhaling deeply.

Posie frowned, tamping down her anger, trying to rise above it. 'Well, sir, we have some new information, don't we? That Amyas was distancing himself from the Roades, and from pretty much *everything* since January. There was even some mention of a divorce. Did you hear that? Seems like he was starting over, as much as he could, with Olga and the prospect of their child.'

'Do you think the doctor was bluffing when he said he'd never met Olga? He didn't seem to know about the child, either, did he?'

'If he *did* know then he's a very good actor as well as one of the best surgeons in the country. I think what it shows is that Amyas kept secrets from everyone, Bill Sawbones included. Especially with regard to the child. I wonder why *this child* – Katia – was so special to him?'

'I don't know. Would you consider Doctor Dawney a suspect? He was on that list from the biscuit tin…'

Posie chewed at her thumbnail, trying to put her personal dislike aside, to remain impartial. 'Well, he's obviously awfully clever. I wouldn't think that putting four hundred geographical miles between Dr Dawney and a man he wanted to murder would be much of an obstacle; he would find a way somehow. But the crucial thing is, I can't see *why* he would want to kill Amyas. What would he gain?'

Lovelace shuffled in the cold air. 'Do you fancy grabbing a bite to eat? Just some bread and cheese and a glass of wine at Gordon's on the Embankment? The hired nanny for Phyllis, Ella Brown, has moved into the downstairs bedroom permanently, so I don't need to rush home to Clapham anymore if I'm busy. It would be good to chat?'

'I'm so sorry, sir, but I need to pack for my holiday…'

Actually, she just needed to walk in the rain and to clear her head and to think. To be alone.

The Inspector smiled mock-cheerfully. 'I understand. I'll see you tomorrow then, Posie, for an eight o'clock briefing in my office with you and the lads on the case. You'll be off on your holidays straight afterwards, eh? Remind me again *why* you chose Whitley Bay? Apart from wanting to see the lovely Inspector Oats every day, that is.'

And when Posie muttered something about having seen it advertised in a fashion magazine, like Inspector Oats' wife, it sounded unconvincing, even to her own ears. She watched Lovelace's face, the disbelief flashing over it.

How could she tell him that Whitley Bay had not been *her* choice?

And then Lovelace simply shrugged and waved, and Posie felt wretched.

She watched him saunter away; his determined walk, head down against the rain, as he travelled home to his sleeping child, with nothing more to look forward to than the anonymous rumbling darkness of the underground tunnels through which his Northern Line train would pass on its way to Clapham Junction.

****

After she'd watched Lovelace walk out onto the half-light of the Kingsway, Posie set off for home, skirting through the side-streets and avoiding touristy Covent Garden and Oxford Street and the theatres of Shaftesbury Avenue. As she walked, she let the rain drench her, the water running in rivulets down her neck and back, the expensive silk of her jacket and dress probably now ruined forever. But she didn't care. She didn't think she could ever wear them again, anyhow. Every time she would be reminded of this dreadful case, the nightmarish murder of Amyas Lyle.

As she walked, Posie tried to reconcile everything she had heard today about Amyas. What was it Selwyn Pickle, the Deputy Head of Chambers, had said? That 'ambition can lead you into strange places; places from which there is no return'. Well, it was true. There was no return for Amyas now, that was for sure. But what was it, Posie asked herself, that they were not seeing in this case so far? Something in the overall picture was lacking. A vital piece was missing.

Why did she feel as if only half the story were being told? And were they really sure that the answer to Amyas' terrible death was to be found in his private life, and not in his work?

Posie shook her head as, sopping wet, she put the keys in the lock of the entrance door to Museum Chambers. The hallway was dark, and Ted, the Head Porter, had already gone home. Posie sighed thankfully – she was in no mood for small talk – and leant her head against the cold white marble of the wall as she waited for the birdcage lift to rattle down.

Some of the words she had read today came back to her, running over in her brain, haunting her, nudging at her thoughts: just as they had surely done to Amyas Lyle himself.

Some tears never dry.

Some secrets last a lifetime.

And Posie was certain. Of course this murder case was nothing to do with work. It was love, or love ignored.

Sure as bread was bread.

* * * *

Sixteen

The Inspector's not-large office had been turned into a scene which might have been better suited to Piccadilly Circus.

As Big Ben was striking eight o'clock, Lovelace sat behind his desk opposite Posie, Sergeant Rainbird and Constable Fox. On his desk was a mound of evidence and paperwork taken from the crime scene and from Amyas' work flat yesterday. Around the door bobbed Dr Poots, the Pathologist, together with a large dark man in a tight navy suit a size too small for him, holding a black leather briefcase, whom Posie had never seen before.

Thankful for the early start – as it meant she would make her train from King's Cross to Newcastle leaving at ten-thirty, rather than await the evening train which would arrive too late – Posie had gone without breakfast in order to be here on time, and now her stomach yowled audibly.

Lovelace, who was on the telephone, must have heard, for he reached under his desk where there was obviously some sort of in-built cupboard and brought out a new, family-sized bar of Fry's Five Boys chocolate. Posie broke some off and ate through an orange fondant section, before offering the chocolate around, but only Constable Fox took her up on the offer.

Lovelace slammed the telephone receiver down into its cradle.

'Well, well, well.' He rubbed his hands together happily. Posie noticed how immaculate he looked today. In fact, his navy-and-white striped tie was very fresh, and his brown suit overall looked cleaner, less bobbly than usual. He had been tidied up, for sure. Was this the influence of Ella Brown, the live-in nanny? Was she looking after Lovelace, as well as the child? Somewhere, something in Posie protested, but she was pleased for Lovelace too, aware of feeling a strange and curious mix of reactions.

'That was the Custody Sergeant. We've got Selwyn Pickle's son, Charlie, down in the cells now. He was picked up this morning at work, after our lads failed to get him yesterday at home. He matches the description George the Head Clerk gave of the Billingsgate Porter he saw delivering the toxic white box to 20 Old Square on Monday lunchtime.'

'What *was* the description of the Porter?' asked Posie.

Lovelace ruffled through papers on his desk, before motioning to Rainbird. 'You have it, don't you, Sergeant?'

Rainbird flicked through his notepad until he came to a well-thumbed page. 'Tall, dark fella in his twenties, sir. Wearing the white overalls of a Porter.'

Posie turned to him. 'What, no bobbin hat?'

Rainbird scowled. 'A what, Miss?'

'You know, the black wide-brimmed leather hat all Billingsgate Porters wear. With a hard flat top so they can stack the crates of fish up on them! You *do* know!'

'No mention of any bobbin hat here, Miss.'

Posie turned back to the Inspector and crossed her arms. 'Well, that's very strange. I thought those bobbin hats were like status symbols to Billingsgate Fish Porters. I don't think you'd catch one out on a delivery without one. It's a badge of honour. And anyway, I don't much like the description of the man you've got. Tall and dark and in his early twenties! That could have been half of London!'

Lovelace, obviously not liking his moment of triumph being snatched away, looked less than pleased. 'Mnnn. I take your point, Posie, but we'll get George the Head Clerk to come in later and see if it's the same lad. And we'll interview Charlie Pickle anyway.'

Posie continued to cross her arms, aware of the displeasure radiating across the desk towards her. But she had to press on. 'Also, if you don't mind my saying so…'

Lovelace groaned. 'Go on.'

'How much can you trust the word of George the Head Clerk, sir? We know he's a thief, and that he was paid to spy for Antonia Lyle, to go through rubbish bins. What if he's simply being paid now? Being paid to protect someone? Or to frame someone? To frame someone like Charlie Pickle. Just a thought to consider.'

'Thank you. I'll consider it. Dr Poots, I know you are short on time. Your post-mortem? Any interesting stuff?'

Everyone swivelled around to listen to Poots. The Pathologist fiddled with his small red dickie bow-tie and then flicked his braces, mannerisms Posie had seen many times over the last few years, especially when he had to take the witness stand in Court. It usually signalled some exciting revelation.

'Interesting? I'll say! Cause of death was multiple organ failure, primarily the heart. Brought about by close contact with or inhalation of nitric acid. Nothing new in that. We knew that yesterday, although it's a dreadful way to kill a man. I've never seen such a thing in all my years on the job. But what is interesting is this: your killer obviously wanted Amyas Lyle dead, but he needn't have bothered with all the drama. Amyas Lyle would have been dead in the next month or so anyway, of natural causes.'

The bombshell dropped, Poots slid his report silently across the desk.

'What the…?' Lovelace was opening the report and scanning it frantically.

But just as Poots was about to speak, Posie put her hand over her chest, tapping her breast-bone, almost unconsciously. 'The heart,' she said softly, into the silence.

'That's right,' snapped Poots, cross at having his thunder stolen. 'Dicky ticker. Bad heart. Would have given out in just a matter of weeks. There's no operation in the world could have fixed him up, poor beggar. Now, if that is all…'

Excusing himself, the Pathologist disappeared, and everyone looked first at Posie, then at the Inspector, who stayed quiet, trying to take on board what, if anything, this news meant.

Lovelace tried to garner the energy back into the room. He motioned to the dark man at the back, who hadn't been introduced so far. 'Mr Cameron, isn't it? The solicitor from Pring and Proudfoot? You've come about the murder victim's Will. What can you tell us?'

The solicitor cleared his throat, his three chins quivering. 'I was Amyas Lyle's recent contact at the firm, although it's his father-in-law, Lord Justice Roade, who knows Mr Proudfoot, the owner of the firm. My understanding is that Lord Justice Roade insisted that Amyas and Lady Antonia had matching Wills when they married. Everything – except the house at Eaton Terrace, *that* stays in her family – was left to each other and the boys. That was how the Wills stayed, until very recently. But Mr Lyle contacted me as I was new to the firm – he wanted someone *different* apparently – earlier this year. He wanted to change his Will.'

Posie took a breath and held it. Was this the 'small legacy' Dr Dawney had spoken of for Olga? Was there anything provided for the baby?

'Amyas Lyle wanted to remove all references to his wife and their sons in his new Will. They were to inherit nothing.'

Everyone in the room stared.

Mr Cameron was well aware of the heavy impact of his

words. 'Mr Lyle wished instead to leave *everything* in his possession at the time of his death, including the house on Fever Street, to a Mrs Olga Karloff and any children they might have together.'

'Thank goodness!' Posie breathed.

Constable Fox piped up. 'Gives the drug-addict wife a belter of a motive, doesn't it, sir? To be struck out like that, out of her own husband's Will?'

Sergeant Rainbird was nodding. 'Blow the Billingsgate Porter, sir! Small fry, if you'll excuse the pun. Do you want us to get on over to Chelsea now, sir? Bring the wife in for questioning, like?'

But into the sudden hive of activity, Mr Cameron coughed awkwardly. He had turned bright red and his eyes were bulging. He was waving his black folder uselessly. 'Please! Everyone! LISTEN!'

At the resulting silence he looked relieved. 'Don't anybody go anywhere. Lady Antonia had no clue her husband was thinking along these lines. Anyhow, crucially, the new Will was only just drawn up. Mr Lyle gave me the final instructions on Monday this week, as it happens. The day he died. I must have been one of the last people to see him, that morning, at my office, before he was murdered.'

He sniffed, indicating his folder. 'I have the new Will here, all drawn up. Amyas was due to sign it today. He hadn't yet signed it…'

Posie stood, frozen in horror. 'Oh, golly. You mean the new Will is absolutely worthless, don't you?'

'Yes, unfortunately. Not worth the paper it's written on. I'm very sorry. Of course, one hears of these things, but it's never actually happened to me in my own career. It will come as a huge blow to this Olga Karloff, no doubt.'

Posie shook her head in disbelief. 'So the old Will still stands? Legally, it's as if Amyas hadn't changed his mind at all?'

'I'm afraid so, Miss. Lady Antonia will inherit everything,

the house at Fever Street included.' Mr Cameron looked at Lovelace. 'I wanted to mention it to you personally, Chief Inspector. In case it shed any light on the case. Amyas Lyle must have had a big change of heart regarding his immediate family; he even cut out Lord Justice Roade as one of the Executors.'

'Who were the new Executors meant to be?' asked Lovelace, looking as if he didn't much care either way.

Mr Cameron flicked through his folder quickly. 'Mr Lyle retained one, a doctor called William Dawney. The other Executor was new. A Miss Posie Parker. Why! That's *you*, Miss, right? Amyas said he needed to talk to you about it before signing.'

Posie stared and stared, ignoring Lovelace who was looking at her in bewilderment and exasperation. Suddenly the strange exchange with Amyas in the middle of Lincoln's Inn Fields made a sort of sense, and she realised what he had wanted to talk to her about at his office.

But why *her*? Had Amyas been wanting Posie to fight Olga's corner if the new Will was disputed? To counter William Dawney and his obvious disapproval of Olga? What obligation did she owe to Amyas Lyle, except a disquieting sense of guilt and unease at having stood him up once, nearly twenty years before? She had never met Olga, either. Why had Amyas thought she was right for this very onerous job? That she would accept the task?

And if Amyas *had* actually signed the new Will, the current situation would have meant that – quite unbelievably – Posie Parker and William Dawney would have become the legal guardians of little Katia Lyle, responsible for making sure Amyas' money was used for her benefit.

And now the weight of this knowledge rested upon Posie like a millstone around her neck. The slight pin-pricks of conscience she had felt when considering the fate of Katia Lyle earlier had now been changed into something entirely different. Doubled. Quadrupled. Somehow Amyas had considered her a safe pair of hands with his unborn daughter's life.

She'd have to make some telephone calls.

'Shall we bring the wife in anyway, sir?' asked Rainbird hopefully, after the solicitor had left. 'She might have got wind of this change of mind and thought she'd act before she was cut out of the husband's new Will, don't you think, sir?'

The Inspector sat down again. 'No,' he said with certainty. 'I don't want any attention brought to this. We'll let things settle for the moment, take in the implications of everything we've heard before we jump to rash conclusions.'

Posie narrowed her eyes, aware that Lovelace was taking things slowly here, obviously not wanting to put any well-connected noses out of joint. Especially any connected with Lord Justice Roade, who was, after all, a friend of the Superintendent. Who was apparently a jolly fine man.

'What *should* we be doing, sir?'

'You go off to Whitley Bay, Posie, and sniff around. See if there's anything doing, although I doubt it. And we'll pursue other leads here in your absence. But softly, softly. We don't want to scare anybody off, do we? Sergeant Rainbird can assist me with interviews. And Constable Fox can start going through the newspapers again, and the Court Reports. *Anything* Amyas Lyle has worked on in the last twelve months, any complaints made against him, anything odd at all. Bring it to my attention. You got it, Constable?'

Fox swallowed and then nodded, obviously not relishing this prospect one bit.

Posie sighed. She didn't want to belittle the Inspector in front of his men, but he was wrong. That last note, the one which had come with the poison...

She whispered it under her breath: '*A* lifetime *of tears is what you caused me.*' A lifetime wasn't referring to just the last twelve months, was it?

Posie checked her watch – nine o'clock – and then glanced across the desk in front of her. The stack of handwritten notes were nowhere to be seen – presumably still with the Forensics team – but heaped altogether were the postcards of the Spanish City. She got up and leant over. 'Can I take one, sir? I'll bring it back.'

'Of course.'

She placed the black-and-white image into her notebook, carefully so as not to bend it at all. She would study it later on the train. For now there was the chance of getting a hot breakfast somewhere, or even just a piping hot coffee at King's Cross Station, without rushing madly across town.

Posie started to pull on her black waterproof overcoat on top of the chic blush pink linen skirt-suit she had chosen to travel in. She glanced at the rain outside, which showed no sign of letting up, and felt thankful for the several jumpers she had packed into her small leather valise, as well as the single bathing costume and hat.

Ready to sidle off without further ado, she had just picked up the valise when there was a knock at the door. A uniformed policeman stood there.

'What is it, lad?' said Lovelace, a little impatiently. 'Trouble with our young fella in the cells, is it? Tell him we'll be along shortly.'

But it was nothing like that. 'A message for Miss Parker, Chief Inspector. Says here it's care of *you*.'

A plain white envelope was handed over, and Posie, trying not to look like it might matter, opened it quickly. She read the note inside once. And then again. And then she had to sit down.

'What is it? What is it, Posie?'

But Lovelace had tugged it from her hand and was reading it too, a look of incredulous despair on his face.

Dear Miss Parker,

Evans here (I'm the Butler at the Lyle house).

You asked if anyone was watching the house yesterday, and it was only after you left I learnt that the Master was dead.

But I saw him just before you arrived. I know I did. Over by the gardens.

I hope you can understand. I think you can, which is why I've sent this.

Please don't inform my Mistress of the contents of this note; I need this job badly because my family relies on my income. They won't get anything if I'm banged up tight in some loony bin, will they? Which she might well arrange.

Yours,
Albert Evans

'What do you make of *that*, then, sir?' But there was no triumph in Posie's voice.

Lovelace waved his men away from around the door where they had been gathering like so many bees around a honeypot.

'I think *you'd* better get away on your holiday before I send *you* off to the loony bin, too. Not ghosts again, Posie. I don't think I can bear it. I don't know what to make of it, yet. Ravings of a poor, mad fella? Get away with you. Go and enjoy the company of Inspector Oats for a few days. I'm not sure which prospect I would dread the most. Oats, or the loony bin.'

And Posie laughed and left the office, trying to push away the disquiet which threatened to engulf her, the strange ideas which Lady Antonia's Butler had suggested in his note. Above all else, the fact he had seen a man yesterday who he had thought was Amyas Lyle, too.

Like Posie had.

But how was that possible? Because at the end of the day, Amyas Lyle was dead.

****

At King's Cross Station, where Posie had promised herself a proper breakfast, she first headed to the main hotel inside the station, and asked to use their public telephone. Ushered into a booth at the back of the reception, she checked the time – quarter-to-ten – and placed a call to the mews house in Pavilion Road, Chelsea, which was the London residence of Rufus and Dolly Cardigeon when they were in town.

The Operator connected her. Fred, the ancient Butler who had been in service to the Cardigeons for years now, picked up. She'd expected the couple to be up, just about, maybe having a slow breakfast, or coffee, but she was wrong.

'I am afraid Lady Cardigeon has already departed this morning, Miss Parker. So you can't speak with her. She's taken the children and the nanny and the maids.'

'Where's she going, Fred?' This all seemed most unlikely. Dolly had mentioned nothing of the sort when they were at the Ritz. And Dolly hated early starts, too.

'They are leaving London, Miss. On a train departing at ten-thirty from King's Cross. Going up to York, then on from York to Rebburn Abbey by hansom cab or motor-taxi, whatever can be arranged.' Realisation dawned on Posie that Dolly would be catching the very same train northwards as she would be, albeit getting off a stop or two earlier along the line.

She would ask Dolly about it in person. Probably a tiff; *another* tiff. Probably Dolly couldn't bear to see Rufus drinking himself to nothingness every day. It would be slowly breaking her heart.

'Er, Fred? Is Rufus there? It's actually *him* I need to speak to.'

'Oh, right you are. I'll just see, Miss.'

'I'm in a hotel phone booth, Fred. If you could hurry, I would very much appreciate it.'

After some shuffling, banging sounds and a muffled shouting, a very snippy-sounding Rufus came on the line. 'Posie? That you? Is Dolly with you?'

Mercifully, he sounded lucid and very on the ball.

'No. I haven't seen her.'

'Mnnn.' He seemed to take a gulp of something, hot black coffee, hopefully. 'What is it? Something more to do with Amyas Lyle? I see his murder is splashed all over the newspapers. I've got *The Times* here with my toast and marmalade. A toxic box of tears, eh? Nitric acid? Well, well, well. I don't like to say it, but he got what was coming to him.'

Posie wondered for a split-second how the press could have got the story so absolutely correct, but then the press always *did*. The pips sounded and she asked the Operator to keep her connected for another three minutes.

'Rufus? I'm going to appeal to your better nature now. Can you hear me out?'

And all in a rush Posie was telling him about Olga Karloff – the woman he had once kept as his own mistress – and her death in childbirth, and about the birth of Katia Lyle, and how she was very sickly and small. Posie finished by explaining about the new Will, which hadn't come into effect and was meaningless. How Amyas was *going* to provide for his child, but at the last hurdle, hadn't managed it.

She explained how she was supposed to be an Executor.

'I don't understand why you're telling me all this, Nosey. It's a sorry little tale and no mistake, but whatcha bothering me with it for?'

'The little girl is alone, Rufey. There's medical treatment, hospital stays, and if she survives, somewhere for her and the Housekeeper to live, all needing to be paid for. I'm assuming Fever Street will go to Lady Antonia, who will sell it. Could you perhaps buy it back? Or come to an agreement with her? Or put some money into a trust for this little girl? You're so rich and she really has no-one. She was Olga's daughter, for goodness' sake. If the roll of that dice hadn't gone as it did, little Katia could be *your* daughter.'

There was an icy silence on the other end of the telephone and Posie's heart sank.

Rufus clicked his tongue twice. 'But she's *not* my daughter, though, is she? I have three of my own perfectly *legitimate* children, thank you very much. This was Amyas Lyle's problem, and if he didn't find a way of providing for her future legally – and he was a legal mastermind, by all accounts – that really isn't my problem. I'm not buying this child a house, or anything, for that matter. What made you think I would?'

'But Rufey, you're one of the richest men in the country! You wouldn't even miss the cash. You wouldn't have to have anything to do with her, if you didn't want to.'

Rufus laughed scornfully. 'Well, you're not doing so badly yourself, are you, Posie? Why don't *you* take her home with you? *You* were the one Amyas obviously expected would pick up the pieces, and here you are doing just that. Oh, and don't for goodness' sake mention anything about this hot little mess to Dolly, will you? That might just be the final straw.'

And then Rufus was hanging up on her, and Posie didn't know whether to laugh or cry.

Snatches of Rufus' words ran around her head, '*Well, you're not doing so badly yourself, are you?*' It was true. Posie, as a result of a bounty payment for her first ever big case, had been made an independently wealthy woman in her own right; not fabulously wealthy, or even rich, but secure, more than secure. Wealthy enough to bring up a child comfortably, even a sickly child.

Posie closed her eyes and leant against the cold glass door of the telephone booth.

She hadn't really imagined her life with a child in it.

Still less a child she hadn't yet met. A child for whom she had no obligations, no love, no ties. She could do it alone, of course she could. If that was the only option left to her and Katia. But it would be far better to get someone else on board.

In a burst of sudden courage and mad hope, Posie found herself placing a second call with the Operator. *Desperate times, desperate measures.*

'The French Hospital, please.'

And then Sheila, Dr Dawney's secretary, was answering.

'Posie Parker here. I need to speak to Dr Dawney. It's urgent, I'm afraid. Is he there?'

A disapproving intake of breath. 'Well, this is most irregular.' Some clattering in the background, a babble of voices. 'You're in luck, as it happens. He's just coming out of the operating theatre now, for a tea-break. He's between operations. Hold on, Miss Parker. I'll get one of his students to fetch him.'

And then a few seconds later, a snatch of the receiver. 'Yes? William Dawney here…'

'You and I have a problem we need to discuss, sir.'

And into this unlikely hurried pause of a tea-break, Posie found herself explaining as succinctly as possible about the failed new Will; about how both she and Dawney would have been the two Executors, working together. And finally, she told him about the two-day old Katia Lyle, who had been born on the day both her parents had died. How she was in the safest possible hands at Great Ormond Street, but still fighting for her life.

What could they do?

Posie breathed into the silence.

Was she crazy making this telephone call? After all, she had no clue as to Dawney's personal finances; all that she knew was that Dawney was a gambling man, and therefore probably had money to spare. But what about the fact that

Dawney was cold and she hadn't much liked him on first meeting? What sort of a guardian would he prove to be? *If* he agreed to anything? For a nasty second Posie thought Dr Dawney had gone, or that the line had been interrupted. She said a silent prayer.

But then she heard the release of his breath, a long, ragged sigh.

'I *thought* something was up with Amyas lately. Now you tell me about this child... it all makes sense. And you're absolutely right, of course. As the old Will stays in place, Antonia and her father will never dream of carving off even one penny for this baby girl: they'll sell the house from right underneath her. They'll want to protect the boys, of course. And that's if the baby lives, which sounds far from certain.'

Posie rushed on, wanting certainty, one way or the other. 'What should we do, sir? Are you happy to work with me on this? Try and forge some sort of future for this child? I'm just about to go away for a few days on holiday, but I couldn't go without resolving things in my mind, one way or the other.'

Dawney's voice was clear and firm, not warm but clinically reassuring. 'Of course I'll help, Miss Parker. Help provide a future. What sort of a man do you take me for if I stand by and don't get involved in this? The child is innocent, after all. You were quite right to bring this to me. Let's meet once you are back from your holiday, and we'll take it from there. Now, I must dash.'

Posie drew a large breath of relief. Somehow, in all this ungodly mess, people would band together to help the child born into the centre of it all. Even unlikely people, who she had found distasteful at first meeting. It was probably time to forget that long-ago childish fight which Richard Parker had tried so hard to conceal.

And now Posie headed train-wards, her appetite long

gone, and her thoughts of Rufus very black indeed, but feeling slightly cheerier anyhow.

* * * *

PART TWO
WHITLEY BAY
Wednesday 9th and Thursday 10th July, 1924

Seventeen

She was finally here. The north.

Whitley Bay.

The skies were bigger than anything Posie could remember, bigger and pinker and filled with an impossible light which bounced off the North Sea and was reflected ten-fold, quite unlike anything you got down south.

It was warmer too, oddly, and the pink evening sky carried the promise of a fine summer's day in store. Posie stood on the promenade, right up against the iron railing, still wearing her travel clothes and eating fish and chips. The tide was in, and the waves crashed against the concrete below her, giving off a fine salt spray, and still she didn't move.

Posie had been happy to board the train with Dolly and her nannies and her children and all the luggage. But then – guiltily – she had been even happier when the Cardigeon party had got out of the first-class carriage at York Central Station.

Three and a half hours of Dolly's railing at her husband, her complaints and her non-stop stream of general unhappiness had been competing with the baby, Raymond, crying, and the little girls, Bunny and Trixie, wailing and being sick. The nannies, the expensive toys, rocking the cumbersome pram, the trips to the restaurant car and the toilet – none of these had seemed to have helped.

Posie found herself feeling completely inadequate, useless at comforting Dolly about Rufus, as Posie also found him greatly changed for the worse, and she was useless at helping with the children. She found herself looking on in a state of helpless bafflement that she could even begin to think of looking after a small child.

Where on earth would I start?

Who knew little children could be so tiring, or demanding?

And then had come the relief of the final hour and a half of journey, alone, blissfully taking in nothing, letting her mind become a blank. Posie had tried not to think about the murder case she was involved in, shutting it out as best she could, although strangely, all day, even at King's Cross, and even on the train, she had felt that someone was watching her, following her, keeping her in their sights. She'd felt that pin-prickly sensation creep over her when she'd accompanied Dolly to the restaurant car, when they'd been sipping coffee, but for the life of her, whenever she turned around there was no-one there.

She had tried to forget about it, put it down to a tired mind in need of sleep. What she wanted to do was to free some space in her head to think about Max.

Beautiful, unavailable, out-of-the-ordinary Max.

Max was her some-time man in a some-time affair. In truth, an affair which was more off than on, mainly due to the confines of his job.

Max was a German, enlisted by the British government to work on security issues. A spy, of the very highest calibre. A man who had trained as a doctor himself, years back, with a speciality in drugs and poisons, and it was this expertise which led him to infiltrate drug rings and drug production circles, sending valuable intelligence to the government. But Max was such a highly-prized asset that he would never be afforded a private life of his own; he had signed such rights away. To all extents and purposes, he didn't exist. He was a ghost.

What Posie knew of the man was minimal, and she yearned to know more, but she had been warned off, by him, time and time again. She had met him initially on one of her first cases, and re-encountered him on yet another, but Max had made it clear that it was unlikely there was a future for their relationship, and yet he continued to send her tokens, letters.

They had met up only twice so far this year, and Posie herself wasn't deluded enough to convince herself that this was *enough*. The whole thing was simply a dalliance, an escape.

Perhaps this would be the last time they would meet. It was so complicated trying to keep up with a spy. And anyway, what did they really have in common? A couple of shared adventures; a keenness to forget the past and to move on, a desire to reinvent themselves. But these weren't *qualities*: more like intangible dreams or wishes.

The note had come two weeks ago.

P,

I'M UP NORTH WORKING.

FANCY A SHORT BREAK? I HAVE SOME TIME OWING ME. THE 9TH JULY ONWARDS? WHITLEY BAY? THE MARGARET HOTEL?

MAX

That had been it. So here she was.

It was seven o'clock and the light, balmy evening was full of tourists, like herself. All eating fish suppers or sipping ice-cream sodas in the hubbub of the fashionable Rendezvous Café with its huge oval windows, halfway along the promenade of the famous Whitley Bay beach. From here you could see the landmark crescent sweep of sand, reaching all the way to St Mary's Lighthouse, curving away to the left in the distance.

The promenade was packed. There were so many people here. The magazine article Mrs Oats had read must have been quite influential in its reach. That, or the place was fashionable anyway. A mix of accents from up and down the country could be heard if you listened in hard enough. There were small groups of musicians dotted about, vying for people's attention, and tourists weaving in and out, laughing as photographers approached them for the current trend of 'walking photographs'. There was a Punch-and-Judy show nearby, too, with excitable children sitting waiting, toffee-apples and ice-creams held aloft. Men were cleaning and polishing up some ancient-looking bathing machines they had dragged up onto the promenade, ready for the next day and the next crowd of cautious, prudish bathers. Posie hated such things, and felt that even in her mother's time they were becoming outmoded, but they obviously catered for all tastes and moralities up here.

So far Posie hadn't walked the length of the beach, or the promenade. She'd come from Newcastle on a local train and taken a motor-taxi straight from the station to the hotel. She hadn't been down to the high street, or to the Spanish City, although she could see its very white dome even from here. She would save it for tomorrow.

She felt happy and wind-swept, and above all, *free*. She would finish her supper and walk slowly back the way she had come, up to the sea-front Margaret Hotel, on the way to St Mary's Lighthouse, where the two rooms next door to each other had been booked and paid for already, and not by her.

The only fly in the ointment so far was the fact that Max hadn't arrived.

But he still had all evening to show up, and Posie wasn't worried.

Not yet.

****

Friday dawned clear and blue with the sun already blisteringly hot.

Posie dressed carefully and packed her navy-and-white striped swimming-bag, hat and parasol. She'd slept well, deeply and without dreams. She hadn't been disturbed in the night by anyone, least of all Max, and now she crept next door and knocked softly several times over. A passing laundry-maid shook her head at Posie: 'There's no-one staying there yet, Miss. I know, cos I just went in to change the linens and there was no need. The room hasn't been used.'

Smiling like this was the best news in the world, Posie headed down to a nine o'clock breakfast and attacked a plate of bacon and eggs and kippers at her table with an appetite she hadn't realised she possessed. She skimmed the local newspaper and took a couple of printed brochures about local attractions with her to read at the beach. She tried to banish a nervous tremble of fear which had now lodged itself inconveniently in her stomach, a fear which was all about Max, or his *absence*.

Hesitating at the foyer about whether to leave a message for Max with the receptionist, she decided not to. After all, they weren't in the business of drawing attention to themselves normally, so why start now? They hadn't chosen the most obvious hotel, for example, although the Margaret was one of the best; plush and discreet and with an air of opulence which befitted a town on the up.

Studying the local map in the foyer, Posie chose to go back to where she had been the previous night. She'd leave those beautiful looking yellow-sand coves of Cullercoats Bay and Long Beach Walk, stretching southwards, for another day. A day spent with Max.

She'd make use of this precious, sun-filled day – it

might be the only one – and sit on the main Whitley Bay beach. If Max still hadn't appeared after lunch, she'd walk to the Spanish City, into the town, and see if she could make any headway with her investigation, such as it was. Digging where William Dawney had already tried and failed. At the last moment Posie returned to her room to get her carpet bag with everything she had brought about Amyas Lyle in it. Just in case.

Later, sun-roasted and sun-oiled and feeling like she had had altogether perhaps enough sun and sand for the day, even though it was only midday, Posie trudged back slowly over the wet sand. She pulled her straw sun-hat down on her face and started to walk in the opposite direction from her hotel. And here she was. At the Spanish City.

It was set back from the promenade but still looked out over the sea. The building was impressive, with a huge white pearl of a dome, studded with windows and adorned with two white towers on either side bearing flags and, at the very top of each, a statuette of a woman dancing. Beneath the towers was a collection of shops and cafés, with a grand arched entrance into the building placed symmetrically in the middle. One of the cafés, an Italian ice-cream parlour – Bertorelli's – with seats set out on the pavement, seemed to be doing a roaring trade.

Posie stepped back, taking a seat on a bench which had its back to the sea and a view of the Spanish City directly opposite. She looked at the place again, taking in the famous Empress Ballroom on the left-hand side, and a funfair stretching back behind it. The road snaking away on the right seemed to be a high street of some sort, with restaurants and tea-rooms right along its length.

It was enchanting, this place. So new, so *now*.

Posie knew from her reading of the local guides that an entrepreneur with a group of touring entertainers called the 'Toreadors' had taken over this patch of land fifteen years before, starting out initially with makeshift canvas tents which he had painted to resemble a Spanish street scene. Over a couple of years the area had become known as the 'Spanish City' and its success had chimed well with the growing tourist boom enjoyed by the town. By 1910 plans were afoot to make something permanent on the site, something spectacular, and in a sixty-day building spree the building she saw in front of her had been erected, to much fanfare. Now times were changing and it was the Empress Ballroom which people flocked to, one of the favourite dance-halls in the country, rather than the Spanish City itself, and fashionable bands competed to play here, sometimes being recorded for broadcast on the wireless.

Posie found her notebook, within which was the postcard sent to Amyas Lyle. She held it up and compared it with the real-life vista in front of her. There were a couple of differences, maybe. One café was now different, with a different name. There was no ice-cream parlour in the postcard, either.

Posie stared at the postcard again. She stared at the blurry figure of a man lingering outside the main entrance arch with his hands in his pockets, a straw boater pulled well down, a striped holiday shirt on, like a French fisherman. He stood in front of the building on his own, his stance proprietorial.

You couldn't take a photograph like that today; there were too many people around. Too many women in fashionable hats, wanting to be seen.

Posie noticed that directly opposite her, in the very same place where the man with the straw boater had been standing in the postcard, a metal stand on a rotating pole had been set up, picture postcards displayed on it. A man in his late fifties sat next to this on a canvas chair, eating his lunch from a greaseproof paper packet.

Posie crossed the street and made her way to the stand. She made a brief show of inspecting the postcards for sale and then chose four at random. Having paid, she pocketed the newly-bought postcards and casually fluttered the postcard sent to Amyas Lyle in front of the man in his chair.

'I wondered if you had any like *this* for sale?' she asked brightly, holding it up for his inspection rather than letting him put his greasy mitts all over it. 'I've looked but I can't see any on your stand here.'

The man looked up at Posie from beneath an old tweed cap. He had a weather-beaten face and sparkling blue eyes. 'Ah, pet, but aren't you a sight for sore eyes?'

At Posie's scowl he sighed and shook his head. 'No, sorry, pet. I've never sold postcards like that. And I'm not likely to get any, am I? Not unless I go back in time, like! This postcard is from last year. I can tell because a few things have changed, see?'

'Are there any other postcard sellers inside the Spanish City who might have this card for sale?'

The man laughed easily. 'Of course there are, pet. Two or three other sellers, actually. You ask away. But you'll only get the same answer. You see, the management orders the postcards it wants every year and sells them to us. All strictly controlled, see? I've never seen that card before.'

A sort of recognition came into the man's eyes suddenly. He frowned. 'I tell a lie. You know, pet, I *have* seen this card before. Just the once. Must have been months ago, six months maybe? It was winter: not many tourists about. A fella – a posh gent with a voice like yours – he was asking the same questions as you are now. Had I sold this card? Did I know who the fella in it was? All that nonsense.'

Dawney. He had been as thorough as he had claimed, then.

'And what did you tell this posh gent?' Posie waved a bright coin near to the man's hand, a coin equivalent to at least a day's earnings, probably two. 'Please?'

'I told him to go inside and ask the management. I said

maybe it was a short print-run or it was a shot which didn't make the final selection? Maybe they'd have a better idea.'

'The management.' Posie passed the coin across. 'That's very helpful. I'll do that.'

'I don't know as it is helpful, actually, Miss.' The man's tone was now much more reverential. 'You see, after I sent him in, this gent came out again about five minutes later, looking out of sorts. When I asked him what was the matter, he said the management was off sick and he couldn't get an answer out of anybody.'

'I see.'

'It often happens, Miss. The management is often away, sick. So I'm told. But you could try, couldn't you? If it's that important to you?'

Thanking the man, and feeling slightly wrong-footed, Posie swung under the great arch of the entrance and up the steps into the main lobby of the place. It was immense. Across the black-and-white tiled floor people sauntered, dipping in and out of the many doors which led off it. Suddenly aware of her rumbling stomach, and that 'management' would probably also be at lunch, she chose the nearest of the doors, leading to a Lyons Corner House, and passed through.

It was the sort of café where you didn't sit down for the waitress to come. Instead, you held a tray and queued at a shiny silver counter with a large glass cabinet all the way along, with an array of cakes and dry-looking sandwiches inside it. Ladies in blue Lyons uniforms hurried behind this glass cabinet, endlessly plucking cakes out with tongs, and re-stocking empty shelves, and working immense tea urns beside the cashier. It all seemed very busy, very hectic. Before she could blink, Posie found herself up by the cashier, pointing at a cheese and salad sandwich she felt panicked into buying, and asking for the wrong sort of tea.

And then as she swung into the main part of the room, where all of the tables were taken, balancing everything on her tray very precariously, her straw hat under her arm and her hair wild with sweat and sun-oil, she saw a pair of blue eyes staring across the room at her. Following her every move.

Blue eyes she knew very well.

* * * *

Eighteen

Blue eyes above a ratty brown moustache. Blue eyes in an angry, twitching face, above a rumpled linen shirt and cream holiday trousers which were way too short.

Inspector Oats, in holiday mode.

He was sitting uncomfortably at a prime table over by the window, the big man shoe-horned into a small space with a very large lady taking up almost all of the available room. Presumably this was his wife, Tilly, reader of the influential magazine.

Posie's heart sank, but she managed a smile and a nod, while frantically looking around for a table anywhere other than near *them*. But to her horror, Inspector Oats was now threading his way through the crowd, his usual aura of authority still clinging about him, people jerking their heads around in fright.

'My missus wondered if you would like to join us.' And before Posie could open her mouth to answer, Inspector Oats had taken up her tray and was weaving back the way he had come.

Out-smarted, and feeling like she was now entering a hell specially of her own making, Posie followed dumbly, almost lost for words.

Mrs Oats was beaming and patting at a third chair she

had procured from somewhere, while Inspector Oats was setting out Posie's tea-things and her sandwich. There was no doubt *here* as to who wore the trousers in the marriage.

Up close Mrs Oats was even more formidable than at first sight; a mountain of a lady, her hair dyed a not very convincing cherry red, a dewy sheen on her face not quite covered up by the lashings of powder she had applied. Obviously a 'looker' in her youth, and keen to hang onto that accolade at any cost, she wore a red poppy-flowered poplin dress which was too young for her and which strained impressively at the bust. She had bright, sharp brown eyes which scanned the tea-room restlessly, making sure she wasn't missing anything.

'Sit yourself down, dearie, and enjoy your lunch. I'm Matilda Oats, by the way.'

'Thank you. Posie Parker. Pleased to meet you.'

'My Bill, he saw you come in, he did. Couldn't believe his eyes! Didn't want to trouble you at first; thought you might like some time on your own. I said *what nonsense! The famous lady detective!*'

Mrs Oats had raised her voice theatrically at this point and several people at nearby tables were looking on with interest. Inspector Oats had turned a dark shade of red and was fiddling with the table-cloth, and Posie hurriedly started to drink her tea, the better to be over the horror of the thing. But she was mindful to be polite; she hadn't forgotten how Inspector Lovelace had brought Oats in on his interview with Selwyn Pickle, the barrister, only two days before, and how courteous and polite Lovelace had been towards his colleague and usual arch-rival.

'I didn't know *you* were coming up here for your holidays, too,' muttered Oats, almost under his breath. He looked very put out and slurped at his own tea in a miserable fashion.

'Yes, well.' Posie tucked her hair behind her ear nervously. 'It was a last-minute thing, you know. It's quite the place here, isn't it? Are you enjoying it?'

And then Mrs Oats was babbling away nineteen-to-the-dozen about boarding-houses and suchlike. Posie was just biting into her dry cheese sandwich when the niceties ran out and Mrs Oats caught her off guard with a question coming hard on the sudden silence:

'My Bill, he wondered if you were up here *working*, like? On an *assignment*, Miss Parker? For the Chief Inspector?'

Inspector Oats was puce in the face. 'Tilly, please…'

Posie put down her sandwich. Curiously, she didn't feel angry or affronted. Instead, there was something refreshing about this woman's bare-faced nosiness. Posie tried to look as important as possible. 'I'm here on a personal break. But you're half-right. I'm supposed to be looking into a possible Whitley Bay connection for the recent murder of Amyas Lyle.' She looked straight at Oats. 'You know, sir, the murder case which Inspector Lovelace involved you with on Wednesday?'

Inspector Oats sat, back ramrod-straight. 'I know the one. Yes.'

'You see, love?' Mrs Oats was excitable, almost winking at her husband.

'Sorry? *What* is there to see?' asked Posie, not understanding. She remembered Oats and his scornful comments to Lovelace that involving her '*always results in a catastrophe*', and something about mildew on cabbages. She felt sure Inspector Oats was about to lash out at her in his customary way, but he seemed to be holding back, biding his time, for some reason.

'Well,' said Mrs Oats, her three chins quivering, licking at her very red-lipsticked mouth. 'My Bill's told me about this 'ere murder of this lawyer fella, and we read about it all in the paper yesterday morning anyhow. It stands to reason, doesn't it, that Chief Inspector Lovelace will be wanting to send all and sundry out to chase possible leads, to finish this case off as soon as possible. He's got to work quickly now, hasn't he?'

Posie stared at Mrs Oats. *What was she going on about?*

It was true: she *had* felt the weight of a time pressure being applied in a way she had not felt on previous cases, Lovelace impatient for clarity and justice. But she had no idea why. Posie opened her mouth to speak, but was interrupted once again.

Mrs Oats was looking triumphant. 'It's going to be announced next week, didn't you say, Bill? The big news?'

Oats was looking embarrassed, but Posie turned back to his wife. 'What news?'

'That Chief Inspector Lovelace is leaving the force! Leaving Scotland Yard and moving away. A long way away! He's been asked to become Commissioner of Police for the whole of New Zealand! Imagine! The top dog!'

New Zealand.

Posie was aware of the world she was inhabiting hurling her through three hundred and sixty degrees of shock, her tight grip on the table her only way of tethering herself.

Of course. It all made sense. Lovelace's current manner, his distraction. His desire to do everything right, to leave the job on a high note. The meetings, the grovelling behaviour towards Lord Justice Roade, who was friends with the Superintendent, who must have got him this job, this opportunity in the first place.

Sergeant Rainbird had been trying to warn her, to tell her. His comment about *sheep*. About how Lovelace would have to get used to them.

Well, yes. Everything Posie had ever heard about New Zealand promised a lot of sheep.

New Zealand.

The other side of the world. Likely no return visits. Once he had gone she would never see Richard Lovelace again, or her god-daughter, Phyllis, for that matter.

Why hadn't he told her? Was he just going to present it as a *fait accompli*?

And then, in among the waves of shock, she remembered

him talking about lunch and then his invitation to dinner two nights previously. Had he wanted to tell her about New Zealand then?

Self-preservation drove her on, and she recovered herself. She smiled coolly, looking as if this information was nothing new. 'Ah, yes. Of course I knew about the offer of the Commissioner's position, Mrs Oats. What an honour! But my understanding was that the Chief Inspector hadn't finalised things just yet?'

Matilda Oats pursed her lips. 'Well, I'm not one to gossip, but I have heard from the other wives at Scotland Yard that he's got himself a nice little set-up now: a lass called Ella Brown who looks after that poor motherless child of his, and Ella has said she'd be only too willing to up sticks and move abroad, if there was a gold ring in it for her.'

'Tilly! Hush your mouth!' yelped an exasperated Inspector Oats. 'You know nothing of the kind!'

'I know the truth when I hear it!' said Matilda Oats with certainty. 'And what we *do* know for absolute certain is that with Lovelace gone, there's a new Chief Inspectorship going begging at the Yard. And who better for it, I ask you, than my Bill?'

Ah! Posie now saw the crux of the thing as it really was.

Things were fitting into place now. Why she had been called over, for starters. She shifted a little in her seat, trying to get things into perspective. So *this* was why Inspector Oats was working so collaboratively with Lovelace for once, anxious to squirm his way into Lovelace's good books, hopeful for a recommendation, a word in the ear of the Superintendent. *This* was why he was looking so shamefaced now, with his wife spilling the beans on his ambition so spectacularly.

But what if it *did* all play out as Matilda Oats wanted? If Oats took the Chief Inspectorship when and if Lovelace moved on? Posie experienced a horrid sinking feeling. Financially stable as she was personally, she often worked with Scotland Yard on cases which involved a bounty payment, or a reward of some kind, without which the Detective Agency on Grape Street would have struggled several times over. Posie needed security. Job possibilities. She didn't want to make her bed and lie in it with the devil, but…

She gritted her teeth. 'I'm sure the Inspector here will be admirably well positioned to gain the promotion.' She watched Inspector Oats' pale eyes widen in surprise. 'I will put in a good word myself with the Chief Inspector, although I'm not sure how much weight those words will carry.'

'Would you, love? Oh, see, Bill? I told you it would be worthwhile havin' her over here, didn't I?'

But now Posie was cutting in, wiping at her mouth with a napkin: 'I'm sure we can make it *worthwhile* all-round, eh, sir? I'm pretty good at working with the police on investigations, undercover-like, when you need a lone girl. As you know, I usually get good results, never a catastrophe in sight. I hope I can look forward to continuing to work with you in the future, Inspector?'

She almost laughed at his desperate-looking face, his way of not wanting to commit to anything at all, and yet his reliance upon her.

'In fact, can you give me your boarding-house address here, sir? I'm following up a lead, and if it results in anything, Inspector Lovelace told me to bring it to you, for you to sort out. I hope that suits you, sir?'

And suddenly nodding vigorously, Oats wrote out his address in Whitley Bay, an address which Posie had no intention of ever using. And with that she said goodbye, strolling out of a curious and unnerving lunch, feeling the Inspector's eyes boring into her back as she left, bluffing a self-confidence she certainly did not feel.

* * * *

Nineteen

Outside and away from prying eyes she felt deflated, as if she had no more get up and go. Posie stopped in the main entrance hall.

Where on earth was Max? And now this business with Inspector Lovelace and New Zealand, and the woman who looked after Phyllis. Had Matilda Oats said that on purpose, to deliberately hurt Posie? Posie who had never been a home-maker in her life. Who hadn't a clue how to iron and starch shirt collars. Who would never, even in a million years, leave London and move to New Zealand. Not even for a gold ring.

But she didn't even *love* Richard Lovelace. So why was she so bothered at this news?

Don't cry, if it's the last thing you do.

She stood up taller.

One of the doors off the central lobby had a small sign in gold lettering saying 'MANAGEMENT' with an arrow leading jaggedly upwards, indicating stairs. Desperate for work, for a lead anywhere, Posie threw open the door, conscious as she went that she was re-tracing Dr Dawney's footsteps, probably in vain. It seemed unlikely he had missed anything, but it was better than standing around thinking depressing thoughts.

Posie found herself walking up a tight spiral stairway into the massive white dome of the Spanish City itself, which had been recently fitted with a suspended ceiling, the extra floor it had created having been turned into a few small offices. The whole construct was new enough that the air still smelt of sawdust. She walked through a cheap-looking wooden door and was confronted with a pair of women, roughly her own age, with matching blunt bobbed hairstyles, sitting at desks, side-by-side, with gleaming typewriters in front of them. Behind them was another cheap door, with a big sign saying 'DIRECTOR' on it. There were no windows here, the only feature of the office being a dark, plush, ruby-coloured carpet.

Both women looked up guiltily.

Posie was obviously the first visitor of the day. She saw stacks of music tickets and waiting envelopes in piles ready to be sent out, obviously untouched for hours. The women had penny magazines propped open in front of them instead, and one had a set of studio photographs of herself, fanned in an arc on her desk, trying to choose a favourite shot. Grocery shopping in string bags was visible under the two desks, fruit and tins spilling out haphazardly.

It was on the tip of Posie's tongue to say '*hard at work?*' when she realised this would be churlish. Who knew the circumstances of these women's lives? Who was she to judge?

The oldest, sharpest-looking woman recovered herself first. She took a spiteful glance at Posie's ring finger and saw it was empty and almost smirked to herself. 'Can I help you, *Miss?*'

'I hope so. Is the Director here?'

The woman drew herself up importantly. ''Fraid not, Miss. Mr Dance is off sick.'

'Oh? That happens a lot, I hear?' Posie paused, smiled, letting the shared knowledge sink in. She often had a knack of inviting confidences, and hoped that might be the case now.

The other, younger, slightly friendlier woman nodded confidentially: 'On account of his *nerves*, Miss. You know? Wilfred Dance came back from the Great War a broken man, and the owners here didn't like to take away his job on top of everything else. But he don't come in much, Miss. If truth be told, he don't do anything really. Not since Christmas when he had another of his funny turns. His worst so far.'

'Freda!' The first woman gasped, scandalised. 'Don't speak about Mr Dance like that to a perfect stranger!'

The second woman shrugged, refusing to back down. 'Well, it's true, isn't it, Violet? As God is my witness I'm not saying anything untrue. Besides, the place runs very well, doesn't it, without him? What with *us* here, and Mr Vannelly here now, too. He's the Acting Director, and he keeps the place going like clockwork. Mr Vannelly is a friend of Mr Dance. In fact, I think it was Mr Dance who suggested to the owners that Mr Vannelly come and work here when Mr Dance went off sick. It was just meant to be temporary but he's stayed on. It's a very solid arrangement; the owners don't realise quite how much Mr Vannelly does.'

As the first woman huffed at her friend's indiscretions, Posie moved towards the wooden door with the word 'DIRECTOR' on it. Up close she could see that beneath this sign other lettering had been stuck up, forming the words 'WILFRED DANCE' and beneath it, in smaller letters, 'AIDEN VANNELLY'. She could also see that the door was unlocked, hanging open on its new, cheap hinges, and that the room inside was in darkness.

'And Mr Vannelly? Is he here to speak to?'

'No, Miss,' said the second woman, Freda, regretfully. 'He's been away this last week. On holiday.'

'I see.' Posie wheeled around, the postcard to Amyas between her fingers. 'Could *you* help me, ladies? Forgive me, but it is quite important. Have you ever seen this postcard before? I've asked the postcard sellers here and apparently it's not one of the images which are authorised for sale.'

She passed the postcard to the women who looked at it, heads bent together.

The younger one, Freda, looked up and for the first time looked suspicious. 'This is very odd. There was another man asking about this postcard in here, oh, *months* back now. He was southern, like you. Handsome, like Ivor Novello. But blonde. You know him?'

Posie shook her head. Well, it was true, wasn't it? She *didn't* know Dr Dawney, not personally.

Freda waved the postcard back at Posie. 'I told him I didn't know anything about it. Never seen it before. He wasn't happy to hear *that*, I can tell you. Stropped around the place, good and proper, talking about "dead ends". I thought he'd lost the plot! Thought he might do some damage to the place; not that there was much up here then, we'd only just moved into this office.'

Her colleague, Violet, was confused. 'I don't remember any of this, Freda. What are you on about, pet?'

'It must have been January? It was freezing cold, we had snow on the ground. You were off with the flu, and I was all on my own. Mr Dance was off, as usual. And Mr Vannelly was in meetings every day that week, booking bands to come and play.'

Posie sighed. Dead ends.

But Violet had got to her feet, gone through into the Director's office where she flicked on an overhead light. She was rifling around somewhere and she came out with a dark-red box, ripping the lid off hastily.

'A shame for your blonde Ivor Novello that he had a wasted journey, then, eh?' she said almost viciously to her colleague. 'A shame *I* wasn't here. I could have helped him.' She pulled out a big handful of the stacked postcards which were inside the red box, all identical to the ones sent to Amyas Lyle. She splayed them over the top of her desk.

Posie held her breath, heart racing, anxious not to betray how important this was. A break-through? Or just some strange coincidence? Although she'd never believed in coincidences.

'Is this the only box of these, do you know? Or are there others on sale elsewhere?'

Violet shook her head. She'd picked one of the postcards up. 'No. This photograph was taken last year, last summer, by Mr Vannelly himself – he's a keen photographer – before he worked here actually, but the owners weren't keen on selling it. Refused to print it. I think they thought it was a bit too arty, not a popular scene which tourists would go for.'

'Why is there a whole box of this same postcard then?'

Violet jabbed at the postcard in her hand. 'It was Mr Dance who paid for this one professional print-run of the postcard, even though I reckon it was jolly expensive. He said he'd keep it for times he needed to send a note or a card with a truly *personal* touch.'

Violet flicked her nail at the blurry man in the picture. 'This is him, see? This is Wilfred Dance, the Director, standing out front of here. All kitted out in his summer gear. Freda just told you he and Aiden Vannelly were friends, didn't she? This must have been a project they did very early one morning, see? There's no-one else about! But what a waste of money, eh? I don't think Mr Dance ever sent many of them. As Freda said, he hasn't been in much. They've just been sitting here gathering dust.'

Posie tried to keep her excitement under wraps. Something was important here, she felt sure of it.

She helped put the scattered postcards into the box again and followed Violet to the door of the Director's office, leaning against its rough-hewn frame. It was a very small room, a few posters for well-known bands tacked to the walls. She watched Violet place the box behind a large dark-wood desk which took central position in the room. It was empty but for a silver-framed photograph of a Great War army training unit; twenty or so men grinning out across the years, hopeful and immaculate before the realities of northern France and the trenches had killed at least two-thirds of them.

Posie was just about to turn back into the outer office again when something caught her eye. Another framed photograph on the second, smaller desk. Posie was conscious now of Violet, wanting to turn out the light. But her heart was now hammering against her rib cage like an angry bird.

'I say!' She pushed her way across to the second desk, to the photograph. She picked it up, bringing it close to her face to study it better. It was a photograph of a man in his early thirties, dark-haired, gorgeous, wearing what looked like a housemaster's gown and mortar-board hat, standing with his arm around the waist of a small, finely-built woman in her fifties, wearing what was obviously her Sunday best. The dark, rather chiselled facial features they shared made it clear they were mother and son.

Violet was behind Posie now. 'That's Mr Vannelly. With his mother. God rest her soul. He was a teacher a while back. Housemaster at St Gillies Prep School...' Her words tailed off into nothingness.

Posie's hands were trembling. *At last!* At last it was all coming together. Or parts of it were. She put down the photograph carefully, tried to act normally.

'Do you have an address for Mr Vannelly, Violet? *Aiden* Vannelly, isn't it?'

Violet was back at her own desk. She was suspicious, almost sullen now. 'No, Miss. I don't have an address.'

Freda, who obviously carried something of a candle for the man who kept things running here so smoothly, chipped in eagerly: 'I don't know the exact address but I can tell you where he lives: it's just out of here; turn left away from the sea and head down Marine Avenue. It's a small terraced house about halfway down the road on the right-hand side, with a bright blue door and blue window boxes outside. There used to be geraniums growing come rain or shine, but now the window boxes are empty.'

Thanking the invaluable Freda for her help, and turning on her heel as fast as she could, she just heard the first woman shouting behind her:

'There's no use going there anyway, pet. Aiden Vannelly's away on holiday. Not due back until next week.'

But Posie knew she would find him there. Sure as bread was bread.

* * * *

Twenty

It took five minutes to find it.

The paint on the blue front door was peeling and a residue of upswept sand and dirt crunched underfoot on the pathway outside the small house. The lace curtains at the windows needed a wash and Freda had been right – the window boxes contained nothing more hopeful than dried earth.

In those five minutes of fast-paced walking, certain things had come together in Posie's mind: *that* desk photograph; the postcards sent to Amyas; various scattered throwaway comments finally now making sense, crystallising and forming into the person she expected would open the door to her.

Aiden Vannelly.

He was the missing puzzle piece.

She rang the bell. After just a few seconds, footsteps could be heard approaching, a blur of a figure looming behind the stained-glass insert of the front door. And here he was.

'Oh! I say!'

If Posie didn't know the truth, she would probably have passed out with shock and fright.

A dead man, brought to life. A ghost.

Aiden Vannelly looked at Posie with a simple, steadfast expression, as if he had been expecting her at any moment.

'You found me.'

And Posie looked straight into the honey-coloured eyes of the man in front of her, a man who, apart from slightly longer hair, and the gentle Tyneside lilt to his voice, was the spitting image of Amyas Lyle.

His identical twin.

'*You* were in London, Mr Vannelly. You found Amyas.'

'Correct.'

The man shook out something he had evidently been reading when Posie had rung the bell. It was a London broadsheet from the day before. The inside first page carried a story about Amyas Lyle and his murder.

'But I was too late, wasn't I? Amyas was already dead. You'd better come in. It's Miss Parker, isn't it? Tea?'

'That's right. And yes. Thank you.'

Stepping neatly around a small canvas travelling bag, left in the hallway with a cream straw boater hat thrown atop it, Posie followed Amyas Lyle's twin down the long, dark main corridor of the house, where old newspapers had been laid underfoot.

'Sorry about the mess, and the luggage. As you know, I've just returned home, or what passes for a home at the moment. I'm stripping the place down, so I've things all over the place.'

Rooms off the corridor were closed up, dark paintwork and wallpaper peeling away. The place felt neglected, sad.

The pin-prickly feelings all made sense now. Posie wasn't going mad. *Just wait until she told Inspector Lovelace.*

Aiden Vannelly was the man she had seen loitering outside 20 Old Square when she had turned up to meet Lovelace on Tuesday at the murder scene, and then she had seen him again later, outside Eaton Terrace, where he had also been spied by Evans, the Butler. Aiden had presumably also been on the same train as Posie the day before, travelling back up north. She'd been aware of Aiden Vannelly as a presence before she had encountered him as a fact.

That Amyas Lyle had a twin made sense now.

Wasn't it fairly common that when twins were separated, or when one died, the other twin felt the absence keenly, even if they hadn't ever been truly aware of being a twin in the first place?

It seemed that Aiden, the missing twin, had been a presence, even if just an absence, within Amyas Lyle's life all along.

In a throw-away comment Rufus had spoken mockingly of a conversation he had overheard between Amyas and the Headmaster at school once, when the boy was very young, with Amyas insisting he had an imaginary friend who was his constant companion. That fitted somehow.

And hadn't Dr Dawney suggested that the ruthless ambition which drove Amyas forwards was because he was *'lacking something… or seeking an audience'*.

And here was the man who would have made Amyas whole.

They had entered a space at the back of the house, a large, bright kitchen, totally at odds with the rest of the dark house.

'This room is the only one I've completed so far. But I live here practically, I love it.'

'I can see why.'

The room was brightly painted in blues and whites and turquoise, giving the immediate impression of being by the seaside. A huge window, taking up at least half the wall above the sink and drying racks, gave a view onto a small back yard with a shed in it, but the eye didn't linger here for long, as the low fence at the back of the yard gave way to an uninterrupted vista of scrubland running down to the golden sands of the coast and a strip of sea. You could just see St Mary's Lighthouse from here, too.

'What a view,' Posie said admiringly, sitting down at the large kitchen table, which evidently served as a desk for Aiden, too. Everything was neatly arranged, stacks of newspapers and letters and bills in careful piles. There were loose photographs, and an age-grizzled grey photograph album. There were a couple of empty bottles of red wine, too, and a used wine glass. A pair of spectacles and a cup of tea had been pushed quickly aside.

Posie watched as Aiden Vannelly lit the gas and heated water for fresh tea. He wore loose linen trousers and some sort of striped foreign-looking shirt. If she hadn't known better she would have said he was an artist.

He turned and leant against the wooden sideboard, where a blue gingham cloth had been hung to cover the boiler and the pipes. He studied Posie carefully, chin in hand. 'This was my mother's house. I lived here too, but now she's dead and it belongs to me. I thought it was time to make some changes. The papers you can see at the table are hers. I'm going through everything, trying to make order.'

He poured Posie tea, and then took a pastel-blue painted chair opposite her. They sat in silence, studying each other intently.

Posie felt a delicious shiver run through her.

Golly, but this man was *divine*.

No wonder the women over at the office in the Spanish City had been fiercely protective of him; had spoken of him in such glowing terms. Here were the handsome good looks of Amyas Lyle, the same unusual eyes and film-star features, but in a softer, more human version. This man seemed gentle. There was nothing of the vampire about him. Nothing that would have made an elder brother warn off his impressionable younger sister. Nor did he seem to be the type of man who would have pushed aside his own happiness to swim in the murky waters of a loveless marriage. *This* man seemed to lack the burning ambition of his twin brother.

'You're working with the police to solve my brother's murder, Miss Parker?'

'Oh, yes. Inspector Lovelace is simply the best detective in London.'

'Except for *you*, so I've heard. So do you know who killed my brother yet?'

Of course she didn't. But a dangerous murderer needed to be caught, and she didn't want this man thinking she was incapable. She gave a shrug. 'We have several leads. One of which was *this*.' She waved the postcard of the Spanish City in the air. 'And *this* is what led me to you. Although we've been tailing each other about, haven't we?'

Aiden took the card from Posie, and the second or so of contact with his skin made her shiver once again. *Get a grip.*

'Ah, yes.' Aiden put on his spectacles. '*I* sent this. That's quite correct. Along with many others. You know I took this photograph?'

'Oh yes. The girls in your office told me. Part of a select print-run for your friend Mr Dance. And yes: I know you sent several. Since January, a couple every month. Always blank. Did you send notes, too? Arrange for them to be hand-delivered?'

She didn't mention their threatening nature.

But Aiden Vannelly was shaking his head, looking confused. 'Notes? No. I never wrote a word on my postcards to my brother, let alone full-blown notes.'

Posie frowned. 'Fine. Can you tell me why you sent the anonymous cards, then?'

And then at his silence, the question she had been burning to ask: 'Did Amyas know about you? That he had a twin brother?'

Aiden Vannelly put the card down and then exhaled noisily. 'The answer to both your questions is "I don't know." But actually, I think the real answer to the second question is no: Amyas didn't know he had a twin brother, or about his real mother. How much do you know about this whole affair, Miss Parker?'

'Next to nothing. Anything is helpful.'

Aiden stood, staring out across the scrubland, looking at the distant sea. Posie let the silence go on, beat after beat. She watched the tension in the gentle lines of the man at the window, a man deciding whether or not to tell a story. The shoulders loosened, the decision made.

He stayed at the window, his back to her. 'It's not a nice story, Miss Parker, but I'll share what I know with you.'

'Thank you.' Posie took out her notebook.

'My mother was a housemaid in one of the big stately homes around here, on the Northumbria Coast, Bane Castle. She was very young and pretty, and she was only seventeen when she got herself *in trouble*. It was all very tricky, because it was the young Master of the House who got her into the predicament. His name was Amyas, by the way.'

Aiden had turned to the table, grabbing at the album. He opened it up and was pushing it towards Posie, pointing at a postcard taped inside. She saw a castle on a remote craggy coastline. And then, below it, a photograph of a thick-set young blonde man wearing the tight waistcoat and high neckerchief of the late Victorian era. He had passed on nothing to his sons other than his eyes, watchful and intense, and probably honey-coloured, although the sepia photograph didn't allow for certainty.

'Your father, I'm guessing?'

'Yes. That's the rotter himself. Amyas Llewellyn-Jones. Although he was a pretty smart sort, by all accounts; too clever by half. This was my mother's treasured book of her life. Her name was Martha, by the way.'

Posie looked up at Aiden and he met her eyes briefly, before flicking on to the next page. 'She was packed off out of that great castle as quickly as possible and paid to go to some nursing home tucked out of the way. And Master

Amyas, he was sent off to India in disgrace, to Delhi, to help run the Empire. He died out there too, pretty soon after, from dysentery. Meanwhile my mother had given birth to twin boys, Amyas and myself. I expect the Llewellyn-Jones family thought it would end there, that obedient little Martha Vannelly would give her babies up and disappear out of their lives forever. But they underestimated my mother, as nearly everyone did.'

Posie was looking at a photograph of two tiny babies, dark, eyes closed and sleeping, end-to-end in a white ruffled cot, in immaculate white lace outfits. 'AMYAS AND AIDEN' was scrawled below the picture. She stared up at Aiden. 'What happened?'

'My mother had no-one of her own, no family who would support her. But she wouldn't give us up. She blackmailed the Llewellyn-Jones family, or rather she asked them to support her. They didn't want anything to do with her, or *us*, but they gave her a one-off payment on the condition she never darkened their door again. My mother took the money and she moved us here, to this very house. She always said she had to be near the sea. And she liked the liveliness of Whitley Bay, the tourists starting to arrive.'

He was turning pages in the album. There were postcards tacked in of Whitley Bay from thirty years before, pamphlets for attractions long gone. A lone photograph of the house Posie was currently sitting in, drinking tea.

'There was enough money to rent this house, with a bit left over for food for a couple of years.'

'Just a couple?'

Aiden paused, his thoughts tracking back almost to the start of his lifetime. 'She looked after us as best she could. But it must have been tough; a young woman of not yet twenty, with two lively little lads on her hands, no help from anyone. They must have been long, hard days. Lonely. But she did her best. I remember my mother taking us in a big wheelbarrow-contraption to the beach. It's melded into one endless memory for me. We must have been two years old, almost three. Almost every day that summer she pushed us along to the beach here at Whitley Bay, or to Cullercoats. And sometimes to King Edwards Bay where the sand gave way beneath your feet and you felt like falling every time the saltwater washed over you. I remember Amyas and I screaming and shouting in the waves, half-crazy with the fear of it, the excitement. Our mother shouting at us to stop…'

And suddenly Posie sat, stock-still, unnerved. *Surely it couldn't be a coincidence?*

The words Aiden Vannelly was using to describe his memories were uncannily similar to one of the threats sent to Amyas Lyle, which Aiden had denied having anything to do with.

Posie flicked through her silver notepad to the back, where she had quickly jotted down the wording from the notes, in the order in which they had arrived.

Yes. Here it was.

Remember the beach where we used to play? The feel of saltwater on your skin? The sand giving way beneath our feet? The constant danger of slipping in? That's how YOU should be feeling right now.

It was too similar to overlook, almost the same description, in fact.

'What's wrong, Miss Parker? You've gone as white as a sheet!'

Posie closed the notepad, a chill overtaking her. She shook her head, not comprehending at all but not wanting to stem the flow of Aiden's story, so freely given. 'Oh, it's nothing, Mr Vannelly. My mistake. Please carry on.'

Aiden shrugged. 'So my mother, Martha, she managed as best she could. But after a while she was running low on money, and she started to take in work: laundry, needle-work, washing for some of the new boarding-houses which were springing up. But it wasn't enough. She swallowed her pride and went back to the Llewellyn-Jones family, asked them for more. But that was her mistake, her downfall.'

'They didn't give her money?'

'No. They sent her packing, but days later, a letter came from them. The Old Master, Sir James Llewellyn-Jones, had heard that a university friend of his, a solicitor from down south, a Mr Lyle, was childless, and was considering adoption. Why should my mother not offer one or both of her twins to them? In fact, to make things easier, they'd already arranged that this couple, the Lyles, would come and call on us here in our house on Marine Avenue, to take one or both of us twins away. If my mother protested, or resisted, the Llewellyn-Jones family promised they had high contacts in the police force here, and they would report my mother as being a lady of the night; then the police would come and get both of us anyway, and put us into an orphanage, or the workhouse.'

Posie gasped. 'But that's terrible! Inhuman!'

Aiden grimaced. He took out a slim cigarette case from his back trouser pocket, shook one out for himself and offered one to Posie. 'Not everyone is born with a silver spoon in their mouths, Miss Parker.' He lit a cigarette and inhaled deeply, shooting Posie a look from between narrowed eyes, as if accusing her of this very thing.

Posie riled. He had *no idea*.

'Don't you dare make assumptions about *me*.'

He grinned and blew out a smoke ring. 'Don't worry, I won't. I'm teasing. I've done my research on you, too, Miss Parker. It wasn't only Amyas who had a good brain on him and a thirst for knowledge. I do realise things weren't always as easy for you as they appear now.'

He shrugged. 'I just mean that my mother, who had been a servant, didn't have any way of fighting off this great family. Who would believe her word against that of the mighty Llewellyn-Jones family? And it was true. They were hand in glove with the police.'

'What happened?'

'It went exactly as they said. They came here, as promised. Mr and Mrs Lyle, together with Sir James Llewellyn-Jones. I don't remember much of it, to be honest. Dark, shadowy people in the house, impossibly old – they must only have been in their forties, I suppose, but compared to my mother who was a slip of a girl they seemed ancient – speaking in low, strange, southern voices. There was a lot of crying, both from my mother and from us. Screaming, maybe. There was the exchange of money, apparently. Enough for another couple of years of living. They took Amyas away. He was screaming. I think my slight memory must have been enriched by my mother's later tales.'

'She felt she had sold Amyas? Even though she had no choice?'

Aiden laughed, and it was almost a snarl. 'My mother was bitter from that moment on. There wasn't one day of her life – not one *minute* – when she didn't regret what had happened. Pored over the details of the thing, again and again. She spoke about it every day. How her son had been ripped from her. How her heart was broken.'

'How dreadful. How dreadful for *you*, too.'

'Oh, it was. You see, the fact she had lost a son was awful. But the fact it was *Amyas* was a hundred times worse.'

'I don't understand.'

Aiden ground out his smoke angrily. 'My mother didn't want them to take Amyas. She offered *me*. I was the choice to be taken away. Amyas was the first-born, and her favourite. She was quite open about that to me, over the years. I don't know why: maybe he was sweeter, better-looking, better behaved, more affectionate, cleverer. Who knows? Call it a mother's instinct, maybe? Maybe she knew what he was capable of, the heights he would scale.'

Posie sat aghast. 'So how come the Lyles took *him*, then?'

Aiden shrugged. 'They must have sensed my mother's favouritism, maybe they thought there was something wrong with me. That I was backwards, or not quite as good as my brother. The Lyles were only after one boy. For all their good connections they didn't have money. They apparently pointed at Amyas and said "He's the one for us." They wouldn't back down, not when my mother screamed and shouted. And so she was faced with a choice: lose Amyas, her favourite child, to people who could offer him a bright future. Or lose both of us to the workhouse.'

'It wasn't much of a choice.'

'No. But we lived with the consequences of it for the rest of her life.'

'I can imagine.'

'I don't think you can, with the greatest respect. You see, every day of my life, she reminded me that I was her least favourite son, that my brother, who had no idea of our existence, was doing better than me. That all of his achievements only drew into sharp relief my lack of them.'

Posie watched Aiden who had closed the photograph album, placing his hands on top carefully, as if he was touching a prayer book, or a Bible. He looked haunted.

'Come, follow me. I've something to show you.'

And he headed back down the dusty brown corridor, reaching the closed door nearest to the front door. A living room, perhaps?

But when Aiden opened the door, walking in and throwing back the heavy velvet curtains, Posie couldn't believe her eyes.

* * * *

Twenty-One

The small room, once a parlour, contained brown velveteen armchairs and a chaise longue in the old style, with antimacassars draped about. Oil lamps were still mounted on the walls, long unused. There was a fireplace too. But there the similarity to a conventional parlour ended.

The walls on three sides were covered in newspaper cuttings, papered up like some crazy wallpaper. A small desk had been set up in the corner, and on it were a pair of scissors, a pot of glue and a pile of newspapers, as yet untouched.

'This was *her* room, Martha's,' Aiden said, looking about distastefully. A thick film of dust covered everything. 'I haven't got around to clearing it yet. Although she died before Christmas, so it has been sitting here like this some seven months.'

Posie walked further in, and started inspecting the walls. Every single story and cutting was about Amyas Lyle, going back years. Most cuttings were about legal cases Amyas had been involved in, or about his Chambers, 20 Old Court. There were photographs cut from the newspapers, too: a fairly recent photograph of Amyas in a wig and gown on the day he had been awarded his KC; a much-younger Amyas, in a hurry, looking like he was crossing the Strand, scowling at the photographer.

The words and pictures made Posie's head reel.

Here was a clipping announcing Amyas had married Lady Antonia Roade, together with a small, blurry wedding portrait. There was an announcement too about the birth of healthy twin boys. Further over, near the fireplace, was a photograph of the Amyas Posie would have recognised in the street at Cambridge, fifteen years ago, wearing his degree gown and hat, on the day he had attained his Law Degree. And then, in pride of place, a photograph of Amyas at school, maybe sixteen or seventeen years old, in the winged stiff-white collar and straw hat which marked him out as one of life's elite. A tight, self-possessed smile lighting the handsome face.

'I think she was proudest of that photograph,' said Aiden from the door, hands louchely in his pockets.

Posie stared, mesmerised. *By this time he was running a gambling racket with his friend William Dawney, and Harold Robertsbridge had died as a consequence. He was disliked and feared by most of his school, nicknamed 'the Vampire'. Did he still chatter to the imaginary friend who was his constant companion when he was younger? The real-life twin he had left behind, to moulder forever up here in the north.*

Posie turned, her heart aching for the man who now held her gaze. She opened her mouth to explain that these fancy photographs hid a deeply troubled soul, but...

Aiden raised a hand. 'It's fine.' He smiled. 'I know you're going to tell me that my brother wasn't the boy my mother thought he was. *I know*, you see. I told you, I'm capable of research too. I know about the bullying, the ambition, the gambling. He was a monster. At least, at school.'

Posie frowned. 'I don't understand. Did your mother keep in touch with Amyas, then? Or with the Lyles? How did she get these photographs? You said Amyas didn't know he had a twin brother?'

'I can't stand being in here.' Aiden closed the curtains, made a show of ushering Posie out.

'The deal was that there would be no contact at all, in exchange for the money, and the Lyles promising not to call Amyas by any other name. *That* was important to my mother. But as the years wore on, my mother wrote. She found their address – it wasn't hard, she knew the town where they lived – and she wrote to them, again and again. She pleaded for them to return Amyas, and then when this didn't happen, she asked if she could visit him. Everything was denied.'

They returned to the kitchen. Aiden picked up his mug of tea, swished it around and drank the dregs. Posie and Aiden stood side-by-side at the window, looking at the afternoon sun reaching long fingers across the green tussocky land and over the sands.

'Have you any idea what that can do to a person? The desire for Amyas became my mother's sole reason for living.'

Posie swallowed. She had never heard such a sorry, bitter tale. The bitterness etched through everything.

She thought of some of the other notes which Amyas had received. '*Some secrets last a lifetime,*' and '*Some tears never dry.*' And then the damning '*She never stopped thinking about you.*'

These notes surely referred to the secrets and tears of Amyas' mother, Martha Vannelly? How wrong the Inspector had been when he had said that the murder was not connected to '*an historical adoption of thirty-five years ago.*'

But how was it connected? How did it fit together?

Aiden continued softly: 'I think Mrs Lyle eventually took pity on my mother. She wrote telling my mother that Amyas was attending the best school in the land, that Amyas would be a great man, and that if my mother interfered with any of their plans, she would be denying him a wonderful future. Mrs Lyle promised to send occasional photographs, and school reports. On the condition my mother wouldn't continue to harass them. Wouldn't contact Amyas.'

'So she backed down?'

'Yes. She turned Amyas into a sort of God in that room of hers. When he married and became a famous lawyer she spent almost all her spare money on having the *Legal Gazette* and fancy London newspapers sent up here every month, so she could indulge in wallpapering that room with Amyas' achievements.'

'Golly. And she never contacted him directly? Not even when the Lyles died?'

'No.'

Posie's brain was racing. The story she was hearing here, although similar, didn't accord with the sheer anger and hatred spewing forth in the handwritten mail Amyas had received. She flipped through her notebook again and surreptitiously looked through the pages for the other messages.

'*You will pay for what you have done*,' repeated twice.

And: '*You cold-hearted excuse for a man. You don't deserve to live.*'

Aiden looked over at Posie's notebook with a sidelong snatch of interest, a half-comic raise of the eyebrow, and then he shook his head.

'No. My mother never contacted Amyas directly. To be honest, as the years went by, I think she became frightened of doing so, of destroying the myth she had created. Mother was often very ill, too. She became frail early on. She had a weak heart, not helped by the fact that she worked very hard, day and night, here at the fairground rides at the Spanish City, taking money from the tourists. I think she may have felt ashamed, too. Ashamed of what she was, what we *were*. Amyas had become an important man, and we were nothing.' Aiden passed a hand across his eyes briefly.

'And Mother got me to promise that I wouldn't contact him, either. It was a promise I honoured in her lifetime.'

Posie watched the golden sun flicker across the man's face. She wanted to say: '*You weren't a nothing. You were miles better than the brother who got away*,' but she held her tongue.

'Didn't you want to contact him? When you were growing up?' She thought of Amyas with his imaginary friend, wanted to recount that strange tale, but again, caution bid her to be quiet. This was not her story. 'I heard that twins, once separated, can ache for the other, like having a missing limb?'

Aiden Vannelly threw back his head and laughed.

'You know, call me heartless, but the only ache I ever got from my brother was a headache. In fact, I hated him. It was my mother's fault, of course, not his. He took all her time, and here I was, a living breathing boy, not able to hold her attention. I didn't do too badly myself. I didn't go to Public School, of course, but I got a scholarship to the local Grammar School, which was no mean feat. I got my teacher's certificate too, and I started teaching at a local boys' school around the same time Amyas was getting his Law Degree at Cambridge. I taught general subjects: maths, literature, sciences, photography. Photography was my passion. But the trouble was, Amyas was always one step ahead of me. My mother never recognised my achievements, and it was rather disheartening to a young man who feels he's done quite well for himself. I almost took to hating my mother too. But then came the Great War, and all that hate was suddenly rendered meaningless. The war made me realise I didn't need my mother's attention, or her respect. I didn't need to hate my successful twin brother. The war washed away everything bad I'd ever felt; made me live for each day as it came. Being there, in France, it made me feel impossibly alive.'

Posie was surprised. '*You* fought in the war? But Amyas couldn't...'

'You mean because of my heart? Yes, I have the same

condition my mother had, like Amyas did. But that wasn't going to stop me signing up, doing *something*. They wouldn't have me to fight, just as they wouldn't have taken Amyas. But that didn't mean I couldn't be useful. I signed up to work as a kitchen hand, an army postman, a goods delivery man. Anything.'

'Good for you.'

'I was assigned to a unit's field kitchen at first, doing everything. Cooking, cleaning, serving up meals. It didn't mean I didn't see the horrors: I saw it all. They were the best of times, and the worst of times. It made me the man I am. That's where I met Wilf Dance, whose job I took here. He was Officer of the unit I was assigned to, one of the best pals a man could hope for. He realised I loved photography and had a knack for it and it was he who recommended me for a new position working for the army photographic corps. You know, putting together maps of the enemy territory and useful bits and bobs like that.'

He was opening the door to the backyard now, fingering the lock gently, frowning slightly, muttering under his breath, jangling a small bunch of keys.

'What's wrong, Mr Vannelly?'

'Oh, nothing. Must be a trick of the light. This lock looks a bit funny, that's all. But it's not broken, and I haven't had anything stolen from the house. There isn't anything to steal! But we *have* had several burglaries around here lately.'

He grimaced and smoothed the lock down and beckoned Posie to follow him outside.

Gulls were wheeling overhead, and some children were playing with a bright red ball on the grass ahead of them in the distance. There was no wind, only sunshine, yellow and forgiving. Posie felt a peaceful silence fall between them. She sensed the man's tranquillity, his peace within himself. It was almost tangible.

'I wanted to come back here after the Great War. The

north, these skies. How could I have gone anywhere else? I went back to my old job, teaching, and then a couple of years later my mother got very sick. Much worse than before. She was still living here, but couldn't pay the rent, so I used up my savings and bought the house for her. And then I gave up my teaching job and I nursed her. For three years, here, at home, right until the end.'

'That was good of you.'

He shrugged easily. 'She *was* my mother, after all. And I owed her that. She was only fifty-two when she died, but all that longing and all that hard work had turned her into an old woman years before her time. My mother wanted to die. She didn't speak about Amyas any more to me, maybe she felt guilty, because *I* was the one here, helping her. But she continued to cut out those wretched stories, those pictures...'

Posie swallowed, treading delicately. 'And when she died? You said you decided to make some changes?'

'That's right. I needed a job, again, for a start. But the job market is teeming with able men, back from the war, with no employment. There were no posts available for teachers; all of them were filled. I was running low on funds, having used up my savings. In fact, I was stony broke. I'd visited Wilfred Dance over the last couple of years when he'd been in and out of psychiatric hospitals, and he offered me his job, under wraps. It was ideal: the Spanish City was nearby, and a challenge. I don't know if I'll do it forever, but it's a good start, and it's decent pay. And this house, I thought I'd do it up. I thought I might try to meet a girl, too. To settle down. It's time. Maybe have a pair of twin boys into the bargain, myself.'

He paused for just a second too long, then smiled. 'It's a day for a walk on the promenade, Miss Parker, if ever I saw one. And a vanilla ice-cream soda at the Rendezvous Café. Not for telling old, sad stories. How 'bout it? Later on? Don't tell me that your nice police Inspector expects you to sit in all by yourself at night, especially now you've tracked down the sender of those postcards.'

'Oh! Oh, well… maybe.'

Posie felt as if she were being torn in two. All of her wanted to run away, run over the grassy scrubland with this amber-eyed man at her side. Run until they came to the water's edge, until they stood beneath the billowing golden clouds of the big northern sky, felt the sea on their bare feet.

But what about Max?

Although she didn't know him *that* well, she knew him enough that he wouldn't just not turn up to a romantic getaway he had taken the trouble of arranging and paying for. He wouldn't have just left her alone in Whitley Bay for no good reason. She owed him constancy, at least, if not a lifelong commitment.

And this man at her side… Well, she didn't know him from Adam. Hadn't a clue if what he was telling her was wrong or right.

She frowned. 'Those postcards you sent. You said you hated Amyas, and that later you didn't care. Why *now*? Why send him something this year? They started up in January.'

There was a pause. Aiden clipped the gate shut softly, as if closing the door on thoughts of ice-creams and promenade walks, and new-born twin boys.

He looked down at Posie. 'The sad truth is that my mother's death at Christmas released me. In many ways. I thought it might be time to begin again. The Lyles were both dead, and so was our mother. It was just *us* left, Amyas and myself, without the complications and guilt of those who had gone before. I thought maybe we could scratch our way towards a meeting. Complete the circle.'

'But you didn't include your name, or any explanation on those cards. What was he supposed to have thought? Or done? How was Amyas supposed to find you?'

Aiden shrugged. '*You* found me, didn't you? As did...
Well, never mind that. But the point is that my brother
Amyas was a very clever man: he could have found me if
he'd tried. I'm not the sort of person to be confrontational,
or aggressive. I didn't want him to think I was after his
money, or wanting revenge. I thought if I sent a gentle
message, the same thing, over and over, maybe it would
stir up memories for Amyas. *Where we are from.* I hoped he
would be intrigued enough to come and track me down.
That he would come back here, to Whitley Bay, and we
would be back where it all started.'

He paused, biting at his lip. 'I suppose I was stupidly
proud of myself, too, in my own small way. I'd landed a job
running a wonderful establishment and I'm proud of that.
Proud of my photograph, too, even if it's not available to
buy. Twisted logic, perhaps, but it *felt right.* That's all I can
say. But Amyas didn't come, did he? I wasn't sure what to
do next, how to proceed.'

'So you came to London, to find him?'

'Yes.' Aiden was still close to Posie, seeking out her face
now, willing her to understand. But his lovely eyes were
troubled.

'Is there something you're not telling me, Mr Vannelly?'

A sigh. 'Oh, call me *Aiden*, please. I've just told you my
life story. Why do you think I would miss something out
now?' But he was evasive, and turned away slightly.

'I came to London because it was *time*. I was due a
holiday and I decided it was now or never. I knew Amyas
never took a holiday, that it would be a good moment to
find him. Talk things over. Then I would move on with my
life, one way or another. You saw me there, didn't you?'

'Yes. On the morning he was found dead, I saw you
under that big tree in Old Square, watching. And again
later, at Eaton Terrace.'

Aiden Vannelly shuffled awkwardly. 'I arrived in London
the morning before, on the Monday, and stayed in a cheap

211

hotel near King's Cross. Amyas was still alive at that point. What terrible timing! I had decided to try and see Amyas at work early on Tuesday morning, but when I got there I saw black vans and policemen everywhere. I listened in carefully and I heard that my twin was dead. Murdered! I couldn't believe it. Was it fate, after all these years? Or else it felt like I'd been set up, arriving to witness this tragedy, although this was a mess all of my own making. I hung about a bit and I got a fella who was with the pathology team to come over and tell me *how* exactly Amyas had been murdered. Nitric acid! My God! What a way to go!'

'I'm surprised anyone in the pathology team told you anything,' said Posie, frowning at the lack of professionalism.

'Mnnn. Well, I lied, actually; I told him I was a doctor and that I had been mistakenly sent for in the hopes that the murder victim was still alive.'

'Clever,' said Posie, meaning it.

'I watched you arrive, Miss Parker, in your glad rags, and then I saw the body carried out, and I scarpered. I suddenly had this awful feeling that if anyone saw me and recognised me – which they would, we were identical twins after all – I would be in the immediate frame for Amyas' murder. The coincidence with my being there was simply too great.'

'So why did you go to Eaton Terrace?'

Aiden sighed. 'I was in shock, really. I was shaking like a leaf all over. I couldn't believe what was happening. I found myself walking aimlessly through the centre of London. I'd never visited the city before but this was hardly the time for sight-seeing. I only had one other address written down, and that was Amyas' family home. I thought I should go and see where he lived. His wife, his children.'

'And what did you think?'

'It was a complete circus. His wife, a drug-addled spoilt brat, and little boys who seemed like strangers to me, all drove up in smart cars from a holiday abroad; no more upset at Amyas' death than as if a distant cousin of theirs had died. The boys then went out and played tennis.'

'They're only young, I suppose,' said Posie, not quite understanding her own desire to defend the Lyle twins. 'Maybe their mother hadn't yet told them.'

'Perhaps.' Amyas jangled his keys again. 'The story was over, though, for me, wasn't it? I spent a dreadful afternoon on Tuesday and a solitary night at my cheap hotel before coming back here yesterday. I had my return ticket already, you see, pre-booked for that train. The same train you took. I saw you with that sad-looking woman with the fancy clothes and too much make-up on.' He gestured towards the wine bottle. 'I'm ashamed to say I drowned my sorrows before getting to bed last night.'

'Understandable.'

'So now things are full-circle and I'm free of them both, my mother and Amyas. Not that I wanted that, you understand. So is there anything further you need from me, do you think? In an official capacity?'

Posie was shaking her head. But there were still so many questions, so few answers. Underneath her very nose this lovely man had explained his side of the story, which was all well and good, except that there was something in his story which wasn't quite right.

They were standing by the shed in the garden now, a blue-painted neat-looking place with a door and a window on one side.

Aiden inclined his head. 'This is my photographic studio, such as it is. It's just a darkroom now, but it used to be my refuge, in my mother's time, when she was very sick, and very demanding. I still keep my teacher's things in there now, in case I ever return to the profession. If we're done, and you have no more questions, I'm going to work on some images. You can leave by the back gate here, if you like. But if you change your mind, and fancy that ice-cream soda later, please come back. If I don't answer the front door, I'll be here in the shed. Knock three times and I'll know it's you.'

'Thank you.'

She walked away, through the gate, without a backwards glance, the sun's glare at full-pelt upon her upturned face, her straw hat still in her hands. She started to walk over the grass, heading for the sea, thinking about Aiden Vannelly.

Posie was usually inclined to trust her gut instinct, and she had liked the man. That was an understatement. But something didn't ring true. He had said he came to London this week '*because it was time*'. But that was just appallingly woolly. He had been sending postcards since the start of January, after his mother had died. So why leave it until now to visit? And what about those angry notes? It would be a logical step to assume they had been written by Aiden Vannelly too. The content was so uniquely personal to the twins' situation, it was uncanny.

Without knowing quite why, Posie retraced her steps, opened the gate into the backyard and turned towards the blue shed. She had been meaning to knock three times, but she had no need, for the door was propped open.

'Aiden?' But she was met by the sound of violent sobbing.

Posie stepped inside the small space, and saw Aiden sitting at a stool, head-down, half keeled-over on the workbench in front of him. It was dim in the shed, with only one lightbulb illuminating things, but even in this strange light Posie saw that things were not good.

A photograph of Amyas in his lawyer's robes was tacked to the wall, scored through with knife marks, so that the face was almost unrecognisable. But there were other things too: notes, maybe twenty of them, dropped all over the floor, in that same black curvy handwriting which the other threats to Amyas had been written in. Posie stooped to pick one up. It was a practice run, for a few words had been scored through and another line written neatly below.

'*You will pay for what you have done.*'

She picked another one up. '*She never stopped thinking about you.*'

In a haze of incomprehension, she looked about herself, hearing, clear as day, Inspector Lovelace's words, ringing out loudly: '*The person or persons who killed Amyas Lyle have no boundaries. What we are up against here is pure evil.*'

Posie took in other things too, in that terrible moment. A duffle bag at her feet, the contents spilling out: a white overall, stained and grubby, a distinctive black Billingsgate Fish Porter's bobbin hat. And rows of chemical solutions on the shelves which ran around the shed, bags and boxes and tins all marked with the warning skull and crossbones motif. A table was set up alongside one wall with various apparatus laid out on it, a chemistry textbook lying open. In that split-second Posie heard the words of that slightly ludicrous barrister, Selwyn Pickle, when he had said that '*anyone could make up a batch of nitric acid, but only a madman or a devil would try and use the end result on a living human being.*'

Was that what had been made here? In this home-made laboratory? Posie looked at Aiden's shaking back. How could she have been so wrong?

Was he a madman? Or a devil? Did it even matter?

She fled.

* * * *

Twenty-Two

Posie hadn't thought it would come to this.

The running along the promenade in the direction of the boarding-house address Inspector Oats had given her. The chance glance to the left, seeing him and his fat wife gathered with a crowd around a Punch-and-Judy show on the promenade itself, the crowd in floods of laughter.

'Inspector!' Her gasping shout parted the crowds, a frown appearing on Inspector Oats' face as he saw her emerge.

'What is it, Parker? Make it snappy! What is it? A police matter?'

And then the relief and excitement on his pale, puffy face when she told him what she had found at Aiden Vannelly's house. She watched Inspector Oats change in front of her, the puppet show paling into insignificance, the crowd rendered meaningless. He became taller, tightly-wound. He pulled Posie and his wife aside from the crowd.

'Give me the information you've got, Parker,' he demanded. She breathlessly gave him Aiden's name and location and then almost doubled over, panting hard, drawing strange looks.

'I'll get the local force onto this,' Oats was muttering, 'under my command, of course. Local press boys will be interested too, I'll warrant. Let's rope this devil in!'

Matilda Oats was almost frothing at the mouth with excitement, and Posie had to make herself heard above her excited chattering.

'Be careful how you go, sir. Aiden Vannelly has a weak heart. I'll call through to Inspector Lovelace now, sir. Tell him what I've found so he's kept updated.'

And then Inspector Oats snapped upright, affronted. 'You'll do no such thing, missie. You mark my words, this is a police matter now, and we're engaged in catching and arresting a dangerous murderer. You don't go messing around anymore. *I'll* call the Chief Inspector, once we know what we're up against. And not a minute before. You got that, missie?'

And before she could remonstrate, or argue that it was her 'messing about' which had got them to this point in the first place, Oats had disappeared at an impressive trot along the promenade, heading for the local police station.

Groaning aloud, and making for the nearest Italian restaurant, Posie burst in and asked to use the telephone. Luckily there was one, but situated in a very public place, with no booth or curtain; in the way of simply everyone who came through the door. But it would have to do.

The connection with Scotland Yard was mercifully quick. And checking the time, five o'clock, Posie realised she would be catching Lovelace just as he was leaving for home, returning to Phyllis and Ella in his Clapham house.

'Sir? You won't believe what's happened...'

It all came out in a rush.

She explained about Aiden, about the separation of the twins. Posie told Lovelace about the postcards of the Spanish City; Aiden's trip to London. She reeled off the scene in the shed she had walked in on, uninvited. Posie was near to tears; a hysterical ball of pent-up rage and fright and sadness was caught somewhere in her throat, threatening to explode.

What a dreadful mess. A tragic mess.

'And now I think I've made a mistake, sir, involving Inspector Oats. You should have seen him just now. Like a bull in a china shop, as vicious and self-important as ever. I fear what he may do, sir. How he may treat Aiden…'

As her final words petered out, the Chief Inspector let out a long, low wolf-whistle.

'I don't believe it. It's all too absurd! But this gets us to the end-point, doesn't it? Suspect and motive and evidence. All wrapped up. Posie Parker, I could kiss you! I'll get on to the local police and give them instructions before Oats ruins things nicely, although at least he's *there*. You were right to tell him the news, don't worry about that. He can start to organise a Forensics team to go in and pull the place apart. He can also accompany this Aiden Vannelly character back down to London for questioning here.'

'Be careful with him, please, sir. Tell the local police he has a weak heart.'

Lovelace groaned. 'Very well. Oh, are you having a nice break, old girl? It sounds as if you've been doing more work than spending time having fun. Have an ice-cream on me, eh? Oh, and no real news from here. Except that Amyas Lyle's body has been released to the undertakers. The funeral is being held next Monday, the 14th. I thought you might like to know. To attend.'

Posie walked back over the beaches, as the tide was very far out. She had the urge to keep walking, to get rid of the headache which threatened to engulf her. But she needed to get back to the Margaret Hotel in case Max was there, waiting upon her return.

Max.

But as soon as Posie had stepped inside the place, the receptionist called her over.

'Miss Parker? We took a telephone message for you while you were out. It's just here. I hope it makes sense?'

Posie took a piece of paper, and read:

MISS THEA ELLERIDGE-
WHITEHALL 8977. PLEASE CALL.

Placing the call with the Operator, and wondering what on earth this was all about, a knot of fear settled in her stomach, adding to the heavy weight of sadness which was already there.

As she waited for the connection, Posie imagined Aiden Vannelly being arrested right about now: the fizz and stink of camera flashes going off all around him; the local police unsure where to take him or which procedures to follow; the way Inspector Oats would man-handle the whole thing.

Was that why she felt so wretchedly guilty and awful about shopping Aiden?

'Miss Parker? Hello? Are you there?' A bright, cut-glass voice at the other end of the line, betraying impatience and busyness behind the politeness, cut into her thoughts.

'Oh, gracious. I'm sorry, I was miles away.'

'No problem. Look, my name is Thea Elleridge. We haven't spoken before and after tomorrow, we probably won't ever again.'

'Tomorrow?'

'That's right. We need you to come back to London. Get your things and take the next train to Newcastle. Wait there for the sleeper train to London which will come through from Edinburgh at ten o'clock tonight. You're needed here, my office, at 66 Whitehall. Tomorrow morning, please. Say ten o'clock?'

'Sorry? London? Tomorrow morning? I can't come. It's quite impossible. I'm waiting for someone here. We're having a holiday together.'

'Is it Max you're waiting for? *That's* who you mean?'

'What the... just who the blazes *are* you?'

'I've told you. My name is Thea Elleridge and I'm Max's

219

handler here in London. I need you to come back and talk to me. I can confirm absolutely that if you decide to hang on there at that little hotel in Whitley Bay you will be there a very long time indeed. Max is not coming. See you tomorrow.'

And the telephone line went dead.

Posie placed the receiver back in its cradle and looked with unseeing eyes at the receptionist, her cheery smile vanished as soon as she saw Posie's face.

'Everything all right, Miss? Can I help?'

'No.' Posie shook her head. 'Everything is very much not all right. And the only thing you can do for me is to order me a motor-taxi, please.'

It felt as if every part of her was numb. As if nothing mattered at all anymore. She was beyond pain, beyond feeling, beyond tears.

'I'm leaving. Much sooner than I'd thought.'

* * * *

PART THREE
LONDON
Friday 11th July
to Monday 14th July, 1924

Twenty-Three

That Max was dead, or, at best, missing, she had had no doubt of. Even before the interview.

He had told her in whispered moments that if ever she was doubtful of his safety – *really* doubtful – she should call a special number.

'*Only in an emergency, ja?*'

Posie had kept it safe inside her coin-purse these last eight months. She had never used it, nor thought about using it. Even at Whitley Bay when he hadn't arrived. She probably would have given it another day before calling it.

And now, holding her umbrella above her head and trudging down the wet pavements of Whitehall, where the fallen plane tree leaves were making the surface slippery as an ice-rink, she thought over the bizarre interview she had just come out of, trying to pick apart its various meanings.

The silent corridors of lacquered walnut panelling and the noise-deadening carpets of 66 Whitehall had not intimidated her. Nor the woman she had met, Thea Elleridge, but of course that wasn't her *real* name, was it? Just as the office they met in wasn't her *real* office.

But the way Max had been spoken of had chilled Posie to the bone.

Thea Elleridge, a woman in her late thirties, had regarded

Posie with interest from over the top of beautifully-crafted tortoiseshell spectacles. She had a shiny black leather folder in front of her, and it was closed.

'I'm not going to beat around the bush, Miss Parker,' the woman began snappily, 'you are here as Max has gone missing. We presume this means he's dead. It's never happened before with him, in all the years he's been our asset. It could mean he's gone deep underground, but we doubt it. We think he's been killed. It's likely we'll never know the truth.'

Posie bowed her head.

She had, in her heart, been expecting this. Been prepared. Goodness, she had even changed hurriedly into a sombre black outfit when she had dashed through her flat this morning after getting in off the sleeper train. Already in mourning, ahead of the news.

'We know Max told you about his employment with us, which is strictly prohibited,' said Thea Elleridge accusingly, to which Posie didn't bother replying. 'He told us about *you* at the start of this year, and frankly we were all surprised. We'd had him as an asset for seven years already and he never gave us a hint that there was anyone special in his life, in all that time. You must have made quite an impression on him. Anyhow, here we both are.'

'Indeed.'

'We understand Max gave you a number to call if you were worried about him. That was *my* number, and you can destroy it now; you won't ever be meeting me again.'

'How did you know where to telephone me? In Whitley Bay?'

'Max always informed us, as far was practical, of his future movements. He was methodical about that. We knew about his holiday with you in Whitley Bay as soon as he mentioned it to you.'

'I see,' Posie said icily.

'Don't be offended, Miss Parker. That's just the way things are done around here. The nature of the work.'

'What was Max working on up in the north which was so dangerous? Can't you send another "asset" in and find out what's happened?'

Thea Elleridge fiddled with her fancy glasses. She placed both hands intertwined together on top of the leather folder and looked at Posie as you might a recalcitrant child. 'You must be aware that Max had certain skills, certain training, which was unique.'

Posie nodded.

'Well, we simply don't have any other asset who could follow Max into the environment in which he was working. None could pull it off.'

'This is all very cosy,' Posie said carefully, which it wasn't, as she hadn't even been offered so much as a cup of tea, let alone a biscuit. 'But why are you telling me all of this? Why have you got me to come here and meet you? Surely that phone call to the hotel in Whitley Bay would have been sufficient? And even *that* was risky, wasn't it? Why didn't you just let me believe Max had left me in the lurch? That I had been stood up? From what I understand of your institution, this – meeting me – is already dangerous territory.'

Then it dawned on her. She was necessary to them. They needed something from her.

'What is it you want from *me*? Because that's what this is about, isn't it? This meeting? It's not about commiserations and sympathy over Max, is it? It's about what you *need*,' she snapped. 'So what the deuce is it?'

Thea Elleridge remained cool, and simply smiled. 'How very perceptive and grown-up you are, Miss Parker, about things. In another life we could have used you, but, well, no. Maybe you are a tad too flamboyant for our tastes. I don't just mean in your choice of umbrellas, but your choice in *gentlemen*, shall we say…'

Posie glowered, picking up her carpet bag and making a show of putting on her black gloves.

'Wait, please. We have reason to believe that Max sent you something. In the post.'

'The post?' Posie swallowed down her anger. 'When was this?'

'The last sighting of Max was on Monday, early morning. He was at a Post Office sending a parcel to you, we think. Have you received anything?'

Why would Max have been sending her something on Monday, if he had been planning to meet with her at Whitley Bay on Wednesday evening? It didn't make sense. He could just have carried whatever it was with him and presented it to her himself.

Unless he had believed himself in danger already. Had already known there was a possibility he wouldn't show up?

'I haven't received anything from Max. Not at the hotel in Whitley Bay, nor at my home address at Museum Chambers. But as you well know, I've only just come from the sleeper train. So maybe he sent me something to the Detective Agency, but I wouldn't yet know. If he sent it on Monday it should have arrived by now.'

'That's what we think. If anything does arrive, please can you telephone me?'

Posie stood to leave, noting the rain lashing down outside, running in rivulets down the casement windows, and she unfurled her umbrella at the ready. 'I'm making no promises to you, Miss Elleridge,' she snapped ungraciously. 'Perhaps I will and perhaps I won't. Perhaps what Max was sending me was of a purely personal nature.'

'Perhaps,' said Thea Elleridge, continuing to sit. 'But remember what he *was*, Miss Parker. Max wasn't a normal man, he was a spy. Chances are that anything he sent was important. Remember your duty, Miss Parker. King and Country, eh?'

King and Country! Hadn't she given enough? Did literally every man she loved have to sacrifice himself for this noble cause?

Posie turned and walked out of the office before she let her anger and frustration and pain overtake her. She wanted to howl.

But suddenly she heard her name being called again behind her. Turning, she saw Thea Elleridge standing at her doorway, holding a white envelope. She waved it at Posie. Surprised, Posie looped back, but she saw immediately that the envelope had '*Chief Inspector Richard Lovelace, New Scotland Yard/Future Commissioner of Police for New Zealand*' written on it.

'What am I, your messenger girl?' But Posie shoved it into her carpet bag crossly. 'I didn't know you knew the Inspector.'

Thea Elleridge smiled. 'We go back a long way. Professionally, of course. We haven't spoken in a while now. You're helping him investigate the death of Amyas Lyle, aren't you?'

Posie caught her breath, looking again at the woman with fresh eyes. 'That's right. What's it to you, though?'

Thea Elleridge crossed her arms defensively. 'It means everything to me, actually. Obviously he wasn't in the same class of asset as Max was, but Amyas Lyle has served his King and Country again and again, over the years. He was very useful to us.'

Posie gasped. She thought of Rufus, and him saying how back in the old days he had thought this would be the perfect occupation for Amyas: it had turned out, unusually, that Rufus had been right.

Many things started to make a kind of sense.

'You mean he was a spy? For you? For the government?'

Thea Elleridge shrugged. 'Call it what you will. In many ways he was the best kind of spy. He advanced himself at the same time as working for us, which was perfect, as we were interested in the elite circles he was moving up through. Those he was with regularly.'

'The Roades?'

'Among others. He was also helping us by reporting on fraudulent gamblers, and the London clubs and casinos which were illegally fixing betting. It helped that he was excellent at almost every game you could care to mention, and he was a regular at most of the clubs in town. We recruited him straight out of University and he has been working tirelessly for us for at least fifteen years, even before we were formally organised here. I asked him once why he had decided to work for us, and he said something about having made mistakes in the past, wanting to atone.'

Harold Robertsbridge.

'I know all about his schoolboy past,' whispered Posie.

'Do you? I didn't much care, to be honest. The plans and secrets which have been blown apart by Amyas Lyle's reports to us are too many to count now. All I knew was that I had a first-class mind reporting for us, especially in the Great War, investigating groups who were sympathetic to the Germans, and reporting on large-scale war racketeers, even turning in his own clients on occasion.'

Posie stared in disbelief, remembering both Lady Antonia and her father saying how busy Amyas had been during those years, how dismissive they had been of him. How dismissive and mocking Rufus had been of the fact Amyas hadn't fought. 'It was good of him, wasn't it, to go undercover but to receive no recognition for it?'

Thea Elleridge raised an eyebrow almost scornfully. 'That's part and parcel of the job. You don't join up here for never-ending public praise. Recently he was helping us by monitoring the British Fascist Party, how it was developing, sending us details. Names, meeting places, dates of meetings.'

How they had underestimated the man, and misjudged him.

Thea Elleridge turned to go. 'It's all in there, Miss Parker, for you to give to Richard. I wanted you to know. Amyas Lyle was an honourable man, if unconventional.

You should know too that he had recently informed us that he no longer wished to work for us; he had had enough. He told us he was starting a new chapter in his life: with his new job as a High Court Judge, but more importantly with a new family, I believe. We were unhappy about it, of course, but what could we do? Oh, and this information must stay between ourselves, Miss Parker, and the Inspector of course. I don't want this getting out. I've lost two assets in a week. Funny, isn't it, how they were both connected ultimately to you?'

She stared at Posie with sparkling black eyes which didn't miss a thing.

'Funny, but I'm not laughing.' She walked away, leaving Posie gobsmacked.

And now, walking through the rain, up to Trafalgar Square, past those old whiskery stone lions guarding the fountains, and past the Coliseum and the shabby-looking theatres, closed up until evening time, she tried her best to deal with this latest news.

Max.

And Amyas.

Two men, unconnected except by Posie, and the fact that, incredibly, they had both been spies, sharing an employer. And they had both, it seemed, stepped off the world forever on the same day, but at opposite ends of the country.

Back at the office all was quiet, and Posie hoped to make it to her own office unobserved, undisturbed, but a flash of movement behind her revealed Prudence, heading back to her own desk with a cup of typically over-brewed coffee in her hands. She smiled and seemed pleased to see Posie.

Something about her seemed different but Posie couldn't tell immediately what it was.

'Miss Parker! I didn't expect you back until at least next week. I hope you enjoyed your trip? Back so soon?'

Posie muttered something about holiday plans not quite working out, and being needed back here for the Amyas Lyle case.

'Oh, yes. I saw in all the newspapers this morning that a man has been arrested for the murder! *His own twin brother!*' Prudence made a show of crossing herself theatrically. 'Would you believe such a thing? What is the world coming to? Will you be attending Mr Lyle's funeral on Monday?'

'I suppose so. How do you know about it?'

'Oh… I just heard.'

'Listen, Prudence. Where is everyone?'

'Len has gone to the seaside, Miss. A long weekend. And Sidney is supposed to be on holiday, Miss; we've given him a week's break, but he turns up every day regardless, like it's his second home. To be honest, Miss, I think he'd rather be here than anywhere in the world. It's dry and warm, for starters. He's been listening in on the radio to the races at the Olympics. He'll be glued to that set later today when Eric Liddell tries to take gold. Anyway, I've kept him busy with little errands. I didn't have the heart to turn him away.'

'Fine. Well, this is very important, Prudence: where's all my post?'

'You've only been gone two days, Miss. Here, in this basket.'

Prudence passed a couple of invoices over, together with a magazine for food at Fortnum & Mason, and a postcard showing gorgeous sun-dappled towers and fields of sunflowers in Tuscany.

'No letters? No parcels? Nothing out of the ordinary?'

'Nothing, Miss. I'll keep an eye out, shall I?'

'Please. There'll be at least two more posts today, won't there?'

'Certainly. Oh, and Miss, I'd like to get something off my chest.'

'Please go ahead.'

'Last time I saw you I spoke out of turn. It's not my place to say how you, or anyone else, mourn their loved ones, Miss. I should have stayed quiet. I forgot my place. I was upset on my own behalf, Miss.'

'Sergeant Binny, was it?'

'That's it, Miss. It had been a year since we got engaged, but we didn't announce it to the world. There's not many men who would have had me at my age and with my sick mum in tow, and, well, I was honoured by his asking me to marry him. I never thought in a million years he would go and die on me! Poor man. Sometimes I'm overcome by sorrow. It's sorrow for him, but also sorrow for *myself*, Miss, although I know it's despicable. I thought I'd be an old maid forever, never able to catch another man's eye as long as I lived, but, well…'

'We all feel like that sometimes,' Posie found herself saying, trying to keep the bleakness from her own voice. 'It's fine. It will all be fine.'

And before she could be roped into further intimacies about men who had died in the course of their work, she hurried through into her own office and closed the door fast.

And it was only then that she realised Prudence had, for the first time in a year, not been wearing black.

She had been wearing a bright, crocus-like purple.

* * * *

Twenty-Four

Posie had got herself through the rest of the day doing boring administration, paying bills, organising advertisements for the Detective Agency in the forthcoming autumn magazines, forcing herself to not think a moment longer about Max, or about the strange meeting at Whitehall.

She tried too not to think of Aiden Vannelly, of how he was bearing up, and the house on Marine Avenue in Whitley Bay being ripped apart right now by a Forensics team. The kitchen, freshly-painted, now a crime scene. Martha Vannelly's prized photographs and tacked-up memories – a lifetime of guilt – being ripped down and packaged into evidence bags.

The telephone had been eerily quiet all day, although it was hardly surprising as both Len and Posie were both supposed to be on holiday. The lunchtime and early afternoon posts brought nothing more exciting than yet more bills, and invitations for various lunches in the autumn. Although right now the autumn seemed a lifetime away.

By four o'clock she couldn't bear it any longer.

She bid goodbye to both Prudence and Sid, who were both avidly listening in to the wireless set, waiting for Eric Liddell to start running the four hundred metres all the way over in France. Sid had obviously been folding old brown postage paper for future use, making neat piles of it, alongside old string and used stamps. The bookshelf in the client waiting room had recently been rearranged, too, into books and magazines running in ascending order of biggest to smallest. That he'd found numerous small ways of filling his day, hoping to be helpful, was obvious, and Posie resolved she would speak to Len about a rise in the lad's wages in the autumn.

She managed to get a motor-taxi on the Kingsway and headed straight for New Scotland Yard.

There was no real hurry; the Inspector had no idea she was coming, and yet Posie felt a dreadful sense that time was very much of the essence. It was all she could do not to beg the driver to *go faster*. Instead, she watched the rain-smeared streets of Kingsway, the Aldwych and the Strand unfold before her.

At New Scotland Yard she barged past the entrance desk, saved from giving any explanations by Sergeant Rainbird who was conveniently chatting with the Desk Sergeant.

'Miss Parker? Did you hear the news? About Eric Liddell? He just won gold! Hang on a minute! Aren't you supposed to be...'

Ignoring him, and stropping up the stairwell, one floor after another of grim, shiny, institutional olive-coloured darkness, she got to the fourth floor and wrenched open the door to Inspector Lovelace's outer office. Posie stopped, panting, putting down her bag and pulling off her mac, suddenly realising that the Inspector was on the telephone. She caught strains of the conversation.

'No, I'm not going to be home early, Ella, I'm sorry. I have a late appointment.' A moment's pause. 'Yes. The same as last night and the night before. You can just put Phyllis to bed, can't you? I don't see what the problem is. I'll be with her all weekend. Yes, that's right. Not that it's any of your dashed business.'

And Posie put her head around the door, seeing him standing with his back to her, by the window, his hand pulling at his hair, his waistcoat thrown across his desk-chair, his body tense. At the noise he turned, and seeing Posie, almost dropped the telephone apparatus. He motioned quickly for her to sit.

'Look, I've got to go.' He threw himself into his seat, moving aside piles of overflowing desk-trays so that they could see each other properly.

'Trouble at home, sir?' Posie asked nonchalantly. 'I expect she'll still be giving you trouble in New Zealand, if you take her with you. As I hear is the plan.'

She let the words fall carefully, aware of the meanness in her voice, the way she was hurting him, taking away his planned time for an explanation. But Posie almost didn't care. She watched how Lovelace had coloured, his expression at once sad and weary.

'Oh, Posie. I'm so sorry you it heard in this way. Who…? No, of course, Bill Oats will have told you. You know, I still haven't made up my mind. Nothing is certain. I told the Superintendent he'd have my final answer by Monday night. At the end of this case, the Amyas Lyle Murder…'

'Well, that's almost wrapped up, isn't it?'

'Yes. Almost. I did want to tell you. Honestly, I did. There just wasn't a good time, and you always seem so busy lately. Or somehow as if you were avoiding me. It was flattering, to be honest, to be asked. And I was thinking about Phyllis too. The great outdoors, all that fresh air. She looked so *healthy* when we brought her home from Rebburn Abbey in Yorkshire after Christmas, didn't she? She's a peaky little thing at the best of times and the London weather doesn't help: all this smog and mists. And what is there here for me, anyhow?'

'I'm sure I don't know, sir. Your job? You're one of the best policemen in the country, aren't you? And there's London town, too. Wouldn't you miss it?'

'Oh, hang London!' He seemed to get a grip on himself. 'But why are *you* here, Posie? You're supposed to be on holiday.'

'I didn't have the stomach for it anymore. Not after yesterday. Not after finding Aiden.'

'Good work on that, Posie. Excellent. I never thought for a moment there could be an explanation like that behind it all.'

Posie still felt uncomfortable about her part in the arrest, didn't quite want to believe it was all as open-and-shut as it currently seemed. 'What's happening, sir? I came across for an update.'

'Of course you did.'

And briskly he told her that Aiden Vannelly had been arrested the evening before, and informed of the charges laid against him. Namely, the premeditated murder of his brother.

Lovelace looked grim. 'The fella obviously had a long-running obsession with his twin, but an obsession verging onto hatred. Bill Oats is in his element, telling all and sundry in the canteen that he's pulled in a dangerous lunatic, that he's wrapped up the whole case. Even if Aiden Vannelly won't stand trial. Of course, there's no mention of *you* in his story.'

But Posie was having trouble reconciling the gentle, patient man she had met yesterday with the words 'lunatic' or 'dangerous'. Sure, Aiden had admitted to hating Amyas in the past, but his explanation about the Great War having robbed him of all his hatred had rung true. She had believed him. She had felt sorry for him.

If in another lifetime she had been available to walk out with him for an ice-cream on the beach, she would have said yes to Aiden Vannelly without a second's hesitation yesterday.

And that image of him in his shed, keeled over and sobbing. It played in her mind, on an uncomfortable, repeating loop. A shiver went down Posie's spine. Then some words she had just heard stuck in her brain, played again: 'Sorry, sir. What do you mean he "*won't stand trial*"?'

Lovelace fiddled with his cufflinks, and looked suddenly uncomfortable. 'I hadn't got around to telling you the bad news. Aiden Vannelly was apprehended and arrested and taken into custody. He travelled with Inspector Oats and a couple of sergeants on the mail train down from Newcastle last night. He seemed fine; very quiet and not talking much. Not denying anything, either, by the way. Refused to speak about his brother, or his part in the murder. But it all kicked off when they tried to get him into one of our holding cells downstairs.'

'Sir?' There was a leaden feeling in Posie's whole body, like she couldn't move. She gripped at Lovelace's desk and saw her knuckles turn very white.

'I think he must have panicked when he saw the size of the cell. And in all the ruckus and fear and alarm which came after, I'm afraid to say Aiden seems to have suffered some sort of seizure. Probably a heart attack, actually.'

Posie gasped at the awfulness of it. 'That's dreadful. I told Inspector Oats about his heart. I told you, too. I *said…*'

'He's being well looked after at Guy's Hospital. They'll be able to confirm in a couple of days whether or not he'll make it through. And, if so, if he's been impaired in any way.'

Posie covered her face with her hands. There were no words for this, and today was getting worse and worse.

Lovelace shrugged, mistaking her horror for dismay at the lack of a conclusion. 'It's rotten luck, Posie. But these things happen. I'm sure we'll have plenty of evidence to nail him for this crime, even if he can't stand trial. And I promise, wherever I end up, that – unlike Oats – I will make sure your name is mentioned prominently as the person who caught the killer.'

Posie was shaking her head in disbelief, but then

remembered about her earlier meeting at Whitehall. The letter for the Inspector she was to deliver. Lovelace was reaching for his hat, getting his coat ready to take outside.

'Oh, sir!' She passed the white envelope over, and watched as the Inspector regarded it quizzically, before tearing it open and shaking it out.

There was nothing inside, not one thing.

'Posie? What the blazes is this, now?'

Her heart sank. Was she to look a complete fool, yet again? Was the past association between Thea Elleridge and the Inspector nothing but a lie, another fabrication, and would he believe the tale about Amyas being employed as a spy for the last fifteen years by their Majesty's government which Posie had been spun?

'Does the name Thea Elleridge mean anything to you, sir?'

He laughed easily, quickly, and Posie felt a rush of relief.

'Oh, yes. Yes, I do.' He shook he envelope. 'Is this her work? Typical! She telephoned me here very early this morning and explained. We had quite a long conversation, as it happens.'

'About Amyas being a spy?'

'Among other things.' Lovelace bit at his lip. 'Bally unbelievable, isn't it? At least some of his behaviour makes sense now. He wasn't such a dreadful chap as we first thought. It seems I was rather needlessly harsh on the fella. Did his bit, eh? Even if he *was* a wrong 'un. Do you have any plans for the weekend, Posie?'

'No, sir.' She stood, hurrying before he could invite her somewhere out of sheer sympathy. She felt sure that the Inspector and Thea Elleridge would have spoken about Max in their long conversation and she couldn't bear to explain her side of it, least of all to Lovelace. 'But *you* have a late appointment to keep, sir, and a tight leash to pull at, so I'll not keep you.'

Lovelace gave a wry smile. 'See you at the funeral,

then? On Monday? It's in the Lincoln's Inn Chapel, right by 20 Old Square, where Amyas worked. Eleven o'clock. I think his Chambers are going to host some sort of lunch reception afterwards. Selwyn Pickle's onto it. You know he got elected as the Head of Chambers by the rest of the staff? So he's happy as Larry. And we let his boy go, too. No connection at all to our crime. Just one of those daft coincidences that he happens to be a Billingsgate Fish Porter, or a *trainee* Fish Porter, I should add. That's why he didn't yet have that wretched bobbin hat you were going on about. He was very specific about that when we asked him about it. Said he couldn't wait until he was allowed to wear one!'

'Isn't life strange, sir. So at least *some* good came out of it all. Old Selwyn Pickle and his son the trainee Fish Porter are reconciled.'

'Did I say that?' The Inspector frowned. 'I don't think that's the case at all. Selwyn Pickle refused to come and even *see* the boy, let alone grant him bail when it looked like he'd need it. No: no love lost there. Seems blood doesn't count for much, sometimes.'

'Mnnn. Or else it counts *too* much, in the case of Martha Vannelly.'

'Families are jolly odd, really.'

'Good job I haven't got any then, isn't it, sir? See you on Monday.'

* * * *

It was a quiet weekend, on purpose. Thoughts of Max and his disappearance were ushered firmly to the corner recesses of Posie's mind, stored for dragging out and crying over at a later, more convenient time.

Saturday involved two hospital visits in the morning.

The first visit, just a stone's throw from her flat, was to Great Ormond Street Hospital where Katia Lyle was being looked after.

Posie stared through the plate-glass window which divided up the normal children's ward with the room for very poorly or very tiny babies. A strange and rather alarming sight met her eyes, as doctors and nurses in white theatre gowns and masks bobbed between glass cots covered in muslin tents, and between a row of glass-boxed incubators. Tiny, tiny forms were just discernible inside the glass boxes, and Posie caught her breath at the sheer helplessness of these little children. Her part in all this, in taking on some sort of responsibility for Katia – a child she couldn't even locate here – also made her feel uncomfortable, nervous. *Just what was she going to do?*

She was suddenly aware of a tear trickling down her cheek, something which very rarely happened.

'All right, dearie? Not seen you here before. Who're you here for?' A small but very wide, fat nurse in a white uniform was standing beside Posie, touching her lightly on the arm in a reassuring, motherly gesture.

'Katia. Katia Lyle, please.'

'And *you* are, Miss?'

'I was a friend of her father.'

'I see. Well, she's this baby here. Nearest to us on the left.' The fat nurse tapped on the glass partition a couple of times, at the nearest baby to them, lying in a glass cot, wrapped in several blankets. All Posie could see was a head of dark hair, and a little hand scrunched up below it.

'She's not out of the woods yet, little Katie. But she's doing nicely, for all she was born so very small. She's already been moved out of the incubator and she's now in a normal cot, although it's being heated specially. I'd say little Katie was a fighter, Miss. She's got every chance of living a perfectly normal life after this.'

'*Katie?*'

The fat nurse smiled. 'That's what we call her here.' She consulted a flip chart she was holding in her hands. 'Although it says here her real name is Ekaterina. Silly foolish name for a girl with no parents! We call her Katie as it will be a nice plain name for whoever comes to take her home with them in the end. *If* she gets taken to a home, I suppose.'

Posie stared at the tiny baby, a burning fire suddenly rushing unexpectedly through her whole being. 'She'll definitely get a home.'

'Aye, I think you're right, Miss. She's a popular little lady, and no mistake. Why, today alone she's had three sets of visitors before you!'

'Three?'

'Yes. An older woman who visits every day, perhaps a relative? Foreign-looking, blue eyes, very sad. And then two men who came separately, each on their own. Professional sorts by the look of things. Maybe from an orphanage?'

Of course, the first visitor was Masha, Olga's Housekeeper from Fever Street. But she couldn't have said with any certainty exactly who the two men were.

The next hospital visit was across the river, to Guy's, where Aiden Vannelly was being cared for. Posie tracked down his hospital room with no problems, but saw that a police guard of two uniformed constables was on the door, allowing nobody to pass. White blinds had been pulled down across the windows and she couldn't see inside.

Just as she was about to turn tail after a seemingly useless journey she saw Sergeant Rainbird bobbing along the corridor, two enamel cups of tea in one hand, a large bar of Fry's Turkish Delight in the other.

'Miss! You've just missed the Chief Inspector.'

'Have I? I thought he was having a quiet family weekend at home?'

'Oh, well. I dunno about that, but he was here, anxious to see how our Mr Vannelly was getting on.'

'And?'

Rainbird made a so-so gesture with his chocolate-laden hand. 'Stable. That's all we're being told. I think that's medical jargon for "it could go either way". But what I *do* know is that Mr Vannelly hasn't woken up since the heart attack, so he's in no position to answer questions, let alone stand trial for murder.'

Rainbird was busy doling out the tea and chocolate to his constables, and then he and Posie walked a little way away from them, out of earshot.

'Because that's what you've got, Miss Parker, isn't it? Extra questions?'

'Am I that obvious?'

'I can see it in your eyes. You're like the boss, Miss, if you don't mind me saying so. You get a particular light in your eyes and it's like you won't let go of a thing until you've got what you came for.'

Posie laughed. But he was right. Somehow, somewhere in all this mess there had been something that Aiden Vannelly had been keeping back from her in his story. But *what*? She couldn't make sense of it yet. Would she ever now?

Posie turned to go. Homewards, alone.

'I'm sorry I didn't get around to telling you, Miss,' called out Rainbird.

'Sorry?' she wheeled around.

'About the boss. About New Zealand. I knew he was putting off telling you and I didn't think it was right. I know how close you two are. I somehow couldn't get the words out.'

'That's fine, Sergeant. I know everything now.'

'I'm glad. If you're in the market for *everything*, Miss, then I ought to tell you this...'

'Oh?' Posie braced herself for yet more bad news. Honestly, what more could be thrown her way now? Or was this the delicate 'news' about Lovelace's Housekeeper,

Ella Brown, accompanying him out to New Zealand?

'It's about your secretary, Prudence Smythe, Miss.'

Surprising. 'Mnnn. Go on.'

'We all knew she was stepping out with old Binny last year, Miss, although they were keeping it pretty hush-hush. We organised a whip-round for her at the Yard after he was killed. We knew she was pretty hard up, just her and her sick old mam.'

'That was very decent of you, Sergeant. I'm sure she appreciated it. But what has this got to do with *me*?'

'I'd always admired her, Miss. But in the circumstances, well, it didn't seem right to press my own advantage. So I waited a year, Miss, which I felt was a good time of mourning, respectable-like, and then I asked her out to tea. Just a couple of days ago.'

'Ah.' Things were starting to appear clearer, and brighter. The purple clothes replacing the black. The sudden change in manner.

Well, every cloud…

'I wanted you to know we are now stepping out, Miss. Officially. And I have only good intentions. Just so you know, Miss.'

'I'm very happy for you, Sergeant. For *both* of you. Truly I am.'

And on this delightfully cheerful note, Posie slunk home for the rest of her solitary weekend.

****

Twenty-Five

Monday, the day of Amyas Lyle's funeral, dawned pearly-grey and cool, with the promise of more rain in the air. The heatwave which had accompanied Eric Liddell's remarkable Olympic success in Paris the week before seemed a thing long gone.

Posie dressed carefully in a black silk shirt-dress with a string of pink glass beads for a dash of colour. She jammed on a black cloche hat with a single large black rose made of grosgrain ribbon, added the lightest of light pink lipsticks, and then set off, her carpet bag and her rarely-used black umbrella tucked firmly under her arm.

It was early, too early to get to the church, and Posie stopped in at the office on the way. There she found Sid, sorting through the early morning post. She took the already-opened mail, sat down on the client's sofa and started to read through it. There was nothing interesting, and certainly nothing from Max.

For a brief second Posie stared up at the bookshelf which Sid had re-ordered, and then looked over at the boy himself.

He was wearing the black suit which Posie had bought him the year before, for another funeral, and he had obviously grown a good deal in a year: the sleeves were way up his arms and the trousers were too short for his gangly fourteen-year-old legs. 'Let's get you a couple of new suits later today, Sid,' promised Posie, wondering how she could have missed such a thing. 'We'll go to the Army & Navy Stores.' And then on impulse:

'Why don't you come with me to the funeral? The Chief Inspector and I could maybe use another pair of keen eyes and ears there. If there's no need for you to stay you can just come back on here for lunch, can't you?'

And they left together, meeting Lovelace outside the Chapel a good half an hour before the service began. The Lincoln's Inn Chapel was a very special place, at first-floor level, raised up high above a series of open stone arches below, which created a low, wide, grey walk-through, a place famous for the leaving of foundling babies, and for the ceaseless sharp winds which nipped around the corners when you were trying to have a quiet smoke.

The priest who would take the funeral was actually a Bishop, a cousin of Lord Justice Roade, and he stood in his plain black cassock with a large purple jewelled cross swinging on a chain, just at the bottom of the steps up to the Chapel, greeting people on their way up.

Upstairs, the church was already crowded and the scent of lilies was overpowering. Leaving Sid to loiter at the back of the Chapel, Posie and Inspector Lovelace sat towards the front, opposite and just behind the key family members. They noted William Dawney, sitting with his smartly-dressed secretary Sheila, and in front of them, in the very first pew, Lady Antonia together with the twin boys and her father, who was looking sharply this way and that, unsettled. Lord Justice Roade caught Lovelace's eye and raised an eyebrow in acknowledgement.

Behind William Dawney was Selwyn Pickle, in full legal regalia of a thick, black gown with a fancy white collar. He was accompanied by a thin, worn-out, pretty-looking woman in a black suit. Pickle was bright-eyed and nodding all around, as the rest of the pews filled up dutifully with a pack of other barristers who worked at 20 Old Square, most recalled from their holidays, all wearing their gowns. Posie saw Masha come in, veiled in black lace, sitting down right at the back, and George, the Head Clerk, who also sat down at the back. He looked uncomfortable and kept folding and re-folding his arms.

It struck Posie suddenly that nobody here, save Masha perhaps, really looked upset at the loss of a man cut off so barbarically, in the very prime of his life. If everyone here had known Amyas' true vocation over the last fifteen years, might their reactions have been different now?

Those who *really* would have mourned Amyas, his adopted parents, his birth mother Martha, his mistress Olga and his secretive boss, Thea Elleridge, were either dead or absent.

Just as the Bishop came in, Posie saw out of the corner of her eye that – surprisingly – Rufus was standing at the back, looking quite handsome in a beautifully-cut black three-piece suit.

A woman came in just as the first hymn – 'Abide With Me' – started up and she settled herself in a pew all by herself, near the back. She was young, with a very severe bob, and she wore expensive but strange clothes; a coat with massive lapels, cut like a clown's, and wide, tweed trousers. Lord Justice Roade had turned slightly in recognition of her presence.

'That's Rotha Lintorn-Orman, the woman behind the British Fascist Movement,' hissed Lovelace, with an edge of anger to his voice. 'We'll have the press turning up here soon if we're not careful, turning this into even more of a circus than it is already. I can see the covers now: "*A Fascist's Funeral*".'

He tutted. 'She obviously never realised Amyas was spying on her new party. But why's she here? You'd have thought she'd have more sense!'

'I don't think sense applies to a woman like that, sir. Not to her clothes, nor to her politics.'

Lovelace suppressed a grin and the funeral unfolded. At one point Posie looked over at the twin sons of Amyas, so alike in their stiff starched school shirts, whose resolute gaze straight ahead seemed to give them a wisdom beyond their tender years. What must it be like? At the age of ten to lose a father who was a stranger to them, anyhow? She remembered Aiden Vannelly describing the boys as seeming like strangers to *him*, despite actually being blood relatives.

Their mother, Antonia, was a pretty picture in glittering black, her blue hair even more vivid than before. Lady Antonia sat, perfectly composed, and Posie assumed that by now she knew the contents of Amyas' Will; the Will which had not been changed in time. So Lady Antonia knew she would inherit everything; meaning that the illegitimate child, Katia, would not be provided for. Had Antonia found a drop of compassion in her heart so that the child would get something? Somehow, Posie felt not. Was *that* what Masha was here for now? Was she here to beg with Amyas' wife for some small grain of hope after the service? Or was she just here to pay her respects to a man who had treated her and her Mistress well over several years?

And turning, Posie saw Masha was in tears, dabbing at her face, her veil askew, dramatically making the sign of the cross. And in the very same moment, Posie heard the Bishop, who was starting to give the eulogy, begin by saying: '*While Amyas Lyle was not a religious man...*'

But Posie didn't continue to listen.

Because the different strands of the case came apart again, flailing and flashing in a mass of tangles like so many ribbons caught by an inconvenient wind; for a moment meaning absolutely nothing, but then the pieces shifted, and things seemed to slip easily – in fact, seamlessly – into place.

And then Posie knew what had happened.

Why it had happened.

'Oh, no,' she moaned under her breath, reviewing everything again. It still fitted.

Yes. It had to be.

She stared behind her, where Sid was standing ramrod-straight, trying to be inconspicuous, near the Baptismal Font. The answer lay with Sid.

She started to scrabble for her bag and the umbrella at her feet.

'Posie? What the blazes?'

Lovelace was looking at her as if she had lost her mind. 'Let me help you,' he hissed. 'What is it? Are you ill?'

But she was up. Up and walking to the back, down the aisle, head down, black grosgrain rose conveniently covering her face. She sought out Sid, dragged him outside into the porch with Inspector Lovelace hard on her heels. Sid looked at Posie quite calmly, as if he'd been expecting this to happen. 'What is it you need, Miss?'

'I need you to think carefully, Sid. It's very important. This week, when I was away, I know you were being very helpful with the post arriving, helping Prudence. Taking off the paper and suchlike.'

'Er, yeah. I thought I'd help out. If truth be told, Miss Prudence has been a bit away with the fairies these last couple of days. In a *good* way, I mean. She seems happy; I've even heard her singin', would you believe it? But she was lettin' all the post mount up, in a big ol' pile, so I took the chance to sort it fer you.'

Posie blew out her cheeks: *what terrible timing for Prudence to have acquired a new beau, and new, lackadaisical habits.*

'Did anything arrive for me while I was away which was a bit odd?'

'No, I can't say it did, Miss.'

Her memory swept over her brief view of the bookshelf in the client's corner at the office.

'Think hard. Was it a *book*? An old book which arrived? A thick, blue, old book?'

Gradual realisation dawned on the boy like a slow sun rising.

'Oh! Oh, yeah, Miss. That's quite right. How clever of you! This funny old stinky book arrived for you on Thursday morning, very early. In fact, the postman said it had been delayed in the post as the sender didn't put enough stamps on it; they must have been in a hurry, like, when they sent it. I showed it to Miss Prudence and we had a good ol' laugh about it together. We thought it must be a grateful client showin' their appreciation and sendin' you a present. An odd present at that… But I expect Miss Prudence won't remember it much; I had to drag her attention away from some magazine she was reading with a bride on the cover. She had her nose in *that* nearly all day long…'

'Fine. Now, think carefully, Sid. Was there anything inside the book at all? *Anything?* No matter how silly you thought it…'

'I dunno, Miss. We didn't open it. I just placed it on the shelf, with the other, much nicer books. That's when I thought I'd re-organise them.'

'Can you get me that book, Sid? Now? But I need you to be careful. Sure as bread is bread there is something inside that book and it's important. More important than any of us know. It's the last words of a dead man. So don't open it up or shake the contents out.'

She glanced quickly out at the rain which had now started up again.

'And don't get it wet. We're going to have to look at the thing ourselves and then get it taken over to Whitehall, to the government.'

Sid had started to look worried at all this weight of sudden responsibility and Lovelace stepped in. 'Posie, I don't know what on earth you're going on about, but you're rarely wrong. I've got a police motor-car waiting outside the gates at Lincoln's Inn here. Why don't we send Sid with a couple of my boys to get this book you need? Then we can rest assured we'll get the thing back here quickly and that it won't get wet.'

And Sid, beaming at this sudden and unexpected adventure, disappeared at a near-sprint, holding one of Lovelace's business cards in his hands by way of instruction to the police driver.

'Posie,' whispered Lovelace, as they watched his retreating back. 'Just what are you playing at, my girl?'

'I'm not quite sure. But I know I'm right.'

The Inspector groaned. Then seemed to make up his mind. 'So what can *I* do?'

'I need you to make sure that we get everyone in the Chapel, excepting the load of barristers, all together in one room at the reception. I need to speak to them all at the same time.'

'What? Including the Bishop? And Lord Justice Roade? And Selwyn Pickle?'

'Yes. And Masha, that older lady at the back in the foreign-looking black veil. She's important. And the Fascist woman, and Rufus.'

'Very well,' said Lovelace determinedly. 'But mark my words, it won't be easy. It will be like herding cats.'

'Is anything worthwhile ever easy, sir?'

'Point taken.'

* * * *

The Chambers at 20 Old Square had been fitted out as if a cocktail party were about to take place, and Posie and Lovelace stood uneasily in the entrance hall, listening to the tolling bell from the Chapel go on and on, ringing out the death of Amyas Lyle. Waitresses stood about already holding trays of white wine, and there were tea and coffee urns placed on a long bench, with several trays of damp-looking cheese and ham sandwiches. Vases of yet more lilies had been placed everywhere.

Lovelace ordered Constable Fox and another plainclothes policeman to move the tea and coffee things and trays of sandwiches up to the main meeting room, which was on the first floor. Lovelace helped carry the heavy urns up the stairs.

Posie, left alone, glanced over at Amyas' old office, trying to suppress a shiver, and noticed that the sign on the door had already been taken down and replaced with 'SELWYN PICKLE, KC, HEAD OF CHAMBERS'.

That fitted.

Personally, Posie wouldn't have wanted to ever use that particular office. Dead men's shoes, and all that.

And now the funeral party were making their way across Old Square through the rain, a bevy of black umbrellas struggling against the unseasonal weather, with what looked like Lady Antonia right at the front, her boys alongside her. There was a crush of people at the doorway, and then Lady Antonia emerged first into the room, eyes a-sparkle and nervous, nervous as hell. Others were following her close behind. Lady Antonia was eyeing up the refreshments, frowning, already taking a cigarette from her handbag and lighting up. She spotted Posie and came over.

'Ah, Miss Parker. Good of you to come.' She flicked an irritated finger at a waitress. 'Where are all the refreshments, girl? There should be much more than *this*.'

Before the girl could answer, Posie cut in: 'They're upstairs, Lady Antonia. We'll be going up there shortly; all the people who need to hear the story.'

Antonia's eyes were roving backwards and forwards through the crowd now assembling. She focussed suddenly on Posie again: 'Sorry? What story? You mean the way Amyas was killed? We all know that already, we don't have to go through it again, do we? Not now you have the twin brother banged up tight for murder. Despicable! That's what I call it! Imagine! A *brother*, able to do that? It gives me the chills!'

'I agree. The whole thing was despicable.'

Posie drew the woman back a little, so they were standing near to the Clerks' Room, out of earshot of most of the gathering. Inspector Lovelace was now coming down the stairs, looking around the room, obviously wondering how he could start to move people upstairs without being obvious. Evidently he gave up on that tactic, and started shouting:

'Everyone who *isn't* a work colleague of Amyas Lyle, come upstairs, *now*, please, with the exception of Selwyn Pickle and his wife. That's a police order. No-one's leaving here. I've got two of my best lads on the door.'

Posie saw the twin boys, standing over near their grandfather, eating hurried mouthfuls of sandwich, looking around anxiously for their mother, perturbed. They were too young to hear the story Posie had to tell, surely?

'Not the Lyle twins,' continued Lovelace, obviously thinking along the same lines. 'They can stay down here.'

People started to move uncertainly towards the stairs. Antonia Lyle was turning, irate, looking as if she might pounce on the Inspector in a mad rage. Posie laid a calming hand on her arm.

'Look, Lady Antonia. I think you should know, before I announce it in front of everyone, that I *know* your secret. I know what this was all about.'

Antonia Lyle was staring at Posie, a look of incomprehension on her face which turned to sudden horror and then to indignation.

And then there was a quick movement. An involuntary howl of pain.

'Ow!'

A flash of bright and dark light, like stars exploding in a night sky danced in front of Posie's eyes. It happened so quickly, Posie couldn't protect herself, or her face. The slap full-face with a bevy of heavy diamond cocktail rings was unexpected, the pain so sudden and so strong that Posie felt physically sick.

She recoiled in shock.

And then strong hands, those of William Dawney, were pulling Antonia Lyle roughly back. Somewhere out beyond the pain, Posie saw Sid arriving in the doorway, a small, nervy-looking figure fluttering like an uncertain butterfly, holding onto a big blue book.

Dawney cradled Posie's face in his hands, gently turning it this way and that, fingers moving experimentally along her nose and cheekbones, a handkerchief being patted on, being taken away again, covered in blood. A grim smile.

'You'll live, Miss Parker, and your face will be just as beautiful. It was a bloody nose, that's all. The starting of a nice black eye, too. But no real marks or scarring. You're jolly lucky the nose wasn't broken, and that she didn't get your eye itself. Those great rocks she wears, most unsuitable… You'll have to forgive Antonia, Miss Parker. We both know she's had far more than Dutch courage in order to see this thing through today, eh? A real shame. Heaven alone knows how much cocaine she's put away.'

He was about to move on, Sheila hot on his heels, when he half-circled back to Posie, whispered carefully:

'Oh, about what we were talking of the other day. The *child*. I spoke to Antonia about it. As I thought: she doesn't want to offer any assistance, for anything. She was most definite. The house Olga lived in will be sold within weeks, Old Man Roade is already onto it. The Housekeeper has already been given her marching orders. We'll discuss this further, obviously, you and me, maybe later this week, but I've already made enquiries at the hospital: seems the child will most likely live. I've paid the hospital bills so far. And I thought you should know, I've put plans in place to safeguard her future.'

'Oh! Oh, thank you, sir. Yes, I'll come and speak about it soon. How kind of you. Shall I write out a cheque for my part of her hospital care so far and give it to you today?'

'Gracious, no. I'm a rich man in my own right, Miss Parker. It's fine, honestly.'

And then everyone was somehow upstairs, and Sid and Posie were left alone. Sid passed her the blue book. Posie was staring at it through a veil of pain.

'What happened to you, Miss? You've got a corker of a black eye blooming.'

But Posie waved the concern away, forgetting the pain, staring at the book which Max had sent her, which had been delayed and almost lost. Another missing puzzle piece.

'This *is* what you wanted, Miss?'

His eyes were expectant, glassy with excitement.

'Yes,' she breathed, flicking through the pages Max had flicked through, carefully turning the pages he had turned, trying to locate whatever it was he had sent her. His last words to her.

Were they *really* going to be his last words to her, ever? 'Here!'

A cream card, such as you might fill in at the Post Office if you were composing a telegram, had been inserted in the book, and here was Max's handwriting. Scrawling, cramped, almost illegible. As if it had been written in a tearing hurry. Which, of course, it had.

Posie took a deep breath and read.

'Dash it all! I knew it! I knew it! I was right.'

And then she went upstairs, double-quick.

* * * *

Twenty-Six

The room, which had long oblong sash windows overlooking Old Square, was silent, with everyone sitting in a large circle, expectant. The only noise was the rain on the glass and the Bishop who was slurping noisily at a cup of tea.

Inspector Lovelace stood, arms crossed, in front of an ornate Victorian fireplace, looking more muscular and menacing than Posie could ever remember. Even the look he threw at Posie was black and stormy. *Don't you dare get this wrong*, he glowered. *Don't let me down.*

But he had also raised an eyebrow in concern at the state of her face, and at her shake of the head he winked. He was bluffing, hamming it up although he didn't know the way this story would conclude. Nobody did.

What if I don't explain this properly? What if nobody believes me?

Lovelace was speaking now, waving Posie to the front. 'My colleague, Miss Posie Parker, would like to say a few words about the life and death of Amyas Lyle, who she was privileged to know personally, albeit a while ago.'

'You say this like there's a choice in us sitting here and listening!' called out Lady Antonia, whose father was sitting, stony-faced, beside her, making no attempt to calm her down. 'We were pretty much frogmarched up here! At my own murdered husband's funeral! It's too much! Frightful conduct!'

Posie tried not to touch her face or twitch her eye which was now smarting horribly. She avoided looking at Lady Antonia, and fixed her attention at the back of the room. In her hands she held onto the big, blue book and somehow, its very presence gave her comfort.

'Thank you, Chief Inspector.'

She cleared her throat. 'Even if you didn't *like* Amyas Lyle, I think there's not one person in this room who would deny that Amyas Lyle was a hugely talented man. He had achieved at thirty-five what most men at seventy have not. It was a talent which came naturally, but it was *ambition* which propelled Amyas to get where he did. I expect you all read the newspapers? Therefore you will now know that Amyas was in fact an identical twin, and his equally talented, although not so ambitious, nor so well-placed, twin brother, Aiden, is currently the number one suspect for Amyas' murder.'

There were nods all around.

Inspector Lovelace stepped forwards, a tad defensively. 'Do you mind, Posie? I'm interrupting but I'd like to explain to the people here that we arrested Aiden Vannelly due to the overwhelming evidence against him. I'd say that with this weight of evidence, if Aiden Vannelly ever stands trial, he will surely hang.'

There was a lot of self-righteous huffing and puffing in the room. Posie couldn't bear it. She continued: 'Which is why we are all gathered here. You deserve to know the truth. Because as well as Amyas Lyle being murdered in a truly appalling way, his killer was quite prepared to add another victim to their murderous tally, to let another man hang for a crime he didn't commit. Yes: let me tell you now that Aiden Vannelly is innocent of the crime of killing his twin brother.'

There were gasps all around the room, an itchy buzzing which threatened to turn into a wild frenzy. Posie ploughed on loudly:

'He has been set up so perfectly and entirely that, as the Chief Inspector just explained, the police had no choice but to arrest him. In fact, Aiden Vannelly began to suspect that he had been set up himself, but he was powerless to argue in the face of such powerful evidence laid against him. As it turned out, the police got the wrong person entirely.'

Inspector Lovelace was following Posie with a calm, unhurried set to his face, as if he was in on the whole thing, a double-act sparking off each other, although his green eyes were searching hers constantly. *This is the first I've heard of this. Are you sure?*

'Amyas Lyle was adopted, and his birth mother had tracked and idolised Amyas for years, all without Amyas knowing. And Aiden, left behind with the birth mother, *had* felt jealous and resentful at his brother, but he had made his peace about it. Once his mother died, he decided to seek out his twin brother on his own terms by sending anonymous postcards; the same one, over and over. Of Whitley Bay. Clues, if you like, to his own life. To see if Amyas would respond.'

'Dashed fool idea!' called out Rufus, who was swigging from a hip-flask at one end of the circle of chairs. 'Who on earth has time for that sort of stupid jinks?'

'Quite!' agreed Selwyn Pickle from right beside Posie.

Posie shrugged. 'This was the only *active* involvement Aiden ever had with his twin; his only "crime". The postcards started up in January this year. Which was a coincidence, because Amyas was walking away from his old life, embracing a new life, or *lives*, in January of this year, too. His mistress, Olga, was pregnant with their first child, and Amyas had moved into the house he maintained for her. Set up home. Making a fresh start.'

Posie tried not to dwell on the chorus of outraged gasps, or to look at Lady Antonia, or the Bishop, or at Lord Justice Roade. Or at Selwyn Pickle who was shaking his head disapprovingly, his pale, tired wife beside him practically glaring at Posie. Upturning social conventions in private was one thing, but to publicly speak of such a thing was unforgivable, even, it seemed, in the pursuit of justice. But Posie couldn't care less.

'They were happy there together. Olga and Amyas. Looking forward to the baby.' Posie looked up at Masha, who nodded in silent agreement.

'Our killer saw all of this, and realised that the route Amyas was taking was absolutely and completely crippling to *their* own state of happiness and their own neatly-planned future, and that Amyas had to die. The postcards which suddenly arrived in the post gave our killer an idea.'

Lovelace butted in: 'Find the sender of the postcards, and then create a trail of incriminating evidence to pin the murder on that person?'

'Exactly, sir. And our killer couldn't believe their luck when they tracked down Aiden, realised that here was a wronged twin with a lifetime of grievances to heap at Amyas Lyle's door.'

'Seems very complicated, Miss Parker,' shrilled Sheila, Dr Dawney's secretary. 'A great deal of time and trouble would be spent tracking the twin down, placing the evidence. I mean, why not make it simpler?'

'Because it was essential that the eyes of the world should look elsewhere, not near home, when placing the blame for the murder of Amyas Lyle. A complicated but believable little side-story was just the kind of thing our killer revelled in. And yes: it was difficult finding Aiden. *I* nearly missed him, and Dr Dawney here,' she met William Dawney's clear brown eyes for a second, 'missed him entirely when he went looking for the sender of those postcards. Which was bad luck, as Amyas died without realising he had a twin.'

William Dawney sighed audibly. 'That's true enough. Poor fellow.'

Posie continued: 'But when our killer located Aiden, they made a point of listening to the old stories, his reminiscences; *that* was important for the authenticity they would later cloak their crime in. They also familiarised themselves with Aiden Vannelly's house. And then, crucially, they started writing a series of nasty, contemptuous little notes. They were handwritten and hand-delivered. Starting off harmless, but building to a level which could be regarded as threatening. Over a period of months, running in tandem with those postcards, which conveniently kept on coming.'

Posie stared at Amyas' wife, whose pale, colourless face was the colour of ash.

'Our killer was very taken with the idea of the sea. I don't blame them: I was captivated myself when I went to Whitley Bay last week. The notes often referred to the sea: to slipping into the water; to saltwater; secrets. And to the birth mother Amyas had left behind, who thought about him every day. It's fair to say that our killer went off on a dramatic frolic of their own here: they got things slightly wrong. Amyas never properly knew his real, birth mother – he had been forcibly taken away from her- so the killer was wrong when they tried to assign guilt in his direction, but our killer hadn't taken in the finer points of the story. They'd only met Aiden Vannelly briefly. They were just after a general impression. A theme.'

'The saltwater theme? So that the killer could use nitric acid?' asked Dr Dawney, head on one side, frowning in concentration.

'Yes,' confirmed Posie. 'It seemed neat enough. When the time came for Amyas to be murdered, the real killer had made sure to get Aiden Vannelly out of his house in Whitley Bay and onto a pre-booked train down to London, and had placed enough damning evidence in Aiden's house

– clothes, chemicals, some extra handwritten threats – in order to pin the crime on the living, surviving twin. The killer was very careful, and very clever.'

'But not clever enough for you, eh, Nosey?' Rufus laughed scornfully across the room.

Posie shrugged. 'Aiden Vannelly told me a good deal, but there were gaps in his story, and I've had to fill them in by myself, especially now that he's in a coma and can't confirm things. Aiden said he had decided to visit Amyas last week *'because it was time'*. But that didn't make any sense: he'd had months to make the trip, since his mother had died, so why now? The reason was that the timing suited *the killer*. The killer was pulling strings, you see, organising the whole trip. I know Aiden was very short of money, as he'd spent the last couple of years nursing his dying mother, whittling down his own savings. I somehow got the feeling that a sum of money had changed hands, and that Aiden was ashamed of it. Perhaps our killer gave money to Aiden for "expenses" in travelling down to London, for staying at a hotel and suchlike? I know – because I checked – that it was *not* Aiden who booked his train tickets for the trip to London. The train tickets were purchased a couple of weeks in advance of the murder, for cash, in London, by a *woman*. That was all the desk clerk at King's Cross could remember.'

Lovelace was staring now, rubbing at the stubble on his chin frantically. *How could he and his men have missed this?*

'And I also know that Aiden Vannelly suspected his house and shed had been broken into while he was away in London.'

'So why didn't he tell all this to the police, Miss Parker?' asked Dr Dawney, looking astonished. 'To save his own skin?'

Posie shrugged. 'Probably because the evidence against him was so completely damning. And also, I think that the killer had made something known to Aiden – something unpalatable about Amyas, of which there was much to choose from – and had implied that this information was easily leaked to the national newspapers. It hung over Aiden like a threat. It would be a slur on the name of Amyas Lyle.'

Posie looked over at Rotha Lintorn-Orman, who stared back in hostile silence. Posie went on very quietly: 'I'm guessing the killer threatened to leak Amyas Lyle's involvement with the British Fascist Party. However lukewarm that involvement might have been.'

Lord Justice Roade suddenly stood up. 'This little show is all very interesting, Chief Inspector, but surely this is just a lot of hot air and conjecture? Frankly, I'd expect more from you. And I'll be telling the Superintendent. We're all busy people here, and I'd like to get down and raise a glass to the memory of Amyas Lyle. God rest his immortal soul.'

Lovelace swallowed and was about to answer but Posie cut in, angrily, spitting out every word: 'Yes, Lord Justice Roade. *God* rest his soul. Because this is about religion, really, isn't it? And it's partly your fault.'

'*My* fault? I say… the bally cheek! You upstart! I'll be dashed!'

Posie didn't care. She ignored the little untidy man with the ferocious reputation. What could he do to her, here? She laughed contemptuously. 'Yes! It was while I was listening to your cousin, or brother, or whichever relation the esteemed Bishop here is to you, when I realised the truth. The Bishop said Amyas was "*not a religious man…*"'

The Bishop, who had been sitting, rapt, now calmly removed his spectacles, rubbed them on his cassock, put them on again, for all the world as if he were at some regular weekly diocesan meeting. He smiled placidly: 'That's quite correct, Miss Parker. Amyas was not – unfortunately – much given to attending church.'

'I don't think I follow you, Posie,' the Inspector said. 'Nor do any of us in the room.'

'We need to go right back to the beginning,' said Posie. 'This is what this case was all about. Not tears, or twins, or secrets, or saltwater. And definitely not Whitley Bay. That was all a smokescreen. It's about ambition, but it's also about religion. The two go together here. Unfortunately.'

* * * *

Twenty-Seven

'It was an open secret that Amyas Lyle's marriage was a sham,' said Posie, trying to avoid looking over at Lady Antonia.

'It was just accepted that this marriage would go on forever. But when we met Dr Dawney for the first time last week, he made a throwaway remark about Amyas mentioning that he wanted a *divorce*. This jumped out at me, and made me realise quite how serious Amyas must have been about his commitment to Olga, and their future baby.'

Lady Antonia whipped around in her seat. 'William? What's all this about a divorce?'

Dr Dawney crossed and re-crossed his arms. 'Calm down, Antonia, it was just a comment, six months or so back. Amyas never acted on it to the best of my knowledge. Never started anything legal.'

Posie looked all about her. 'Yes, that's quite correct. His solicitors hadn't been informed of any such action. But it *was* obviously on Amyas' mind. As was changing his Will. In fact, he had already arranged a new Will, in favour of Olga and their child, cutting out his wife and their sons entirely.'

At the gasp which echoed around the room, Posie laughed: 'Don't worry. Lady Antonia here is still sitting pretty for cash: Amyas didn't get around to signing the new Will. He was killed before he could do so. I think the killer had realised that Amyas was seriously stepping away from his old life. The changing of the Will, and the steps which would follow, which would surely include a divorce, meant that the killer had to act *now*. To kill. To set up Aiden Vannelly. The time was *now*.'

'What's so wrong with a divorce?' asked Rotha Lintorn-Orman mock-casually. 'Everyone's doing it nowadays.'

'There's nothing much wrong with a divorce,' answered Posie, matter-of-factly, 'except when you have secrets already covered up. And when it's going to smash apart all your plans for the future.'

Lovelace had given up any polite semblance at being a double-act. 'Go on, Posie. What secrets?'

He looked over at Lady Antonia, who had covered her face with her hands. Posie stared at her without any grain of remorse or sympathy.

'I wondered several times over why Amyas was getting so excited about this baby with Olga; why he was beginning to think about his own birth family, when before he hadn't ever bothered. I think he was keen to trace them now, to find out about the heart defect he knew he carried; about whether it was genetic. If there was a chance it would be passed on to his own children. To be prepared…'

Rufus was scratching at his head: 'But surely he would have been interested in this when his twins were born? Ten years back?'

'You'd have thought so.' Posie smiled. 'Several times in this case I've had the feeling we've not been seeing the complete picture; that things were being hidden. And it was when Aiden Vannelly said he had seen the twins – his nephews – and they were like "strangers" to him that I realised the truth. They *were* strangers. The Lyle twin boys were *not* Amyas' sons. And therefore he didn't need to worry about their hearts…'

Posie saw the old Lord Justice chewing at his lip, looking nervously around, looking like he wanted to bolt. He was casting anxious looks in the direction of the Bishop, who was by now on the edge of his seat.

Posie flicked through her notebook. 'When we spoke to Lady Antonia, she said Amyas had done the "honourable thing" and married her when she got herself in the family way. But he was doing more than that: the babies were not even his, and he was doing the honourable thing anyway. And this is where we see the full gamut of Amyas' ambition. He realised an opportunity and he took it. He didn't love Antonia Roade, but he took the pregnant girl as his wife, and he made the situation good, in exchange for a glittering career which Lord Justice Roade promised him on a plate. It was all enshrined in a contract. The loveless marriage, the lack of interest in the twin boys... I think it can all be explained from this starting-point.'

The Bishop shook his head in disbelief. 'But why couldn't Antonia have married the true father of the boys? Was he some sort of rascal? A bad lot?'

Posie shook her head. 'Not at all. In many ways he was ideal. He mixed in the same social circles, he had a bright future ahead of him. He adored Antonia, and would do whatever she asked. In fact, he still does.'

'So?' demanded the Bishop, fingering his purple jewel crossly. 'Why didn't he jolly well marry her?'

'*Religion*. Wasn't it, Lord Justice Roade?' Posie turned to the old Judge, hunched down in his chair, breathing deeply, his face puce. 'You are famous for coming from a long line of Protestant churchmen, aren't you?'

'And what of it?' hissed the Judge. 'Antonia is my only daughter. Of course I'd have liked it if she'd married the father of the boys. I'd have let her marry anyone, if she wanted it, regardless of religion. And *she* did want to marry him. But he...'

'Was a Catholic,' said Posie, simply. 'With very Catholic

parents, who would never in a million years have accepted the Protestant-born Antonia Roade as a daughter-in-law.'

Posie looked around the dead-quiet room, past Lady Antonia who was still sitting with her hands covering her face, and she fixed her gaze on Rufus, whose eyes seemed suddenly clearer, focused.

'By Gad! It's you, William Dawney! You're the twin boys' father?'

And everyone turned to the centre of the circle, where Sheila had laid a protective hand on Dr Dawney's arm. She was looking from Posie to Lovelace as if assessing the lesser of the two evils, and finding both about equally matched. Dawney was shaking his head. He turned, calling back to his old school acquaintance. 'No, Cardigeon. You're all wrong on that. As usual.'

But Posie was clutching the blue book she had been sent and she was moving closer to Lovelace all the time. She spoke to the room, confident of her facts.

'I'm very much afraid that the Earl of Cardigeon is absolutely right. William Dawney, as Amyas Lyle's old school chum and gambling buddy, was often at parties held by young lawyers. And he met Antonia Roade at one such party, and she got pregnant by him. His parents forbade the match, and he watched from the side-lines as the woman he worshipped became trapped in a dreadful marriage. He later married a suitable woman, a fellow Catholic, Kate. But he was always near; visiting Antonia on a Sunday, after he'd attended the nearby Brompton Oratory, checking in on her and his twin boys, in the handy guise of visiting Amyas. William would have done anything for Antonia. When she wanted cocaine to try and forget the loveless marriage she was part of, that was what William Dawney did; he got her the drugs. More drugs and then yet more drugs. I'm guessing that he liked what was happening: she was becoming totally reliant on him for her addiction.'

Lovelace was staring from Posie back to Dawney, who

shook his head in disbelief. 'Miss Parker, with all due respect, this is nonsense.'

'After all,' continued Posie, ignoring him completely, 'getting cocaine was easy for a man like Dr Dawney. He runs one of the biggest drug-rackets in the country, all concealed by a ring of crooked doctors, meeting up season by season in different hospitals, so as not to get caught. Dawney needs money to feed his gambling habit, and the drugs and the gambling together have made him a very rich man. He told me that tonight.'

'That's hardly a crime, is it? Being a rich man?' called out Sheila, rigid with anger.

'Of course not. But this went much further. I'm supposing that Dr Dawney had got it in mind that, now his own parents were dead, he would be free to marry again. To marry the drug-addled Antonia and be the father to his boys he should have been from the start. To make everything right.'

'But wouldn't he need to get Amyas out of the way first?' called Rufus.

'Exactly. I expect he planned on killing Amyas in a quiet manner, with a "fake" heart attack; after all, he knew his old friend's medical history. But this plan was all a little vague. Something to arrange over the next couple of years.'

'So why did he have to act *now*?' asked the Inspector, staring at Dawney in horror and incomprehension.

'Because, as I said before, he hadn't realised how Amyas had pulled himself free. How he was beginning to extricate himself from the marriage to Antonia. How at the beginning of the year Amyas started talking of divorce. Would probably start proceedings soon...'

Lovelace groaned. 'Of course. A Catholic can marry a person who's been widowed, but not a person who's been divorced... and time was beginning to tick.'

Posie looked at Dawney, who sighed. 'Your logic is completely correct,' he said quite casually. 'But this whole thing doesn't apply to me. How on earth would I have pulled it off?'

'Very easily,' answered Posie. 'You told me you went up north, after your wife had died, at the start of this year, looking for Amyas' family, and that you had no luck in Whitley Bay. This was all borne out when I went to visit the Spanish City; a couple of people remembered you sniffing about with a postcard, and they said you'd not managed to get the information you wanted. But then I asked myself: what if you hadn't managed to get information, but you'd tracked down Aiden Vannelly anyway? As luck would have it I saw a photograph of Aiden on a desk in the offices at the Spanish City and I realised that Amyas had been a twin all along. Why shouldn't that have happened to you too? At any rate, you tracked the twin down and overawed Aiden with your fancy ways; your professional status. You promised him, no doubt, that Amyas was now searching for his family; that you would pay him money to make the journey south at a convenient point. You listened to his memories, took a tour of the house, saw the little photography hut with its pathetic attempt at a chemistry lab. Aiden was too ashamed to admit to me that he had taken your money, even when he started to realise you had made him a scapegoat in your murderous plan.'

Lovelace was shaking his head. 'I don't know, Posie. Dawney would have needed accomplices when Lyle was murdered. He was supposed to be in Edinburgh, wasn't he?'

'I *was* in Edinburgh,' said the doctor with a deep fuming breath of exasperation.

Posie stared at Sheila. 'I don't see a problem with accomplices, sir. Sheila here was probably the woman who bought Aiden's train tickets.' Sheila was shaking her head resolutely, her hand still on her boss' arm.

'And Dr Dawney has no end of medical students at the French Hospital who would do anything for him, just to get ahead. I'm thinking, sir, that if you track them all down, one of them will admit to mixing up the batch of nitric acid in sea-water in the lab there. The same fellow will probably admit to dressing up as a Billingsgate Porter, and delivering the box. I expect Dr Dawney sold it to him as a joke on an old school chum. The same lad may even have written the series of notes, seen it all as a good laugh…'

Lovelace was mentally trying to fit it all together. 'And you think Dawney himself placed all those things in Aiden's house and shed?'

'Certain of it, sir. It would be just a couple of hours out of his normal route, to get off the train at Newcastle and get a taxi to Whitley Bay, then back again and on to Edinburgh.'

Lady Antonia seemed to have recovered somewhat. She was pale but determined. 'Now you've aired our dirty laundry for all and sundry to rake through, you're going to accuse William of *this*? Murder! It doesn't make sense! He and Amyas were *friends*, you poor, deluded girl. Call yourself a detective!'

Posie looked at the woman in front of her, felt the chill from the icy shards of self-protection which she was desperately trying to clothe herself in. She shook her head:

'No. You're wrong. Both William Dawney and your husband only kept friends if it aided them. True, they shared a history, but not a good one. Amyas had spent his whole adult life trying to free himself of that history, as it happens. And I have reason to believe that he may only have stayed friends with William Dawney because he was monitoring him: his gambling, his drugs racket.'

She didn't add for *whom* Amyas had been monitoring William, instead she bit her lip hard and dashed on: 'Besides, the old ties to Amyas were as nothing compared to the love William had for you.'

At this Posie saw a fierce lick of jealousy splash across Sheila's face, an almost cat-like snarl light up her composed neat features. 'Is this true, Bill?' she was asking. 'What about *me*?'

'I'm afraid you've been well used, Sheila,' said Posie sadly. 'But at least you are still alive. You're sitting next to a very dangerous man, and one day you'll count yourself lucky you escaped.'

Lady Antonia shrieked with laughter. '*Dangerous*? Now you really are talking rot. William fixes people. He doesn't kill them!'

'I beg to differ.'

And Posie passed across the blue book at last, felt its weight as Lovelace took it, frowning. It was open at a particular page, marked with the cream telegram card.

She whispered in a low undertone: 'Max sent it to me. He went missing right afterwards. Last Monday. Whitehall have informed me he is most likely dead. They will want this book, and the card. As evidence.'

Lovelace looked urgently at the door to the room, checked that Constable Fox was still guarding it, and then looked quickly at the cover of the book.

The blue book wasn't actually that old. Just three years. But it was well-thumbed and looked distressed through use. The title 'MEDICAL PRACTITIONERS IN ENGLAND, SCOTLAND AND WALES' had once been embossed in gold but was now faded. On the fly-sheet the crest and motto of the Royal Infirmary, Edinburgh, was displayed prominently, and another flowery, fancy stamp made it clear that the blue book was a reference book belonging to the hospital library in Edinburgh. It had been taken out illegally.

Not quite understanding, Lovelace flicked through to where he had seen the card. And after he read what was written on the card, he then swallowed. Read again:

POSIE,

MY LIFE IS IN DANGER AND MY COVER BLOWN. I'VE JUST TIME TO SEND THIS. I WAS FOLLOWED HERE.

I'VE BEEN IN EDINBURGH AMONG A CIRCLE OF DOCTORS, ONE OF THE CLEVEREST DRUGS RACKETS I'VE EVER SEEN. MAINLY COCAINE BUT HEROIN TOO. CARRIED UP AND DOWN THE COUNTRY IN MEDICAL BAGS.

FIND THE BIG BOSS AND BRING HIM DOWN.

HE'S ONE OF THE MOST EVIL MEN I'VE MET.

I HEARD HIM BRAGGING ONE NIGHT ABOUT HOW HE KILLED HIS OWN WIFE, WITH A NARCOTIC WHICH WOULD BE ALMOST IMPOSSIBLE TO TRACE IN THE BODY AFTERWARDS. ALL FOR THE SAKE OF SOME WOMAN HE FEELS HE IS IN LOVE WITH FROM YEARS AGO.

SORT THIS OUT, POSIE. AND GIVE THIS TO THEA ELLERIDGE AFTERWARDS.

M

And then Lovelace checked the actual page the card had been placed in, and he saw it was a section of names starting with a 'D'. And there, on the left-hand page, taking up a good half of it with all the accolades about the Great

War, was an entry for Dr William Dawney, Chief Medical Practitioner and Surgeon at the French Hospital, London.

The Chief Inspector snapped the book shut. He looked over at Constable Fox, gave him the merest flicker of a nod, and then, with a sweep of an interrogatory glare that took in the whole group, but which rested eventually on Dr Dawney, he spoke carefully:

'William Dawney, fresh evidence placed before me means that I am indeed arresting you today for the premeditated murder of Amyas Lyle, and also for the murder of your wife Kate Dawney, and for perverting the course of justice with regards to implicating Aiden Vannelly in a crime he did not commit.' Lovelace cleared his throat, and avoided Posie's eye. 'And lastly, for the manslaughter of an undercover Agent for the British Government, missing in action, presumed killed last Monday, in Edinburgh.'

Even in death Max had no name, no real identity.

'And you will also be charged for crimes in relation to drugs trafficking, and the supplying of illegal drugs. Anything you say may be taken in evidence.'

The last part of the charge fell on deaf ears, as the room was swaying, swerving under the weight of the allegations raining down on one of its members. People were only just catching up with the Inspector's words, the heavy implications. Dr Dawney sat still, silent, a calm at the centre of the storm. But Lady Antonia was flailing in her seat, pulling at Dawney's arm in jagged bursts:

'*You* killed Kate? You killed her? But she died in agony, those last few days. How could you? You did this for *me*? You wanted to marry me? After all this time?'

And Dawney turned at last, perhaps the only smile Posie had ever seen breaking across his handsome, ethereal face. 'Of course I did, my darling. Things weren't just changing for Amyas. We were almost free of everyone who had ever kept us apart. It wouldn't have been long and I would have found a way to get rid of your wretched father, too.'

'You monster of a man!'

Lord Justice Roade was up on his feet. 'You got my daughter into the state she's in, and your supply of drugs means she could never get clear of you.' His voice grew louder and wilder with every word, the impressive voice now just a husky bawl: 'You should be ashamed of yourself, Dawney. May you rot in hell.'

But Dawney just smiled, and as Constable Fox surged forwards with handcuffs at the ready, Lady Antonia began to weep:

'What makes you think I would have married you, anyway, William?'

'Of course you would have done, my darling. You're the mother of my children. And you know I always know what's best for you.'

But then two things happened. And Posie hadn't foreseen either of them.

****

Twenty-Eight

The first was that as Constable Fox approached, Dawney stood up, the picture of contrition, arms outstretched, as if ready for the handcuffs.

But in a split-second he had pulled a tiny, silver service revolver from his pocket. People were screaming, then blubbering themselves into a deathly quiet. You could hear a pin drop.

Posie had seen such revolvers before; they were standard army provision for any non-fighting Officer in the trenches, and they must have been issued to doctors of a certain rank as standard issue.

Dawney cocked the gun and aimed it straight at Constable Fox, who immediately dropped the cuffs and put his hands up in a gesture of surrender. Dawney was smiling assuredly. 'Let me go,' he said, smoothly, moving the revolver from Fox to Inspector Lovelace, who crossed his arms angrily, the blue book still clutched to his chest.

'I'll walk out of here now and disappear, Chief Inspector. Give me ten minutes of a head start, otherwise I promise there will be carnage here. Less a funeral, rather a massacre. Starting with *you*.'

'No can do.' Lovelace shook his head calmly and Posie found herself fixing her gaze upon him, upon his strength, his way of seeming to keep the room with him, with no-one panicking.

'The game's up, old fellow,' called out Rufus from the back of the room.

But the second thing to happen of consequence was that Sheila, the composed secretary, stood up. And then she started screaming, raving, grabbing at her employer's arm to shake off the gun. Masha, who was next to her in the row of chairs, tried to grab at Sheila's black tweed skirts, to hold her back, but Sheila had become a force of anger, a woman scorned.

'What about *me*?' she screamed at Dawney. 'Everything you promised *me*? Marriage, children. You said you needed some months alone after your wife's death to grieve, but now I realise you were lying! Lying about everything. You killed your own wife, Bill! Shame on you. That's dreadful!'

'Get out of my way, Sheila.'

And the woman was screaming at the Chief Inspector now, too, a flurry of bitterness within which the truth was held. 'And Miss Parker is absolutely right. I *did* have to book a set of tickets for Aiden Vannelly, with the instruction I paid in cash and kept myself well covered up, so no-one would be able to identify me later.'

Her voice was getting higher and higher, almost a shriek: 'And I can tell you something else, too, Chief Inspector: the medical student you are looking for who helped Bill with those horrid notes and to make up the chemicals and deliver them is one of his most devoted students at the French Hospital, Dan Chivers. But Dan had no idea he was getting involved in a murder. None of us did. Dan thought he was taking part in a practical joke…and also…'

But before she could continue Dawney had turned and mercilessly fired the gun at close range and Sheila fell, her body spiralling into a bloodied crumpled mass across the carpet. Antonia Lyle was screaming now, the Bishop crossing himself.

And then, as Dawney straightened up and took aim again at the Inspector, and Posie thought her world might actually end, there and then, there was a sudden whirring, whizzing noise from the very back of the room and in front of them William Dawney went down, screaming, collapsing on the floor next to his dead secretary, his gun and his hand shot quite away, blood pumping from his arm in what seemed like waves.

Lovelace was staring at the back of the room, while Posie was holding onto a trembling Constable Fox, and all eyes were fixed on Rufus.

He had a small, black, service Luger in his hands. And he was tucking it away in a pocket of his beautifully-tailored black jacket. He looked enormously pleased with himself.

'There!' he said proudly. 'Still a first-class shot! That's the first thing I've done right in weeks!' He looked over at Posie.

'I hope you're going to tell *that* to Dolly.'

* * * *

EPILOGUE

A week had passed, and it felt as if summer had definitely gone, although the evenings were still long and the temperature was warm. But fingers of rain licked London incessantly, and the leaves spun from the trees as if it were September.

People were making their way back to London from the wet seaside resorts, cancelling their holidays, and with long school summer holidays still stretching ahead, the London museums were fit to bursting with aggrieved parents and nursemaids and very tetchy children. London was coming back to life.

Len was back at work, and generally there were more and more black-suited men and women crowding onto the buses and trams and Underground trains than was usual at this time of year. Jobs beckoned; colleagues were sought out for consoling canteen lunches; projects picked up and shuffled once again.

William Dawney had been taken to hospital after Rufus had shot him, but had contracted septicaemia from the loss of his hand and it was anybody's guess whether he would regain consciousness and whether he would live or die. Let alone whether he would ever be brought to trial.

Lovelace had intimated that he privately thought

William Dawney might be found to be clinically insane.

Formal statements exonerating Aiden Vannelly of the murder of his twin brother had been published in as many newspapers as possible by Scotland Yard, but whether Aiden too would live or die was yet to be seen.

Posie had visited Aiden twice more at Guy's, looking through the slightly-raised white blinds at the man she had met very briefly. And even here, where he floated in this half-world of living and dying, he looked like he had found a sort of peace.

The blue book with its card inside had been duly submitted to 66 Whitehall and the authority of Thea Elleridge, who had promised to investigate the drugs racket and the other doctors who were part of it. So far, there was no word from Max, and Posie had prepared herself never to hear from him again.

Posie couldn't settle to anything.

Sergeant Rainbird and Prudence Smythe announced their engagement, and a small party at a modest hotel on the Strand was planned to celebrate the event. But Posie, although ecstatic at the news, couldn't find it in her heart to look forward to the party, or to celebrate very much at all.

A couple of suitable cases had come across her desk in the last week. One regarding a missing fashion model, and the other being a strange request to look into the case of a haunted newly-built house on the south coast. Both were good options, with clients prepared to pay proper fees.

The postcard from San Gimignano in Tuscany, an invitation to come and stay from an acquaintance, Jacinta Glaysayer, still lay tantalisingly on Posie's desk, and Posie began to think that maybe getting out of London and having a change of scenery might be for the best after all.

By day she couldn't settle, and by night she dreamt.

The same dream, constantly. She was in Cambridge yet again, at age eighteen, but this time the date with Amyas

Lyle had worked out. Posie was walking along the King's Parade, arm in arm with Amyas Lyle, and her brother Richard was shouting something behind them which she couldn't hear, no matter how hard she tried.

She would wake in a real-life cold sweat every morning, in her expensive Egyptian-cotton bedsheets, wondering what those words were. What was Richard trying to tell her? *If anything*? Posie puzzled over the dream in the daytime too, fancying she could still hear Richard's half-muffled warnings. His voice seemed to echo down corridors, come up through the lift-shaft, whisper at her in the street.

She was so tired.

Posie hadn't been near Scotland Yard all week, hadn't seen the Chief Inspector. She was waiting any day now for a formal announcement about his move to New Zealand, for a telephone call which didn't come.

She thought about the child, too, little Katia. All that was left of Amyas Lyle in the whole world.

Posie had left a message with Rufus' Butler again, several times now, asking about meeting in order to help finance the little girl's future, to try and persuade Rufus to change his mind. But she hadn't heard back. And now she didn't think she would.

Posie had resolved in her own mind that she would have to take responsibility for Katia and raise her alone, as she had done so much else in her life. It was *right*, somehow. A girl with no family, helping another girl with no family. She would have to find a way of making it all formal, she supposed. Making it work.

After an unpromising Monday, Posie finished early, calling farewells to Len, Prudence and Sid; the latter of whom was sorting out some of Len's recent photographs into smart folders for clients. She crossed the wet streets, skirting around the gates of the British Museum as the bells of St George's Church nearby were chiming five o'clock. She hurried around Russell Square and down to Great Ormond Street Hospital.

Posie trailed the corridors, her umbrella tapping on the floor, dripping wet things in her wake, and made her way to the same children's ward she had visited before. There was a coat-stand just outside the ward, and as she was hanging her damp things up, the fat nurse from before saw her there.

'Oh, hullo, dearie, here to see little Katie, are you?'

'That's right.'

'She's attracting quite a bit of attention lately, you know. One set of papers was signed for her last weekend, and it seems they're all being unpicked now. A whole lot of *other* papers were signed this afternoon. We were right, weren't we? *Lots* of interest in little Katie.'

Posie stared. It seemed she was too late. Was this Masha? Had she somehow raised the funds to support the little girl and applied to be her guardian? Or was it Rufus, after all, doing his best to atone for the last few months, now on a crusade of all-out good, doing it all with minimal fanfare?

But when she got up to the plate glass of the incubation room, Posie saw Inspector Lovelace was standing there, holding a small girl in his arms, whose face and hands were pressed up tight against the glass.

'Sir? Phyllis?'

Lovelace turned, almost doing a double-take. 'Posie!' He beamed. 'How lovely to see you, and how unexpected.'

'Likewise. What are you doing here, sir?'

'I've been here most evenings, and at the weekend too. With Phyllis.'

Posie grinned. 'She's got under your skin, little Katia, hasn't she? Me, too, if I'm honest. I feel a weight of responsibility for her. I know nothing about children, and will probably never have any of my own, but I feel I ought to step in and provide for her. Goodness knows how I'll do it, but I'll manage. Finances aren't a problem, of course, but the actual parenting… Well, I might be too late, anyhow. The nurse coming off duty said that there had been some paperwork signed for the baby today, and lots of interest.'

Lovelace almost snarled. 'You know that wretch Dawney, he'd paid for the baby's hospital care, and he'd also arranged for her to be taken into an orphanage at the earliest opportunity. A state orphanage, little better than the workhouse. The devil take him…'

Posie shook her head in disbelief. She had at least thought there was a small glimmer of good in what Dawney had done, or said he had done for Katia. She should have known better.

Phyllis was passed over to Posie, who winced under the sudden weight of the bulky, wriggly little girl in her sweet pink smocked dress.

'That's going to be my sister,' Phyllis said proudly, pointing at the baby nearest them. 'Her name is Katie, and we're taking her home with us.'

Posie raised an eyebrow incredulously and the Inspector laughed. 'It's true. I've been unpicking Dawney's paperwork today, on the grounds that he was a criminal and his actions had no legal weight.'

Posie gasped aloud: 'And *you're* adopting her?'

'In as far as is possible in this mess of a system. When she's stronger, bigger, she'll come home with us. I've engaged Masha to be my Housekeeper, and look after both girls. It's time Phyllis had a sister; someone to play with. It's not good to be alone. I won't be able to provide them with riches or privileges, just an honest copper's salary, but it will be enough.'

'But I thought you were going to New Zealand, sir? Are they all going with you? And what about Ella Brown?'

Lovelace pulled at his shirt collar self-consciously. 'She got too, er, *proprietorial*. I had to let her go. I don't like my shirts so starched anyway. And New Zealand, well, after some thought, I realised it was just too far away.'

Phyllis kicked at Posie's side with her sharp little shoes, and Posie suddenly realised her eyes were full of tears. She brushed them away but she couldn't stop them coursing down her face.

Here was a good man, prepared to put the happiness of a tiny, unwanted girl right at the forefront of his life, when others, with riches beyond compare, couldn't be bothered.

'Too far away from what, sir?'

Lovelace turned from the glass and grinned, his green eyes full of mischief. But there was something else there, too. A haunted, knowing emptiness. A restless passion which never gave up hoping.

'Too far from London, Posie. And other things, of course.'

Richard Lovelace let out a low, strangled cough, which could have been a sob. Posie suddenly reached for his hand, held it fast in hers.

'Maybe we can make a go of this together, Posie, eh? Show the world how to do things when we haven't got a clue. We'll make it up as we go along.'

'Raising Katia, sir? Together?'

He didn't miss a beat, didn't falter. Smiled a smile which was confident of not much more than the asking. 'No, Posie. I thought *we* could perhaps be together. At last.' He cleared his throat, looked straight ahead through the thick glass. 'You must know I love you?'

'Oh! Oh, sir!'

For the first time in a week, her brother Richard's voice, so insistent in her dreams, and blurry in the background of her daily life, ceased. All she could hear was silence. The bleeping machines. A peace. Little Katia, or Katie Lovelace, or whoever she would one day be, growing stronger. *Going home.*

But where would 'home' be?

Never mind.

And they stood there together. The three, soon to be four. An unconventional tangle.

Posie swallowed. She was continuing to hold Richard Lovelace's hand. It felt so right. She felt for the first time in ages as if she wasn't scared, wasn't hurting. There were no ghosts here, no complications; no spies living umpteen, double lives. No Amyas Lyle. No Max.

Yes: this was *right*.

Richard Lovelace looked down at Posie. 'My darling? What do you think?'

'I think it sounds good, sir. We'll manage.'

He gripped her tighter, and his lip was trembling.

'Of course we will. And isn't it about time you stopped calling me "sir"?'

* * * *

Historical Note

All of the characters in this book are fictional, unless specifically mentioned below. However, timings, general political events, weather conditions and places (and descriptions of places) are historically accurate to the best of my knowledge, save for the exceptions and details which are listed below.

A key character, Amyas Lyle, is (by profession) a barrister in this novel. This is the English term for a court attorney, or an attorney-at-law. He is the Head of a fictional Set of Chambers in London (20 Old Square) which is an office for a group of barristers who each work alone, but have decided to share facilities and a physical building together. I would like to point out that 20 Old Square is completely fictional, although Lincoln's Inn and Old Square itself are both real.

The reference to a 'KC' throughout the book is to a 'King's Counsel' (George V was on the throne in 1924) while today it would be a 'QC', a 'Queen's Counsel'. It is the highest legal privilege which can be awarded in recognition of legal excellence.

As in the other Posie Parker books, I refer to the First World War of 1914–1918 as the 'Great War' throughout, which is simpler for the modern reader although it would not have been referred to in this way in 1924.

The eagle-eyed among you will note that in the book I usually refer to Richard Lovelace as 'Inspector Lovelace' or simply 'Lovelace'. Followers of Posie's adventures so far will know that in fact he is already a Chief Inspector, but to constantly refer to him as such seems to me unnecessarily clunky and detracting from the text, particularly in the middle of dialogue.

As ever, both Posie's work address in London (Grape Street, Bloomsbury, WC1) and her home address around the corner (Museum Chambers, WC1) are both very real, although you might have to do a bit of imagining to find her there.

1. (Generally) As depicted in this novel the first third of July 1924 in England (and nearby Paris, where the Olympics were taking place) was very hot and sticky, with soaring high temperatures reaching up to 40 degrees Celsius. The second two-thirds of July were cold, rainy and thundery; more like autumn weather.

2. (Prologue) Tennis was certainly played in the central portion of Lincoln's Inn Fields (the park itself) in the 1920s. There is a delightful stock photo (of which I do not own the copyright) of four girls limbering up for a game in this very place on a balmy summer's day in the 1920s. (See: https://media.gettyimages.com/photos/between-1920-and-1930-in-england-the-girls-begin-a-game-of-tennis-in-picture-id105212691?s=2048x2048)

3. (Prologue) Ede & Ravenscroft are the makers and suppliers of legal wigs and gowns in London, today as in the 1920s.

4. (Chapter One) The Copper Kettle in Cambridge, on King's Parade (where Posie should have met

Amyas Lyle before the Great War), did not actually exist in 1924 but it is now a Cambridge institution in its own right.

5.   (Prologue and mentioned in various later chapters) The Paris Olympics referred to occasionally in this story (as background) took place from 4 May to 27 July 1924 at the Stade Olympique Yves-du-Manoir, Paris. The British runners Harold Abrahams and Eric Liddell were champions, winning gold respectively in the 100m and 400m races. Their participation and their stories have been immortalised in the film *Chariots of Fire*.

6.   (Chapter Three) The formation of MI5 during this time is mentioned at note six of the Historical Notes to *Murder at Maypole Manor* (*A Posie Parker Mystery* #3).

7.   (Chapter Three and throughout the book) The British Fascist Party was formed in 1924 (the year of this novel) by Rotha Lintorn-Orman, in the wake of the Italian fascists' march on Rome, led by Benito Mussolini. Originally called the *British Fascisti*, its far-right policies were poorly defined, with its early membership formed from Britain's highest society, including (interestingly) many aristocratic women. At the time of this novel it was very loosely-defined in aims and the meetings were fairly irregular. By 1927 the party started to move towards a defined form of fascism, and after 1931 adopted the model and aims of Mussolini's National Fascist Party.

8.   (Chapter Three) As mentioned by Inspector Lovelace, Hitler's trial for treason (with nine others) in February 1924 in Munich ended up

being a twenty-four-day free publicity spree for Adolf Hitler and his freshly-formed fascist (Nazi) party. Hitler and his party comrades had tried and failed in November of 1923 to bring down the existing German political order, the Weimar Republic. The trial in February 1924 enabled Hitler to showcase himself as a statesman-in-the-making, and this was picked up on by the German right-wing press, who were eager to find themselves a new hero. As Lovelace explains here, fascist groups everywhere were now slavishly following Hitler's every move, and governments and government agencies sought to monitor followers.

9.   (Chapter Five) Fever Street is completely fictional.

10. (Chapter Six) 'Silly season' in the press is an English expression for the summer holiday season, when there is little news to report (Parliament and Courts all being closed) and any type of story is deemed newsworthy, with the newspapers usually full of second-rate reports, gossip and hoaxes.

11. (Chapter Nine) In the 1920s sheep were really introduced by law into the parks, commons and green spaces of central London as a way of reducing mowing costs. For a fascinating collection of photographs detailing this, see: https://mashable.com/2015/08/02/london-sheep.

12. (Chapter Eleven) Posie's yellow silk umbrella is from Thomas Brigg and Son's, the finest makers of umbrellas in 1920s London. It is now Swaine Adeney Brigg. For more see: https://www.swaineadeneybrigg.com

13. (Chapter Twelve) The Royal Waterloo Hospital for Children and Women (where Olga Karloff is admitted) is located just over Waterloo Bridge, near Waterloo Station. It is no longer a hospital, having closed in 1976.

14. (Chapter Thirteen, and later) The French Hospital in London, where Dr Dawney is the Chief Surgeon (Dawney is a fictional character) was a real hospital with a fascinating history. Set up in Victorian times for the benefit of 'distressed foreigners of all nations requiring medical relief' it occupied a very central location in London, at Shaftesbury Avenue. Updated in 1910 to include modern wards and a state-of-the-art operating theatre and laboratory, it became a receiving hospital during the Great War. During its history most of its patients came from France and its colonies, but others came from Switzerland, Italy, Belgium and occasionally the United Kingdom. It closed in 1966.

15. (Chapter Fourteen) As Inspector Lovelace states here, the adoption process in the United Kingdom was a complete mess at this time, and 'adoption' gave neither the child nor adoptive parents any rights at all, the whole process bound up in secrecy. 'Adoption' *was* going on, but there were no safeguards in place at all and by the early 1920s there were calls for this to be changed, with a 1921 Child Adoption Committee recommending that adoption should be legalised. However, it was not until 1926 that the Adoption of Children Act was passed.

16. (Chapter Fifteen) Gordon's Wine Bar by the Embankment (where Lovelace suggests going

for dinner with Posie) is one of the best and most historical wine bars in London (see: https://gordonswinebar.com).

17. (Chapter Sixteen) The Fish Porters of Billingsgate, East London had a distinctive uniform of white overalls and apron and a very unique, thick black leather hat which included a flat leather top, for balancing crates of fish upon. This hat was known as a 'bobbin hat' and was made specially by John Williams Fain, a hat-maker in Lovat Lane, near Billingsgate Market. The Billingsgate Fish Porters are no more, having had their licences revoked by the City of London in 2012.

18. (Chapter Seventeen and Eighteen) For Whitley Bay, generally, see: https://www.visitnorthtyneside.com/

19. (Chapter Seventeen) For the justly famous art deco Rendezvous Café, please see: http://amorendezvous.com. Please note that I have played with timings here and used artistic licence. The Rendezvous Café was not built until 1930 and was not named the Rendezvous Café until 1957.

20. (Chapter Seventeen) The Margaret Hotel is fictional. The best hotel in Whitley Bay at this time would have been the Rex Hotel.

21. (Chapter Seventeen, Eighteen and Nineteen) For the beautifully-restored Spanish City, see: www.spanishcity.co.uk.

The history of the place as recounted by Posie is correct. At the time this novel is set, in 1924, the Spanish City really was at its hey-day, attracting musical groups and famous ballroom dancers to its renowned Empress Ballroom, from where radio broadcasts were often transmitted.

The Spanish City went on to suffer a chequered history of highs and lows, famous essentially after the Second World War for its fairground and Pleasure Gardens. It was sadly very run-down in the period of the 1990s through to very recently, when it has been lovingly restored to something like how it would have looked in Posie Parker's time. Please note that my storyline about the management of the Spanish City in 1924 is entirely fictional, as are the Directors I am writing about. I have, however, tried to stick as near as possible to plans of the interior of the building and the space where I have located the offices of the management (up in the dome itself, which had been segmented by use of a 'hanging' floor) existed at this time. The Spanish City was also immortalised in the Dire Straits song 'Tunnel of Love' from the album *Making Movies*.

22. Bane Castle in Chapter Twenty is fictional, although for an example of the wonderful castles on the craggy Northumbria coastline see Bamburgh Castle.

23. (Chapter Twenty-Five) The Lincoln's Inn Chapel where Amyas Lyle's funeral takes place is indeed an interesting church, famous for being designed by Inigo Jones and consecrated in 1623. It has always had a reputation as being a place for foundling babies to be left, and is likely the inspiration for John Donne's poem, 'No Man is an Island'. The custom of the bell being rung at midday for a dead barrister is correct, although on the day of *death*,

rather than on the day of the funeral, as I have amended it to here.

* * * *

Thank you for joining Posie Parker and her friends.

Enjoyed *The Saltwater Murder*
(A Posie Parker Mystery #7)?
Here's what you can do next.

If you loved this book and have a tiny moment to spare
I would really appreciate a short review on the page
where you bought the book. Your help in spreading
the word about the series is invaluable and really
appreciated, and reviews make a big difference to
helping new readers find the series.

Posie's other cases are available in e-book and
paperback formats from Amazon, as well as in selected
bookstores. You can find all of the other books, available
for purchase, listed here in chronological order:

http://www.amazon.com/L.B.-Hathaway/e/
B00LDXGKE8

and

http://www.amazon.co.uk/L.B.-Hathaway/e/
B00LDXGKE8

You can sign up to be notified of new releases, pre-
release specials, free short stories and the chance to win
Amazon gift-vouchers here:

http://www.lbhathaway.com/contact/newsletter/

About the Author

Cambridge-educated, British-born L.B. Hathaway writes historical fiction. She worked as a lawyer at Lincoln's Inn in London for almost a decade before becoming a full-time writer. She is a lifelong fan of detective novels set in the Golden Age of Crime, and is an ardent Agatha Christie devotee.

Her other interests, in no particular order, are: very fast downhill skiing, theatre-going, drinking strong tea, Tudor history, exploring castles and generally trying to cram as much into life as possible. She lives in Switzerland with her husband and young family.

The Posie Parker series of cosy crime novels span the 1920s. They each combine a core central mystery, an exploration of the reckless glamour of the age and a feisty protagonist who you would love to have as your best friend.

To find out more and for news of new releases and giveaways, go to:

http://www.lbhathaway.com

Connect with L.B. Hathaway online:
- (e) author@lbhathaway.com
- (t) @LbHathaway
- (f) https://www.facebook.com/pages/
  L-B-Hathaway-books/1423516601228019
- (g) http://www.goodreads.com/author/
  show/8339051.L_B_Hathaway

42674004R00185

Made in the USA
Lexington, KY
19 June 2019